DARK VOICES 4
The Pan Book of Horror

David Sutton was born in 1947 and has been writing and editing in the fantasy and horror genre for more than twenty years. He has edited, produced, and contributed to a wide range of small-press publications, most notably for The British Fantasy Society, and is the winner of the World Fantasy Award and eight British Fantasy Awards. His short fiction has been published in such books and magazines as *Best New Horror 2*, *Final Shadows*, *Cold Fear*, *Taste of Fear*, and *Skeleton Crew*, amongst many others. He is the editor of the anthologies *New Writings in Horror and the Supernatural* volumes 1 and 2 and *The Satyr's Head and Other Tales of Terror*, and co-compiler of *The Best Horror from Fantasy Tales*, three volumes of *Dark Voices: The Pan Book of Horror*, and the *Fantasy Tales* series. He has completed two horror novels, *Earthchild* and *Feng Shui*.

Stephen Jones was born in 1953 and is the winner of two World Fantasy Awards, the Horror Writers of America Bram Stoker Award and nine-time recipient of the British Fantasy Award. A full-time columnist, television producer/director, and genre movie publicist (all three *Hellraiser* films, *Nightbreed*, *Split Second*, etc.), he is co-editor of *Horror: 100 Best Books*, *The Best Horror from Fantasy Tales*, *Gaslight & Ghosts*, *Now We Are Sick*, and the *Best New Horror*, *Fantasy Tales*, and *Dark Voices* series, and compiler of *Clive Barker's The Nightbreed Chronicles*, *The Mammoth Book of Terror*, *Clive Barker's Shadows in Eden*, *James Herbert: By Horror Haunted*, and *The Mammoth Book of Vampires*.

Also available in this series

DARK VOICES
The Best from the Pan Book of Horror Stories

DARK VOICES 2
The Pan Book of Horror

DARK VOICES 3
The Pan Book of Horror

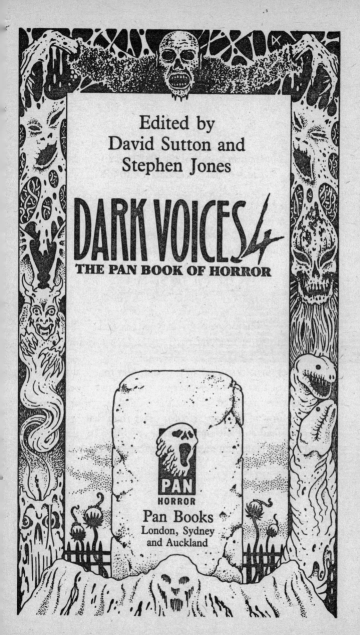

Edited by
David Sutton and
Stephen Jones

DARK VOICES 4

THE PAN BOOK OF HORROR

PAN
HORROR

Pan Books
London, Sydney
and Auckland

This collection first published 1992 by Pan Books Ltd
Cavaye Place, London SW10 9PG

1 3 5 7 9 8 6 4 2

ISBN 0 330 32476 4

Phototypeset by Intype, London
Printed in England by Clays Ltd, St Ives plc

Contents

Acknowledgements

'On Edge', © Christopher Fowler 1992

'Absence of Beast', © Graham Masterton 1992

'The Little Green Ones', © Les Daniels 1992, with grateful thanks to Stanley Wiater, editor of *After the Darkness*

'Razor White', © Charles A. Gramlich 1992

'Propeller', © Peter James Partnership 1992

'They Take', © Brunner Fact & Fiction Ltd 1992

'The Last Drop', © Nicholas Royle 1992

'Pick Me Up', © David J. Schow 1991, from *Psycho-Paths*. Reprinted by permission of the author.

'The Frankenstein Syndrome', © R. Chetwynd-Hayes 1992

'High-Flying, Adored', © Chaz Brenchley 1992

'A Night With Claudette', © Bernard Donoghue 1992

'Casey, Where He Lies', © Stephen Gallagher 1991, from *Imagination*. Reprinted by permission of the author.

'The Visitor', © Peter Crowther 1992

'Book End', © Tony J. Forder 1992

'Week Woman', © Kim Newman 1992

'Necrophiliac', © Tony Callow 1992

O silent grave to thee I trust,
This precious form of worthy dust,
Keep it safe O sacred tomb,
Until a daughter asks for room.

Old London Gravestone

On Edge

CHRISTOPHER FOWLER

A BRAZIL NUT, thought Thurlow, of all the damned things. That'll teach me. He leaned back tentatively in the plastic chair and studied the posters which had been taped to the walls around him.

Confidential HIV testing.

Unwanted Pregnancies.

Mind That Child He May Be Deaf.

He thought: No wonder people avoid coming here. Sitting in the waiting room gave you a chance to consider your fate at leisure.

He checked his watch, then listened. From behind a distant door came the whine of an electric drill. Determined to blot the sound from his brain, he checked through the magazines on the table before him. Inevitably there were two battered copies of the *Tatler*, some ancient issues of *Punch* and a magazine called *British Interiors*. With the drill howling faintly at the back of his brain, he flicked idly through the lifestyle magazine. A *pied-à-terre* in Kensington decorated in onyx and gold. A Berkshire retreat with a marble bas-relief in the kitchen depicting

13

scenes from *The Aeneid*. The people who lived in these places were presumably drug barons. Surely their children occasionally knocked over the bundles of artfully arranged dried flowers, or vanished into priest's holes to be lost within the walls?

As he threw the magazine down in disgust the drill squealed at a higher pitch, suggesting that greater force had been used to penetrate some resistant obstacle.

A damned brazil nut. Next time he'd use the crackers instead of his teeth. God, it hurt! The entire molar had split in half. Torn skin, blood all over the place. He was sure there was still a piece of nutshell lodged between the gum and the tooth, somewhere deep near the nerve. The pain seared through his jaw like a white-hot knife every time he moved his head.

The receptionist – her name was something common that he never quite caught – had sighed when she saw him approach. She had studied her appointment book with a doubtful shake of her head. He had been forced to point out that, as a private patient, his needs surely took precedence over others. After all, what else was the system for? He had been coming here regularly for many years. Or to put it more accurately, he had arranged appointments in this manner whenever there was a problem with his teeth. Apparently Dr Samuelson was away on a seminar in Florida, so he'd be seeing someone new, and he might have to wait a while. With the pain in his tooth driving him crazy, Thurlow didn't mind waiting at all.

There were two other people in the room. He could tell the private patient at a glance. The woman opposite, foreign-looking, too-black hair, too much gold, obviously had money. The skinny teenaged girl in jeans and a T-shirt had council house written all over her. Thurlow sniffed, and the knife rocketed up into his skull, causing him to clutch at his head. When the pain had subsided once more to a persistent dull throb, he examined his watch again. He'd been sitting here for nearly forty minutes! This was ridiculous! He rose from his seat and opened the door which led to the reception desk. Finding no one there, he turned into the white-tiled corridor beyond. Somebody would have to see him if he kicked up a fuss.

In the first room he reached, an overweight woman was pinned on her back with her legs thrown either side of the couch while the dentist hunched over her, reaching into her mouth like a man attempting to retrieve keys from a drain. In the second room he discovered the source of the drilling. Here, an exhausted teenaged man gripped the armrests of the chair with bony white knuckles while his dentist checked the end of the drill and drove it back into his mouth, metal grinding into enamel with the wincing squeal of a fork on a dry plate.

'You're not supposed to be back here, you know.'

Thurlow turned around and found a lean young man in a white coat looking crossly at him.

'I've been waiting for nearly an hour,' said Thurlow, feeling he had earned the exaggeration.

'And you are . . . ?'

'Mr Thurlow. Broken tooth. I was eating a brazil nut . . .'

'Let's not discuss it in the corridor. You'd better come in.'

Thurlow would have been annoyed by the brusqueness of the dentist's manner had he not heard the upper-class inflections in his voice, and noted the smart knot of his university tie. At least this way he would be dealt with by a professional.

Thurlow entered the room, removed his jacket, then waited by the red plastic couch while the dentist made an entry in his computer.

'I normally have Dr Samuelson,' he explained, looking about.

'Well, he's not here, he's . . .'

'I know. Florida. All right for some. You're new, I suppose. You're very young.'

'Everyone looks young when you start getting older, Mr Thurlow. I'm Dr Matthews.' He continued tapping the keyboard, then raised his eyes to the screen. 'You haven't had a check-up for well over a year.'

'Not for a check-up, no,' said Thurlow, climbing on to the couch. 'I had a thing, a lump.' He waggled his finger at his cheek. 'I thought it was a cyst.'

'When was the appointment?' Matthews was clearly unable to find the reference on his screen.

'I didn't have one. Anyway, it wasn't a cyst. It was a spot.'

'And the time before that?'

'I lost a filling. Ginger-nuts. Same thing the year before that. Peppermints.'

'So you haven't seen the hygienist for a while?'

'And I don't need to see one now,' said Thurlow. 'They always try to fob you off with dental floss and sticks with rubber prongs on. What is this anyway, going on about check-ups? Are you on commission?'

Dr Matthews ignored his remark and approached the

couch. As Thurlow made himself comfortable, the dentist slipped a paper bib around his neck and fastened it.

'Don't you have an assistant?'

'I used to have one, but she didn't like my methods so I murdered her,' said Matthews. 'Ha ha.' He adjusted the chair from a control pad by his foot, then switched on the water-rinse pump. 'I always like to make jokes. It takes the edge off. Mouth open, please.' He swung a tray of dental tools over Thurlow's chest.

Thurlow opened wide, and the light from the dentist's pencil torch filled his vision. He watched as the hooked probe went in, tapping along the left side of his molars, and glimpsed the little circular mirror at the corner of his vision. Saliva quickly began to build in his mouth. The tapping continued. He knew he would have to swallow soon. Quickly sensing his unease, Matthews placed a spit-pump in the corner of his mouth. It made a loud draining sound, like water going down a sink.

Suddenly Thurlow felt the sharp point of the probe touch down on the bare nerve in his split tooth. It was as if an electric current had been passed through his head. If it had remained in contact for a second longer he would have screamed and bitten the tool clean in half. Matthews observed the sudden twitch of his patient's body and quickly withdrew the instrument.

'I think we can safely say that we've located the problem area,' he said drily, shining the torch around, then lowering the large overhead light. 'That's pretty nasty. Wouldn't be so bad if it was an incisor. It's split all the way from the crown to the root. The gum is starting to swell and redden, so I imagine it's infected. I'll have to cut part of it away.'

Thurlow pulled the spit-pump from his mouth. 'I don't want to hear the details,' he said, 'it's making me sick.' He replaced the pump and lay back, closing his eyes.

'Fine. I'll give you a jab and we'll get started.' Matthews prepared a syringe, removed the plastic cap from the tip and cleared the air from the needle. Then he inserted it into the fleshy lower part of Thurlow's left gum. There was a tiny pop of flesh as the skin surface was broken and the cool metal slipped into his jaw, centimetre by centimetre. Thurlow felt the numbing fluid flood through his mouth, slowly removing all sensation from his infected tooth.

'As you're squeamish, I'll give you an additional Valium shot. Then I can work on without upsetting you.' He rolled back Thurlow's shirt sleeve and inserted a second syringe, emptying it slowly. 'It's funny when you think of it,' he said, watching the calibrations on the side of the tube. 'Considering all the food that has to be cut and crushed by your deciduous and permanent canines, incisors and molars, it's a miracle there's anything left in your mouth at all. Of course, humans have comparatively tiny teeth. It's a sign of our superiority over the animals.'

Thurlow finally began to relax. Was it the drug that was making him feel so safe and comfortable in Matthews' hands, or merely the dentist's air of confident authority? He hummed softly as he worked, laying out instruments in familiar order while he waited for the drugs to take effect. A feeling of well-being crept over Thurlow. His arms and legs had grown too heavy for him to move. His heart was beating more slowly in his chest. The lower half of his face was completely numb. Suspended between sleep and wakefulness, he tried to identify the tune that Matthews was humming, but concentration slipped away.

The dentist had placed two other metal instruments in his mouth; when did he do that? One was definitely there to hold his jaws apart. Although the overhead light was back-reflected and diffuse, it shone through Thurlow's eyelids with a warm red glow. There was a metallic clatter on the tray.

'I'm going to cut away part of the damaged gum tissue now,' said Matthews. Hadn't he demanded to be spared the details? The long-nosed scissors glinted against the light then vanished into his mouth, to clip through flesh and gristle. His mind drifted, trying not to think of the excavation progressing below.

'I don't think there'll be enough left to cap,' said Matthews. 'The one next to it is cracked pretty badly, too. What the hell was in that nut?'

When the drill started, Thurlow opened his eyes once more. Time seemed to have lapsed, for now there seemed to be several more instruments in his mouth. The drill howled on, the acrid smell of burning bone filling his nostrils. However, thanks to the effect of the Valium dose, he remained unconcerned. The drill was removed, and Matthews' fingers probed the spot. There was a sharp crack, and he held up the offending tooth for Thurlow to see, first one half, then the other.

'You want this as a souvenir? I thought not. Now, to do this properly I should really clear out your root canal and drive a metal post into the gum,' he said. 'But that's a long, painful process. Let's see how we can work around it without tearing your entire jaw off. Ha ha.'

The drill started up again and entered his mouth.

Thurlow could not tell which of his teeth it was touching, but by the familiar burning smell he guessed it was drilling deep into the enamel of a molar.

'That's better,' said Matthews. 'I can see daylight through the hole. Now that we have room to manoeuvre, let's bring in the big guns.' He produced a large semicircular metal clip and attached it to the side of Thurlow's lower lip. A new instrument appeared before the light, a large curved razor blade with a serrated tip, like a cheese grater with teeth. The dentist placed it in his mouth and began drawing it across the stump of the damaged molar. The rasping vibrated through Thurlow's head, back and forth, back and forth, until he began to wonder if it would ever stop.

'This is no good, no good at all.' He withdrew the instrument, checked the blunted tip and tossed it on to the tray in disgust.

'I need something else. Something modern, something – technological.' He vanished from view, and Thurlow heard him thumping around at the side of the room. 'One day,' he called, 'all dentistry will be performed by laser. Just think of the fun we'll have then!' He returned with a large piece of electrical equipment that boasted a red flashing LED on top. Matthews' grinning face suddenly filled his vision.

'You're a lucky man,' he said. 'Not many people get to have this baby in their mouths.' He patted the side of the machine, from which extended a ribbed metal tube with a tiny rotating steel saw. When he flicked it on, the noise was so great that he had to shout. 'You see, the main part of the tooth is made of a substance called dentine, but below the gum line it becomes bone-like cement, which is softer . . .'

He missed the next part as the saw entered his mouth and connected with tooth enamel. One of the pipes wedged between his lower incisors was spraying water on to the operating zone, while another was noisily sucking up saliva. His mouth had become a hardhat area. Suddenly something wet and warm began to pour down his throat. Matthews turned off the saw and hastily withdrew it. 'Darn,' he said loudly, 'that's my fault, not watching what I'm doing. I've been a little tense lately.'

He reached behind him and grabbed a wad of tissue, which he stuffed into Thurlow's mouth and padded at the operation site, only to withdraw it red, filled, and dripping. 'Sorry about that, I was busy thinking about something else. Good job I'm not a crane driver, I'd be dropping girders all over the place.'

Now there seemed to be something lodged in Thurlow's oesophagus. Through the anaesthetic he began to experience a stinging sensation. Bile rose in his throat as he started to gag.

'Wait, wait, I know what that is.' Matthews reached in his gloved hand and withdrew something, throwing it on to the tray. 'You've been a brave boy. A hundred years ago this would have been a horribly painful experience, performed without an anaesthetic, but thanks to modern techniques I'll have you finished in just a few more hours. Ha ha. Just kidding.'

He reached back to the tray and produced another steel frame, this one constructed like a filament wire in a light bulb. Carefully unscrewing it, he arranged the contraption at the side of his patient's mouth. Thurlow was starting to feel less calm. Perhaps the Valium was wearing off. Suppose his sensations returned in the middle of the drilling? Yes, he could definitely feel his jaw now. A dull pain began to throb at the base of his nose. The dentist was stirring something in a small plastic dish when he saw Thurlow shifting in his chair.

'Looks like I didn't give you a large enough dose,' he said, concerned. He removed the plastic cap from another syringe and jabbed it into Thurlow's arm.

'There,' he said, cheerfully depressing the plunger. 'Drug cocktail happy hour! You want a little umbrella in this one?'

Thurlow stared back at him with narrowed eyes, unamused. Matthews grew serious. 'Don't worry, when you wake up I'll have finished. I think you've been through enough for one day, so I'm giving you a temporary filling for now, and we'll do that root canal on your next appointment.'

As he began to spoon the cement into Thurlow's mouth on the end of a rubber spatula, Thurlow felt himself drifting off into an ethereal state of semi-wakefulness.

While he floated in this hazy dream-state, his imagination unfettered itself, strange visions uncoiling before him in rolling prisms of light. The humming of the dentists became a distant litany, a warm and familiar soundtrack, like the work-song of a seamstress. Colours blended into one another, bitter scents of jasmine and disinfectant. He was home and safe, a child again. Then these half-formed memories were replaced by the growing clarity of the present, and he realized that he was surfacing back to reality.

'Oh good,' said Matthews as his eyes flickered open.

'Back in the land of the living. For a minute I thought I'd overdosed you. Ha ha. We're just waiting for the last part to dry.' He reached into Thurlow's mouth and probed around with a steel scraper, scratching away the last of the filler. Thurlow suddenly became aware of the restraining strap fixed across his lap, holding him in place. How long had that been there?

'You know, we had a nasty case of "tooth squeeze" in here last week, ever hear of that? Of course, you can't answer with all this junk in your mouth, can you? He was an airline pilot. His plane depressurized, and it turned out he had an air bubble trapped beneath the filling. When the cabin atmosphere decreased, the air expanded. His tooth literally blew up in his mouth. Bits were embedded in his tongue. What a mess.' Matthews peered into his mouth, one eye screwed tight. 'It happens to deep-sea divers, too, only their teeth implode. And I've seen worse. There was one patient, a kid who rollerskated into a drinking fountain . . .' As he checked his handiwork he mercifully lost his train of thought. 'Well, that last batch seems to have done the trick.' The sensation was slowly returning to Thurlow's face. Something was very sore, very sore indeed. He raised his hands, hoping to see if he could locate the source of the pain, but Matthews swatted them down. 'Don't touch anything for a while. You must give it a chance to set. I still have some finishing off to do.'

The pain was increasing with every passing second. It was starting to hurt very badly, far worse than when he had arrived for treatment. Something had gone wrong, he was sure of it. He could only breathe through his nose, and then with difficulty. He tried to speak, but no sound came out. When he tried to pull himself upright, Matthews' arm came around the chair and pushed him back down. Now the dentist stepped fully into his view. Thurlow gasped.

It looked as if someone had exploded a blood transfusion bag in front of him. He was dripping crimson from head to foot. It was splashed across his chest and stomach, draining from his plastic apron to form a spreading pool at his feet. The white-tiled floor was slick with blood. Streaks marred the walls in sweeping arcs, like rampaging nosebleeds. Thurlow's head reeled back against the rest. What in God's name had happened? Pain and panic overwhelmed him as his hands clawed the air and he fought to stand, chromatic sparkles scattering before his eyes. The soporific drugs were still in his system, affecting his vision.

'You shouldn't be up and about yet,' said Matthews. 'I've not finished.'

'You're no dentist,' Thurlow tried to say, the white-hot knives shrieking through his brain, but his words came out as a series of hysterical rasps.

The dentist seemed to understand him. 'You're right, you're right, I'm no dentist.' He shrugged, his hands held out. *So sue me*. 'I always wanted to be one but I couldn't get my certificate. I just can't pass exams. I get angry too easily. Still, it's a vocation for me, a calling. I know what I'm doing is right. I'm simply ahead of my time. Let's finish up here.'

He thrust his hands into his patient's mouth and made a tightening motion. A starburst of pain detonated between Thurlow's eyes. The dentist held his head back against the rest while he pulled at something. There was a *ting* of

24

metal, and he extracted a twisted spring. On one end a small silver screw was embedded in a bloody scrap of bright red gum.

'You don't need this bit,' said Matthews jovially. He picked up a Phillips screwdriver and inserted it in Thurlow's mouth, ratcheting away happily, as if he was fixing a car. 'I like to think of this as homoeopathic medicine,' he explained, 'except that I'm more of an artist. I went to art school but I didn't pass the exam because – you guessed it – ' he nodded his head dumbly, *silly old me* – 'I got angry again. They took me out of circulation for a while.' He removed the screwdriver and wiped it on his apron, then peered inside Thurlow's aching mouth with a benign smile. 'Still, every once in a while I like to try out a few of my ideas. I choose a town and I search through the Yellow Pages, then I visit all the private dentists that are listed. Sometimes I find one with a vacant operating room, and then I just wait for custom. I carry the part, you see, white coat, smart tie, good speaking voice. Biros in the top pocket.' He pointed to his jacket. 'And I keep the door locked while I work. No one ever tries to stop me, and nothing would ever come out in the papers if they did, because private dentists are too scared of losing their customers. You'd never think it could be that simple, would you?'

He went to the desk beside the operating chair and detached a large circular mirror. 'Let's face it, when was the last time you asked to see a dentist's credentials? It's not like the police. Now, let's see how you turned out.'

Thurlow could barely breathe through the ever-increasing pain, but as the dentist tilted the mirror in his direction, the next sight that met his eyes almost threw him into a faint.

'Good, isn't it?' said Matthews. 'Art in dentistry.'

Thurlow's face was unrecognizable. His lips had been cut and peeled back in fleshy strips, then pinned to his cheeks with steel pins. Most of his teeth had been filed into angular shapes, some pointed, others merely slanting. His upper gums had been opened to expose the pale bone beneath. A number of screws had been driven into his flayed jaws, and were attached by cables. The last two inches of his tongue – the lump he had felt in his throat – were missing completely. He watched as the leaking stump jerked obscenely back and forth like a severed snake. Around his mouth a contraption of polished steel had been fitted to function as an insane brace, a complex network of wires and springs, cogs and filaments. The skin beneath his eyes had turned black with the pummelling his mouth had taken.

'I know what you're thinking,' whispered Matthews. 'It's special, but not spectacular. You haven't seen the best bit yet. This isn't merely art, it's – kinetic dental futurism. Watch.'

Matthews reached up and turned a tiny silver handle on the left of Thurlow's jaw. The springs and wires pulled taut. The cogs turned. Thurlow's mouth grimaced and winked, the flaps of his lips contorting back and forth as his face was twisted into a series of wide-mouthed grins and tight sour frowns. On a separate spring, the end of his tongue flickered in and out of his own ear. The pain was unbearable. Fresh wounds tore in his gums and cheeks as the mechanism yanked his mouth into an absurd rictus of a laugh. Matthews released his grip on the silver handle and smiled, pleased with himself.

'Is there somebody in there?' The receptionist was calling through the door.

'This stuff won't catch on for years yet,' said the dentist, ignoring the rattling doorknob behind him. He tilted the mirror from side to side before Thurlow's horrified face. Finally, he set the mirror down and released the restraining strap from the operating couch. Blinkered by the heavy steel contraption that had been screwed into his jaw, Thurlow was barely able to stand. As he tipped his head forward the weight pulled him further, and blood began to pour from his mouth. He wanted to scream, but he knew it would hurt too much to pull open his jaws without the help of the contraption. The receptionist began to bang on the door.

'Don't worry,' said the dentist, with a reassuring smile. 'It'll seem strange at first, but you'll gradually get used to it. I'm sure all my patients do eventually.' He turned around and looked out of the window. 'That's the beauty of these old buildings; there's always a fire escape.'

He unclipped the security catch on the casement and pushed it open, raising his legs and sliding through the gap. Blood smeared from his saturated trousers on to the white sill. 'I nearly forgot,' he called back as Thurlow blundered blindly into the door, spraying it with his blood. 'Whatever you do – for God's sake – don't forget to floss.'

His laughter echoed hard in Thurlow's ears as a descending crimson mist replaced his tortured sight.

Absence of Beast

GRAHAM MASTERTON

ROBERT KNELT ON the window seat with his hands pressed against the windowpane, watching the leaves scurrying across the lawn below him. The clouds hurried across the sky at a delirious, unnatural speed, and the trees thrashed as if they were trying to uproot themselves in sheer panic.

The gale had been blowing up all afternoon, and now it was shrieking softly under the doors, buffeting the chimney-stacks, and roaring hollow-mouthed in the fireplaces.

It was the trees that alarmed Robert the most. Not because of their helpless bowing and waving, but because of the strange shapes that kept appearing between their leafless branches. Every tree seemed to be crowded with witches and trolls and indescribable demons, their gaping mouths formed by the way in which two twigs crossed over each other, their eyes by a few shivering leaves which had managed to cling on, despite October's storms.

And at the far end of the long curving driveway stood the giant oak, in whose uppermost branches raged the monster that Robert feared above all. A complicated arrangement of twigs and offshoots formed a spiny-backed beast like a huge wild boar, with four curving tusks, and a tiny bright malevolent eye that – in actual fact – was a rain-filled puddle almost two hundred yards further away. But when the wind blew stronger, the eye winked and the beast churned its hunched-up back, and Robert wanted nothing more in the world than to take his eyes away from it, and not to see it.

But it was there; and he couldn't take his eyes away – any more than he could fail to see the blind Venetian mask in the tapestry curtains, or the small grinning dog in the pattern of the cushions, or the scores of purple-cloaked strangers who appeared in the wallpaper, their backs mysteriously and obdurately turned to the world of reality. Robert lived among secret faces, and living patterns, and inexplicable maps.

He was still kneeling on the window seat when his grandfather came into the room, with a plate of toast and a glass of cold milk. His grandfather sat beside him and watched him for a long time without saying anything, and eventually reached out with a papery-skinned hand and touched his shoulder, as if he were trying to comfort him.

'Your mother rang,' said his grandfather. 'She said she'd try to come down tomorrow afternoon.'

Robert looked at his grandfather sideways. Robert was a thin, pale boy, with an unfashionably short haircut, and protruding ears, and a small, finely featured face. His eyes shone pale as agates. He wore a grey school jumper and grey shorts and black lace-up shoes.

'I brought you some toast,' said his grandfather. White-haired, stooped; but still retaining a certain elegance. Anybody walking into the library at that moment would have realized at once that they were grandfather and grandson. Perhaps it was the ears. Perhaps it was more than that. Sometimes empathy can skip a generation: so that young and old can form a very special closeness, a closeness that even mothers are unable to share.

Robert took a piece of toast and began to nibble at one corner.

'You didn't eat very much lunch, I thought you might be hungry,' his grandfather added. 'Oh, for goodness' sake don't feel guilty about it. I don't like steak-and-kidney pie either, especially when it's all kidney and no steak, and the pastry's burned. But cook will insist on making it.'

Robert frowned. He had never heard an adult talking about food like this before. He had always imagined that adults liked everything, no matter how disgusting it was. After all, they kept telling *him* to eat fish and cauliflower and kidney beans and fatty lamb, even though his gorge rose at the very sight of them. His mother always made him clear his plate, even if he had to sit in front of it for hours and hours after everybody else had finished, with the dining-room gradually growing darker and the clock ticking on the wall.

But here was his grandfather not only telling him that steak-and-kidney pie was horrible, but he didn't have to eat it. It was extraordinary. It gave him the first feeling for a long time that everything might turn out for the better.

Because, of course, Robert hadn't had much to be happy about – not since Christmas, and the Christmas Eve dinner party. His father had raged, his mother had wept, and all their guests had swayed and murmured in hideous embarrassment. Next morning, when Robert woke up, his mother had packed her suitcases and gone, and his grandfather had come to collect him from home. He had sat in his grandfather's leather-smelling Daimler watching the clear raindrops trickle indecisively down the windscreen, while his father and his grandfather had talked in the porch with an earnestness that needed no subtitles.

'You probably haven't realized it, but for quite a long time your mother and father haven't been very happy together,' his grandfather had told him, as they drove through Pinner and Northwood in the rain. 'It just happens sometimes, that people simply stop loving each other. It's very sad, but there's nothing that anybody can do about it.'

Robert had said nothing, but stared out at the rows of suburban houses with their wet orange-tiled roofs and their mean and scrubby gardens. He had felt an ache that he couldn't describe, but it was almost more than he could bear. When they stopped at the Bell on Pinner Green so that grandfather could have a small whisky and a sandwich, and Robert could have a Coca-Cola and a packet of crisps, there were tears running down his cheeks and he didn't even know.

He had now spent almost three weeks at Falworth Park. His great-grandfather had once owned all of it, the house and farm and thirty-six acres; but death duties had taken most of it, and now his grandfather was reduced to living in eight rooms on the eastern side of the house, while another two families occupied the west and south wings.

'You're not bored, are you?' his grandfather asked him,

as they sat side by side on the window seat. 'I think I could find you some jigsaws.'

Robert shook his head.

'You've been here for hours.'

Robert looked at him quickly. 'I like looking at the trees.'

'Yes,' said his grandfather. 'Sometimes you can see faces in them, can't you?'

Robert stared at his grandfather with his mouth open. He didn't know whether to be frightened or exhilarated. How could his grandfather have possibly known that he saw faces in the trees? He had never mentioned it to anybody, in case he was laughed at. Either his grandfather could read his mind, or else—

'See there?' his grandfather said, almost casually, pointing to the young oaks that lined the last curve of the driveway. 'The snarl-cats live in those trees; up in the high branches. And the hobgobblings live underneath them; always hunched up, always sour and sly.'

'But there's nothing there,' said Robert. 'Only branches.'

His grandfather smiled, and patted his shoulder. 'You can't fool me, young Robert. It's what you see *between* the branches that matters.'

'But there's nothing there, not really. Only sky.'

His grandfather turned back and stared at the trees. 'The world has an outside as well as an inside, you know. How do I know you're sitting here next to me? Because I can see you, because you have a positive shape. But you also have a *negative* shape, which is the shape which is formed by where you're *not*, rather than where you are.'

'I don't understand,' Robert frowned.

'It's not difficult,' his grandfather told him. 'All you have to do is look for the things that aren't there, instead of the things that are. Look at that oak tree, the big one, right at the end of the driveway. I can see a beast in that oak tree, can't you? Or rather, the negative shape of a beast. An *absence* of beast. But in its own way, that beast is just as real as you are. It has a recognizable shape, it has teeth and claws. You can see it. And if you can see it . . . how can it be any less real than you are?'

Robert didn't know what to say. His grandfather sounded so matter-of-fact. Was he teasing him, or did he really mean it? The wind blew and the rain pattered against the window, and in the young oaks close to the house the snarl-cats swayed in their precarious branches and the hunched hobgobblings shuffled and dodged.

'Let me tell you something,' said his grandfather. 'Back in the 1950s, when I was looking for minerals in Australia, I came across a very deep ravine in the Olgas in which I could see what looked like copper deposits. I wanted to explore the ravine, but my Aborigine guide refused to go with me. When I asked him why, he said a creature lived there – a terrible creature called Woolrabunning, which means "You were here but now you have gone away again".

'Well, of course I didn't believe him. Who would? So late one afternoon I went down into that ravine alone. It was very quiet, except for the wind. I lost my way, and it was almost dark when I found the markers that I had left for myself. I was right down at the bottom of the ravine, deep in shadow. I heard a noise like an animal growling. I looked up, and I *saw* the creature, as clearly as I can see you. It was like a huge wolf, except that its head was larger than a wolf, and its shoulders were heavier. It was formed not from flesh or fur but entirely from the sky in between the trees and the overhanging rocks.'

Robert stared at his grandfather, pale faced. 'What did you do?' he whispered.

'I did the only thing I could do. I ran. But do you know something? It chased me. I don't know how, to this day. But as I was scaling the ravine, I could hear its claws on the rocks close behind me, and I could hear it panting, and I swear that I could feel its hot breath on the back of my neck.

'I fell, and I gashed my leg. Well . . . I don't know whether the Woolrabunning gashed my leg, or whether I cut it on a rock or a thorn-bush. But look . . . you can judge for yourself.'

He lifted his left trouser-leg and bared his white, skinny calf. Robert leaned forward, and saw a deep bluish scar that ran down from his knee, and disappeared into the top of his Argyle sock.

'Thirty stitches, I had to have in that,' said his grandfather. 'I was lucky I didn't bleed to death. You can touch it if you want to. It doesn't hurt.'

Robert didn't want to touch it, but he stared at it for a long time in awe and fascination. *Not a beast*, he thought to himself, *but an absence of beast. Look for the things that aren't there, rather than the things that are.*

'Do you know what my guide said?' asked his grandfather. 'He said I should have given the Woolrabunning something to eat. Then the blighter would have left me alone.'

The next day, after lunch, Robert went for a walk on his

own. The gale had suddenly died down, and although the lawns and the rose-gardens were strewn with leaves and twigs, the trees were silent and frigidly still. Robert could hear nothing but his own footsteps, crunching on the shingle driveway, and the distant echoing rattle of a train.

He passed the two stone pillars that marked the beginning of the avenue. There was a rampant stone lion on each of them, with a shield that bore a coat of arms. One of the lions had lost its right ear and part of its cheek, and both were heavily cloaked in moss. Robert had always loved them when he was smaller. He had christened them Pride and Wounded. They had been walking between them – his mother, his father, and him – when his mother had said to his father, 'All you worry about is your wounded pride.' Then he had learned at nursery school that a group of lions is called a pride, and somehow his mother's words and the lions had become inextricably intermingled in his mind.

He laid his hand on Wounded's broken ear, as if to comfort him. Then he turned to Pride, and stroked his cold stone nose. If only they could come alive, and walk through the park beside him, these two, their breath punctuating the air in little foggy clouds. Perhaps he could train them to run and fetch sticks.

He walked up the avenue alone. The snarl-cats perched in the upper branches of the trees, watching him spitefully with leaf-shaped eyes. The hobgobblings hid themselves in the crooks and crotches of the lower branches. Sometimes he glimpsed one of them, behind a tree trunk, but as soon as he moved around to take a closer look, of course the hobgobbling had vanished; and the shape that had formed its face had become something else altogether, or just a pattern, or nothing at all.

He stopped for a while, alone in the park, a small boy in a traditional tweed coat with a velvet collar, surrounded by the beasts of his own imagination. He felt frightened: and as he walked on, he kept glancing quickly over his shoulder to make sure that the snarl-cats and the hobgobblings hadn't climbed down from the trees and started to sneak up behind him, tip-toeing on their claws so that they wouldn't make too much of a scratching noise on the shingle.

But he had to go to the big oak, to see the hump-backed creature that dominated all the rest – the Woolrabunning of Falworth Park. You were here, and now you have gone again. But all the time you're still here, because I can see the shape of you.

At last the big oak stood directly in front of him. The hog-like beast looked different from this angle, leaner, with a more attenuated skull. *Meaner*, if anything. Its hunched-up shoulders were still recognizable, and if anything its jaws were crammed even more alarmingly with teeth. Robert stood staring at it for a long time, until the gentle whisper of fresh-falling drizzle began to cross the park.

'Please don't chase after me,' said Robert, to the beast that was nothing but sky-shaped in the branches of a tree. 'Here . . . I've brought you something to eat.'

Carefully, he took a white paper napkin out of his coat pocket, and laid it in the grass at the foot of the oak. He unfolded it, to show the beast his offering. A pork chipolata, smuggled from lunch. Pork chipolatas were his favourite, especially the way that grandfather insisted they had to be cooked, all burst and crunchy and overdone, and so Robert was making a considerable sacrifice.

'All hail,' he said to the beast. He bowed his head. Then he turned around and began to walk back to the house, at a slow and measured pace.

This time, he didn't dare to turn around. Would the beast ignore his offering, and chase after him, the way that the Woolrabunning had chased after grandfather, and ripped his leg? Should he start running, so that he would at least have a chance of reaching the house and shutting the door before the beast could catch up with him? Or would that only arouse the beast's hunting instincts, and start him running, too?

He walked faster and faster between the trees where the snarl-cats lived, listening as hard as he could for the first heavy loping of claws. Soon he was walking so fast that to all intents and purposes he was running with his arms swinging and his legs straight. He hurried between Pride and Wounded, and it was then that he heard the shingle crunching behind him and the soft deep roaring of—

A gold-coloured Jaguar XJS, making its way slowly towards the house.

Because of the afternoon gloom, the Jaguar had its headlights on, so that at first it was impossible for Robert to see past the dazzle and make out who was driving. Then the car swept past him, and he saw a hand waving, and a familiar smile, and he ran behind it until it had pulled up beside the front door.

'Mummy!' he cried, as she stepped out of the passenger-seat. He flung his arms around her waist and held her tight. She felt so warm and familiar and lovely that he could scarcely believe that she had ever left him.

She ruffled his hair and kissed him. She was wearing a coat with a fur collar that he hadn't ever seen her wearing before, and she smelled of a different perfume. A rich lady's perfume. She had a new brooch, too, that sparkled and scratched his cheek when she bent forward to kiss him.

'That was a funny way to run,' she told him. 'Gerry said you looked like a clockwork soldier.'

Gerry?

'This is Gerry,' said his mother. 'I brought him along so that you could meet him.'

Robert looked up, frowning. He sensed his mother's tension. He sensed that something wasn't quite right. A tall man with dark combed-back hair came around the front of the car with his hand held out. He had a sooty-black three o'clock shadow and eyes that were bright blue like two pieces of Mediterranean sky cut out of a travel-brochure.

'Hallo, Robert,' he said, still holding his hand out. 'My name's Gerry. I've heard a lot about you.'

'Have you?' swallowed Robert. He glanced at his mother for some sort of guidance, some sort of expla-nation; but all his mother seemed to be capable of doing was smiling and nodding.

'I hear you're keen on making model aeroplanes,' said Gerry.

Robert blushed. His aeroplane models were very private to him: partly because he didn't think that he was very good at making them (although his mother always thought he was, even when he stuck too much polystyrene cement on the wings, or broke the decals, or stuck down the cockpit canopy without bothering to paint the pilot.) And partly because – well – they were *private*, that's all. He couldn't understand how Gerry could have known about them. Not unless his mother had told Gerry almost everything about him.

Why would she have done that? Who was this 'Gerry'? Robert had never even seen him before, but 'Gerry' seemed to think that he had a divine right to know all about Robert's model aeroplanes, and drive Robert's mother around in his rotten XJS, and behave as if he practically owned the place.

Robert's grandfather came out of the house. He was wearing his mustard Fair Isle jumper. He had an odd look on his face that Robert had never seen before. Agitated, ill-at-ease, but defiant, too.

'Oh, *Daddy*, so marvellous to see you,' said Robert's mother, and kissed him. 'This is Gerry. Gerry – this is Daddy.'

'Sorry we're early,' smiled Gerry, shaking hands. 'We made *much* better time on the M40 than I thought we would. Lots of traffic, but fairly fast-moving.'

Robert's grandfather stared at the XJS with suspicion and animosity. 'Well, I expect you can travel quite quickly in a thing like that.'

'Well, it's funny, you know,' said Gerry. 'I never think of her as a "thing". I always think of her as a "she". '

Robert's grandfather looked away from the XJS and (with considerable ostentatiousness) didn't turn his eyes towards it again. In a thin voice, almost as if he were speaking to himself, he said, 'A thing is an "it" and only a woman is a "she". I've always thought that men who lump women in with ships and cars and other assorted junk deserve nothing more than ships and cars and other assorted junk.'

'Well,' flustered Gerry. '*Chacun à son goût.*' At the same time, he gave Robert's mother one of those looks which meant, *You said he was going to be difficult. You weren't joking, were you?* Robert's mother, in return, shrugged and tried bravely to look as if this wasn't going to be the worst weekend in living memory. She had warned Gerry, after all. But Gerry had insisted on 'meeting the sprog, and grandad, too . . . it all comes with the territory'.

Robert stood close to the Jaguar's boot as Gerry tugged out the suitcases.

'What do you think of these, then?' Gerry asked him. 'Hand-distressed pigskin, with solid brass locks. Special offer from Diner's Club.'

Robert sniffed. 'They smell like sick.'

Gerry put down the cases and closed the boot. He looked at Robert long and hard. Perhaps he thought he was being impressive, but Robert found his silence and his staring to be nothing but boring, and looked away, at Wounded and Pride, and thought about running beside them through the trees.

'I *had* hoped that we could be friends,' said Gerry.

Friends? How could we be friends? I'm nine and you're about a hundred. Besides, I don't want any friends, not at the moment. I've got Wounded and Pride and grandfather, and mummy, too. Why should I want to be friends with you?

'What about it?' Gerry persisted. 'Friends? Yes? Fan-ites?'

'You're too old,' said Robert, plainly.

'What the hell do you mean, too old? I'm thirty-eight.

41

I'm not even forty. Your mother's thirty-six, for God's sake.'

Robert gave a loud, impatient sigh. 'You're too *old* to be friends with me, that's what I meant.'

Gerry hunkered down, so that his large sooty-shaven face was on the same level as Robert's. He leaned one elbow against the XJS with the arrogance of ownership, but also to stop himself from toppling over. 'I don't mean that sort of friends. I mean friends like father and son.'

Robert was fascinated by the wart that nestled in the crease in Gerry's nose. He wondered why Gerry hadn't thought of having it cut off. Couldn't he see it? He must have seen it, every morning when he looked in the mirror. It was so warty. If *I* had a wart like that, I'd cut it off myself. But supposing it bled for ever, and never stopped? Supposing I cut it off, and nothing would stop the blood pumping out? What was better, dying at the age of nine, or having a wart as big as Gerry's wart for ever and ever?

'Do you think that's possible?' Gerry coaxed him.

'What?' asked Robert, in confusion.

'Do you think that could be possible? Do you think that you could try to do that for me? Or at least for your mother, if not for me?'

'But mummy hasn't got a wart.'

It seemed for a moment as if the whole universe had gone silent. Then Robert saw Gerry's hand coming towards him, and the next thing he knew he was lying on his side on the shingle, stunned, seeing stars, and Gerry was saying in an echoing voice, 'I picked up the suitcase . . . I didn't realize he was there . . . he just came running towards me. He must have caught his face on the solid-brass corner.'

He refused to come down for supper and stayed in bed and read *The Jumblies* by Edward Lear. '*They went to sea in a sieve they did . . . in a sieve they went to sea.*' He liked the lines about ' *. . . the Lakes, and the Terrible Zone, and the hills of the Chankly Bore.*' It all sounded so strange and sad and forbidding, and yet he longed to go there. He longed to go anywhere, rather than here, with his mother's laughter coming up the stairs, flat and high, not like his mother's laugh at all. What had Gerry done to her, to make her so perfumed and deaf and unfamiliar? She had even believed him about hitting his face on the suitcase. And what could Robert say, while his mother was cuddling him and stroking his hair? *Gerry hit me?*

Children could say lots of things but they couldn't say things like that. Saying *Gerry hit me* would have taken more composure and strength than Robert could ever have summoned up.

His grandfather came up with a tray of shepherd's pie and a glass of Coca-Cola with a straw.

'Are you all right?' he asked, sitting on the end of Robert's bed and watching him eat. Outside it was dark, but the bedroom curtains were drawn tight, and even though the wallpaper was filled with mysterious cloaked men who refused to turn around, no matter what, Robert felt reassured that they never would; or at least, not tonight. The night was still silent. The Coca-Cola made a prickling noise.

Robert said, 'I hate Gerry.'

His grandfather's tissue-wrinkled hand rested on his knee. 'Yes,' he said. 'Of course you do.'

'He's got a wart.'

'So have I.'

43

'Not a big one, right on the side of your nose.'

'No – not a big one, right on the side of my nose.'

Robert forked up shepherd's pie while his grandfather watched him with unaccustomed sadness. 'I've got to tell you something, Robert.'

'What is it?'

'Your mother . . . well, your mother's very friendly with Gerry. She likes him a lot. He makes her happy.'

Robert slowly stopped chewing. He swallowed once, and then silently put down his fork. His grandfather said, uncomfortably,'Your mother wants to marry him, Robert. She wants to divorce your father and marry Gerry.'

'How can she marry him?' asked Robert, aghast.

There was a suspicious sparkle in the corner of his grandfather's eye. He squeezed Robert's knee, and said, 'I'm sorry. She loves him. She really loves him, and he makes her happy. You can't run other people's lives for them, you know. You can't tell people who to love and who not to love.'

'But he's got a wart!'

Robert's grandfather lifted the tray of supper away, and laid it on the floor. Then he took hold of Robert in his arms and the two of them embraced, saying nothing, but sharing a common anguish.

After a long time, Robert's grandfather said, quite unexpectedly, 'What did you want that sausage for?'

Robert felt himself blush. 'What sausage?'

'The sausage you sneaked off your plate at lunchtime and wrapped in a napkin and put in your pocket.'

At first Robert couldn't speak. His grandfather knew so much that it seemed to make him breathless. But eventually he managed to say, 'I gave it to the beast. The beast in the big oak tree. I asked him not to chase me.'

His grandfather stroked his forehead two or three times, so gently that Robert could scarcely feel it. Then he said, 'You're a good boy, Robert. You deserve a good life. You should do whatever you think fit.'

'I don't know what you mean.'

His grandfather stroked his forehead again, almost dreamily. 'What I mean is, you shouldn't let a good sausage go to waste.'

Not long after midnight, the gales suddenly rose up again. The trees shook out their skirts, and began to dance dervish-like and furious in the dark. Robert woke up, and lay stiffly listening – trying to hear the rushing of feet along the shingle driveway, or the scratching of claws against the window. He had a terrible feeling that tonight was the night – that all the snarl-cats and the hobgobblings would leap from the trees and come tearing through the house – whirled by the gale, whipped by the wind – all teeth and reddened eyes and bark-brown breath.

Tonight was the night!

He heard a window bang, and bang again. Then he heard his mother screaming. Oh, God! Gerry was murdering her! Tonight was the night, and Gerry was murdering her! He scrambled out of bed, and found his slippers, and pulled open the door, and then he was running slap-slap-slap along the corridor screaming *Mummy – Mummy – Mummy—*

And collided into his mother's bedroom door. And saw by the lamplight. Gerry's big white bottom, with black black hair in the crack; and his red, shining cock plunging in and out. And his mother's face. Transfigured. Staring at him. Sweaty and flushed and distressed. A sweaty saint. But despairing too.

Robert. Her voice sounded as if she were drowning in the bath.

He ran out again. *Robert*, his mother called, but he wouldn't stop running. Downstairs, across the hallway, and the front door bursting open, and the gale blowing wildly in. Then he was rushing across the shingle, past Wounded and Pride, and all the dancing snarl-cats and hobgobblings.

The night was so noisy that he couldn't think. Not that he wanted to think. All he could hear was blustering wind and whining trees and doors that banged like cannon-fire. He ran and he ran and his pyjama trousers flapped, and his blood bellowed in his ears. At last – out of the darkness at the end of the avenue – the big oak appeared, bowing and dipping a little in deference to the wind, but not much more than a full-scale wooden warship would have bowed and dipped, in the days when these woods were used for ocean-going timber.

He stood in front of it, gasping. He could see the beast, leaping and dipping in the branches. '*Woolrabunning!*' he screamed at it. '*Woolrabunning!*'

Beneath his feet, the shingle seemed to surge. The wind shouted back at him with a hundred different voices. '*Woolrabunning!*' he screamed, yet again. Tears streaked his cheeks. '*Help me, Woolrabunning!*'

The big oak tossed and swayed as if something very heavy had suddenly dropped down from its branches. Robert strained his eyes in the wind and the darkness, but he couldn't see anything at all. He was about to scream out to the Woolrabunning one more time, when something *huge* came crashing toward him, something huge and invisible that spattered the shingle and claw-tore the turf.

He didn't have time to get out of the way. He didn't have time even to cry out. Something bristly and solid knocked him sideways, spun him on to his back, and then rushed past him with a swirl of freezing, fetid air. Something invisible. Something he couldn't see. A beast. Or an absence of beast.

He climbed to his feet, shocked and bruised. The wind lifted up his hair. He could hear the creature running towards the house. Hear it, but not see it. Only the shingle, tossed up by heavy, hurrying claws. Only the faintest warping of the night.

He couldn't move. He didn't dare to think what would happen now. He heard the front door of the house racketing open. He heard glass breaking, furniture falling. He heard banging and shouting and then a scream like no scream that he had ever heard before, or ever wanted to hear again.

Then there was silence. Then he started to run.

The bedroom was decorated with blood. It slid slowly down the walls in viscous curtains. And worse than the blood were the torn ribbons of flesh that hung everywhere like a saint's day carnival. And the ripest of smells, like slaughtered pigs. Robert stood in the doorway and he could scarcely understand what he was looking at.

Eventually his grandfather laid his hand on his shoulder. Neither of them spoke. They had no idea what would happen now.

They walked hand in hand along the windy driveway,

between Wounded and Pride, between the trees where the snarl-cats and the hobgobblings roosted.

As they passed Wounded and Pride, the two stone lions stiffly turned their heads, and shook off their mantles of moss, and dropped down from their plinths with soft intent, and followed them.

Then snarl-cats jumped down from the trees, and followed them, too; and humpbacked hobgobblings, and dwarves, and elves, and men in purple cloaks. They walked together, a huge and strangely assorted company, until they reached the big oak, where they stopped, and bowed their heads.

Up above them, in the branches, the Woolrabunning roared and roared; a huge cry of triumph and blood-lust that echoed all the way across Falworth Park, and beyond.

Robert held his grandfather's hand as tight as tight. 'Absence of beast!' he whispered, thrilled. 'Absence of beast!'

And his grandfather touched his face in the way that a man touches the face of somebody he truly loves. He kept the bloody carving-knife concealed behind his back; quite unsure if he could use it, either on Robert or on himself. But he had always planned to cut his throat beneath the big oak in Falworth Park, one day; so perhaps this was as good a night as any.

Even when their positive shapes were gone, their negative shapes would still remain, him and Robert and the snarl-cats and the sly hobgobblings; and perhaps that was all that anybody could ever ask.

The Little Green Ones

LES DANIELS

HE NEVER KNEW who it was that he followed into the cemetery, much less why. His mind was on something else entirely as he wandered down the leafy London street, and evidently he had fallen into step behind some stranger, for when he looked up he was just inside the gate. He felt as if he were teetering on the edge of a dream. Behind him was a modern street, and he knew that if he turned his head he would see a photocopy shop with a bright orange sign, but in front of him was a shady expanse of ancient trees and weathered stone.

'The Public Are Permitted to Walk in the Cemetery Daily,' proclaimed a sign, as if it were the most natural thing in the world for people to stroll through rows of corpses for their pleasure, and in fact he saw figures in the distance, moving slowly through the autumn haze. He couldn't see their faces. He wondered what his friends in Phoenix would say if they saw him go inside himself; it certainly wasn't like him to be morbid, but somehow this spot aroused his curiosity. He felt that this was the real London, that the cars and television sets outside were

49

only a façade hiding something much less modern. Even the cemetery, apparently Victorian, was only a few layers deeper into the layers of disguise that covered something almost sinister in the city, something unutterably old.

He didn't like that, and he wanted to go home.

He had come on business, but there wasn't much business: he wouldn't have been walking around if someone hadn't cancelled an appointment. He didn't even have a room at the convention hotel: some mix-up had shunted him off to a dingy, dark place where the elevator creaked and his room was a box just barely big enough to hold a bed. He was beginning to think he didn't even care if franchises for Cowboy Bob's Bar-B-Q sprang up all over London or not. All that glass and plastic and concrete would be just another trick to fool the eye; the real London stretched out before him.

He stepped through the stone arch in the wall and went into the cemetery. It was quiet, and so big he couldn't see the end of it. Dead leaves littered the pathway, crunching unpleasantly under his feet, but there was still green in the trees overhead. He noticed a squirrel fleeing frantically from his intrusion, and scrambling up the side of a small mausoleum. The motion drew his eyes to the words 'Devoted and Gentle Son', and to the pale stone face of a youth beside them. He looked to be about twenty, but his countenance was blackened in spots by time, especially around the eyes. The sculpture was giving way to some sort of rot, like the decay that long ago had turned the face inside the tomb to putrid fruit.

He felt the first hint of a shudder, looked away, and saw the children. There were two of them, standing on the other side of the path, and they were green.

He realized almost at once that they were statues, but somehow he was not reassured. Both of them, the girl and the boy, were staring at him with that disconcerting directness which only small children can summon; they appeared to be about seven, and they had been made life-size. Except for their colour, which really was quite odd, they looked like figures from an antiquated textbook, a typical pair of typical children from several generations ago. The girl wore a dress that hung straight down from her shoulders to her knees; her shoes had little straps and there was a big bow in her short hair. The boy wore a sailor suit, complete with cap and kerchief; he had short pants and long stockings. They had their heads thrust forward, as if to increase the intensity of their gaze, and they had their arms behind their backs. They stood straight, almost at attention, yet time had tilted each one slightly away from the other, as if they might at any moment fall rigid to the ground. Their faces were earnestly expressionless.

He was only a few paces from the gate, yet in the presence of these little ones he felt terribly alone; he decided on the spot that he would not venture any further into the realm they seemed to guard. After all, he had no business in a graveyard anyway. Still, he stepped across the path to take a closer look at them. He couldn't quite resist the pull of these odd little figures, which seemed so commonplace and yet so horrible. Evidently someone's kids had died, and been commemorated in a fashion that was perhaps not in the best of taste, especially since the statues had turned green. He never would have contemplated such a thing if anything had happened to his two boys, who of course were safe at home, and certain to outlive him in any case. There was no connection with his family anyway; these really quite atrocious little figures were from another time and place.

The girl and boy stood watch over a slab of granite, conventionally grey and shaped somewhat like a coffin. There was an inscription on either side of it, and he discovered to his astonishment that the people buried here were a married couple who had died in middle age. She had given up the ghost in 1927, and he had followed her less than a year later. These were not the graves of children after all.

Then what was the significance of these little green ones who gazed at him so balefully, their loathsome, almost iridescent colour a match for the few leaves clinging to a tumorous old tree behind them? Why were they looking at him, and why was he looking back?

What weird sentiment had inspired these nasty little statues? Who had commissioned them? Was it some whimsical relative, or perhaps the grieving husband, who realized that his time was near and chose to commemorate their early days as childhood sweethearts? Had he killed himself to join her? Had he been hanged for killing her? And why were they so damned green?

It was a sickly, milky green, like lichen or moss, although it might have been oxidation if the things were made of metal. He could have found out easily enough, but he was damned if he was going to touch them. It was too easy to imagine them crumbling beneath his touch, held together by nothing but the strange stuff that encrusted them. Worse yet, his hand might sink into a mass of fungus. People thought green was the colour of life, but this was a festering life that fed on death.

He hurried away from there, hardly taking time to notice another sign beside the gate: 'Persons in Charge of Children Are Required to Control Them.'

His nerves were shot, no doubt. The trip wasn't going well, and he hadn't been sleeping much: jet-lag. But it was this city, too, and the whole country, really. It was on the wrong side of the world. The gravity was wrong here, and so was the light. He longed to be back in God's country, where things stood new and clean against a desert sky, where nothing was old and nothing was green.

On his way back to the hotel, he had to wait for a hateful and ridiculous traffic signal. Instead of an honest and direct 'WALK' or 'DON'T WALK', the electric sign displayed a slumped red figure to keep pedestrians immobile, and a strutting, glowing green figure when it was time to march. He stared at something green taking its first step and felt his eyelids twitch.

He was bone weary, no doubt about that, and he would be expected to perform like a happy salesman at the reception that was only a few hours away. He stumbled into his hotel, made his way to his room, locked the door behind him and fell into his little bed. He told himself he was taking a nap. After all, your health is more important. The room grew dark around him while he lay like a man who had been poleaxed.

Half asleep in his overpriced coffin, he heard a quiet voice, something between a groan and a sigh. It was right there in the cramped confines of his room. He jerked upright like an old-fashioned mechanical toy and peered into the twilight. Was someone there? Or had he made that noise himself?

He got up, more drained than ever, and turned on the

light. There was nothing to be seen, but the bathroom door was closed and he decided to leave it that way. He went out to the convention without bothering to shave or shower or change his clothes.

The party was noisier and stupider than he would have thought possible. He drank heavily and tried not to talk to anyone. A man got up on a table and took his pants down. The future of Cowboy Bob's Bar-B-Q was in his hands. Amazingly, nobody seemed to object. Even the English seemed crude and crass, oblivious to the verdant mysteries that slept beneath their soil. Christ, even Robin Hood had dressed in green. Was everybody blind?

He took a cab back to his hotel and wondered whether his wife was going to leave him. He was in London, but there wasn't even any goddam fog. He could see every landmark they passed, even Brompton Cemetery. The gates, thank God, were locked, and the little green ones safe inside – unless they'd been out for hours. Do you know where your children are tonight?

The cab dropped him off, and every building he could see around him was the work of men long dead. The sky was gigantic. Everyone was going to die, no matter what they did, and something small was going to come around the corner unless he got inside. Why was this happening to him? He hadn't done anything – he'd only looked.

He stood outside his room, so sure the little green ones were inside that he couldn't even bring himself to open the door. He thought about them for a long time, then said the hell with it and went inside, which was a reasonable plan since they didn't visit him until after he was asleep. It wasn't sleep, really, just the fitful snooze of the ageing and the afraid, but it was good enough until he

saw the kids again, their arms locked behind their backs
as if they were tied. They didn't reach out for him, and
they didn't come toward him; instead they went into the
bathroom and stood in the shower. They made no sound,
but all at once the silence seemed shrill, as if someone
had turned up the volume on an unplugged radio. The
boy and the girl waited under the running water, their
little faces bland and boring and reproachful, and the
green that covered them dribbled away, filling the tub and
overflowing on to the floor. It slopped toward him, while
the children, washed free of it, gave forth a blistering
white light that streamed into his eyes and woke him up.

It was sunlight, of course, and it was his last day in
London. All he had to do was survive this, and he would
be safe.

A phoney banquet at the big hotel. International food
franchise folks, eat this. It couldn't have been worse.
Everything was green.

He had walked past the cemetery on his way, and had
peered in for long enough to see the kiddies still standing
there, but he sensed that they were not through with him,
and every course he ate confirmed it. Watercress soup.
Avocado salad. Lamb with mint sauce, the green flecks
swimming up through the innocuous oil. Green beans,
potatoes sprinkled with parsley. Lime mousse for dessert,
and mints wrapped in green foil. It was all fucking green,
and he didn't eat much. Green Perrier bottles were all
around him, but he was slugging back cheap Scotch.

He ran for the plane.

Whatever it was that there was dropped behind him as
he soared into the sky, but not before he looked out of
the window and saw the whole accursed island spread out

below him. It was green, green from stem to stern, green for hundreds of miles in every direction, as far as the eye could see. An alien empire, drifting into insignificance. Christopher Robin's dead.

It was hard to shake them, of course. Their grave little features were engraved on each one of the peas in his plastic plate, and when the plane hit an air pocket he would see their small, sad faces.

They were gone, however, by the time he got to Phoenix, and Death was something that grew in the old world.

He told himself that, even when his wife showed up in a green rented car and asked him for a divorce. She had spent his money on green contact lenses, which transformed her eyes into something glassy, cold, and enigmatic. Maybe she was right, but how could fake and hate bring happiness? It was all nonsense, right up to the last moment, the land around him brown and clean and honest and American. The dead kids were a thousand, thousand miles away. There was nothing to remind him of them.

Dead was dead, and green was green, and that was the end of it.

Yet when his own children ran out to greet him at the door, he saw to his dismay that they were not alone.

Razor White

CHARLES A. GRAMLICH

SEPTEMBER 9TH   SUNDAY

HE CLIMBED TOWARD wakefulness through scarlet-tinted dreams, rising up to a morning sky that burned pink outside his window, like watermelon flesh. A hundred images cracked and ran as the dream period ended and heavy lids shuttered back over eyes that were yellow-brown scars in an otherwise pale face. The empty pupils dilated suddenly with pleasure as he slid from beneath sticky wet sheets and stood looking down, his body finger-painted red.

One hand slid up over the matted hair of his groin as he eyed the human shape that remained in the bed, the touching and the looking triggering the sharp sting of an almost painful arousal. His other hand went out to stroke the pearl and silver hilt of the knife that nailed the woman's head to the pillow. The blade was caught among shattered teeth and he tore it loose, spilling a sliver of dried tongue out on to the bed as the weapon came free of the open mouth. His lips dripped shadows as he smiled, as he reached in the candy jar on the bedside table and took out a handful of lolly drops. He chewed them hard, cracking and splintering their sweetness while he quickly relieved his tension with his fist.

The twice-desecrated sheets served as a nice shroud as he wrapped the body up and carried it down the steps to his basement. There, he selected a straight razor from the collection that he kept in an old army-surplus locker and used it to remove the dead woman's hair as close to the scalp as possible. The shaved head looked alien beneath the fluorescent lights and he turned away, preferring to remember the long and living blonde mane as it had looked spread out on the sheets while they fucked.

He slipped the cuttings into large Ziploc storage bags and slid them into the locker beneath the trays of razors and other utensils. He then used a hacksaw to take off the woman's hands at the wrists before carrying them over and nailing them to the wall beside the other three pairs. The blood that had dripped down from the sawn flesh had scrawled abstract images on the white plaster, and he stared for a while at the surreal designs before pulling a tarp down from the ceiling to hide them. He had often thought it was a pity that no one besides himself would ever see those paintings. Sometimes, he even fantasized about bringing one of the women down here and doing it to her while she shrieked at those red-tipped wings. But that was not how he hunted. He liked them all dewy-eyed with love when he laid them waste. He licked it up.

Cutting up the rest of the body was always difficult, though the heavy saws and cleavers that he had bought from a defunct slaughterhouse helped. Still, he was drenched with sweat by the time he had finished hiding the plastic-wrapped pieces beneath the false floor of the cellar. Some scattered throw rugs helped to cover the places where he had taken up the boards, and half a can of Lysol knocked most of the thick blood-scent out of the air. He knew that he was going to have to get more ventilation in here eventually, though.

There was a sink in one corner of the basement and he used it to wash up his tools before locking them away in the surplus trunk where they were kept. The soiled linens were left in the sink to soak while he went upstairs to shower, standing long in the heated water until it flushed the sweat and blood from his skin and carried it down the drain. The swirling of the pinkish fluid triggered his memory, and the sex and the killing played over and over in his mind, linked for ever by hippocampal threads. He would dream about the way that the soft flesh had parted from the bone.

SEPTEMBER 15TH   SATURDAY

For a week he had the dreams that he wanted. They fed him and warmed him, wrapping him up in soft lips and cool tresses, in bone and in blood. Across the years, there had been times when he felt that he could live for ever in the world that he created out of the murders. But the pleasure had always faded, worn down and swept away by the stresses of whatever job he held at the time and by his constant need to live well. Sometimes a killing fed him for months, sometimes only for days, but it had never been too long before he felt the need to hunt again. And the intervals between needs had been getting shorter and shorter of late. On Saturday evening, one week after his last kill, he dressed in a suit and tie and put the long knife away into the sheath that he had sewn beneath the arm of the jacket. Then he left to stalk, humming the tune to Moon River under his breath.

It was cool in Boston's Combat Zone but the hookers were out anyway in their silks and leathers. He passed them by for now, knowing that one of them would be an easy mark. He had money for a lure, and if he couldn't find anything better then he might have to use it on a whore. Normally, though, he didn't like to do hookers. They were too harsh, and sometimes too stoned or brain-burned to really know what it was that destroyed them. Some didn't even seem to care. He much preferred a sweeter prey, and they should all be unwary. After all, there had been no talk of killing. And he had only done four . . . here. Before that? Well, he had spent most of last year wandering through Mexico, until he tired of women with dusky skins. It was pale flesh that he craved now.

He turned down a side street, letting himself drift along the edges of the crowd that strolled, and walked, and drank. He bought beers himself occasionally, as camouflage, but he only sipped at them. Even though his mouth was dry he wanted his head clear. Once, he sensed someone following him and turned to see a tall youth approaching almost casually through the tourists. He slowed to a stop at an untenanted corner and slid a hand inside his coat. He even smiled and licked his lips as the man came by, but the would-be pickpocket read him for what he was and hurried on past, quickly disappearing among the other people on the street.

The corner lamppost made a convenient place to lean

as he closed his eyes and imagined what it would have been like, the knife going in beneath the soft pad of the waist and ripping upward. The terror in the thief's face would have been a nice taste of meat, and it would not have mattered that he had killed a man. He had killed them before, when the need had grown too great and there were no females about. Such was not the case here, however. There were enough women for his taste.

He pushed away from the post and walked on. Thoughts of killing the man had put an edge to his hunger, but that would only make the coming feast more pleasant. And on the next street over he saw her. She was not alone at first, though soon her companion had gone. He followed her for three blocks before he was sure that she was the one, older, late thirties perhaps, a little overweight. Such were always the best. They were often lonely and wanted so much to find a friend. He could be a friend. His throat constricted as he tried to swallow the laughter that bubbled up at the thought.

He moved in smoothly, a skill of long practice. Within fifteen minutes he had made her acquaintance. In thirty more he was her friend and had her laughing. Three hours later he slaughtered her in the midst of their sex. This time he did it from behind, driving the thin blade into the spinal cord at the base of the skull while her head was thrown back in ecstasy. She grunted and jerked, and he held her tight, feeling almost as if his cock were inside of her at two places, as if he were fucking her in two places at the same time. Then his own orgasm rippled his spine and he let go of the knife so that her head flopped forward to let the blood run out of her mouth. He withdrew from her body and pushed it away, falling back on the bed and gasping for breath. It was some time before he could sleep.

SEPTEMBER 16TH   SUNDAY AGAIN

Sunday morning came out of violent dreams that were his to enjoy. He woke from them reluctantly, rising and stretching until his joints snapped and popped. The woman in the bed with him was frozen and rigid, and, as with the others, he took her downstairs to be ruined in the cellar. He whistled while he sharpened his razors, but when he went to remove the hair he stopped, his fingers clenched in the thick mane. For the first time he noticed the black roots and realized that the woman was not a natural blonde.

No wonder she wanted the lights off, he thought.

He slammed her head down on the floor in anger and kicked at the inert body until it rocked like a sack of feed. All his work wasted. *Wasted!* He did not like being fooled. He'd have to hide her. *The bitch!* But he would put the whole damn pile of her under the ground, right down in the dirt where she belonged. He wouldn't even put her hands on the wall. And then he would show them. Even though the weekend was over and the hunting would be hard, he would show them. He waited only for the night to come before leaving the house.

The streets were more crowded than he expected and he was pleased at first. It made him think that it was going to be easy, but he found out it was not. Most of the women he saw were with someone, and the one or two that he made attempts at did not bite. It angered him that his charm was failing. It had never done so before. But maybe the hunger was too apparent in his eyes, or maybe there was something else making them wary.

It was almost like the times when his mother used to go out and scare away the local cats and dogs that came to the garbage pile out back of their house. She only did it so that his daddy couldn't play with them. She had never liked daddy's idea of fun, the hot-peppered eggs and the fish-hooked pieces of meat. She had certainly hated it when her son joined in, at daddy's urging. But daddy had taken momma out at the end. And he could remember himself as a little boy watching the holiness of his father's face during the swinging, and the swinging, and the swinging. He remembered even better the hard candy that daddy had given him afterward, the pieces all sweet and sugary, and at the same time all red and sticky. He wanted some of it now, and something else for the electric dampness between his legs.

At last, in desperation, he approached a blonde prostitute who lounged at the foot of a stairwell in metallic gold shorts and a silken gold shirt that was tied up around her midriff. She had not been there before, or else his hunt would have been over earlier. Despite his aversion to hookers, this one was too lovely to pass up. Her hair was heavy and thick, hanging pure and pale to the shoulders, and her eyes were green, the exact shade of emerald that he loved. It was almost hard for him to believe that such a beautiful woman could be a street-whore, but the look that she gave him when he mentioned money left no doubt. His mouth began to dry up and his teeth started to ache. It was all he could do not to touch himself. He wanted this one badly, and he knew that he could have her as he reached for his wallet.

'How about my sister?' the little minx interjected, as she saw the flash of green that filled his palm. She put out a hand to toy with his tie. 'The two of us are nearly as cheap as one.'

'What sister?' he asked.

The woman gestured to the shadows within the stairwell behind her and a second whore stepped out. She seemed identical to the first, except for being dressed in silver shorts and a silver blouse. They were twins and he had never done twins before. Even though they were hookers, even though they would be easy, the thought of killing them both was almost more than he could handle. His erection was so painful that he could hardly stand up straight, and he only nodded at their encouraging words and passed out his cash. He could scarcely wait until he could get them home and unwrap them from their pretty packages.

It wasn't for nothing that he had rented a house so near the Combat Zone, though, with the girls striding along beside him, it seemed to take for ever to cover the few short blocks to his place. He was sweating and shaking with impatience by the time he got his front door unlocked and ushered the two of them into the living-room. They wasted no time once they were there.

The whore in gold kissed him hard on the mouth and then slid down his body, pulling open his shirt and licking at the hair and sweat beneath. On her knees, she nuzzled her face into his crotch and tongued open the hard zipper of his pants. A red-nailed hand slid up across the sweep of fabric at his front and unsnapped his trousers. He sprang out at her and she took him into her mouth, hollowing her cheeks as she drew on him.

The second whore slid a tongue into his ear, lapping softly at the delicate whorls. The pink tip probed deeper as she pushed up behind him and ground her mons into his backside, her hands sliding down across his waist to toy with the place where his cock was going in and out through her sister's lips. He twitched and groaned, almost unable to believe the pleasure. But it was all too fast. In another moment he would come, and he had to finish it. He had to finish it now.

His hand slipped beneath his jacket and brought out the knife. His heart thudded with need. But before he could strike, both women had stepped back and away, suddenly out of reach. He blinked, then palmed the blade before either whore could see it and tucked it up inside his sleeve. Only then did he realize how cold his cock was outside the woman's mouth, and how much he wanted desperately to be back inside that warmth.

'What's wrong?' he asked. His voice was rough and vibrating, but the women heard the almost whining undertone that threaded through his words.

'It's all right. Nothing's the matter,' the one in gold said. 'We just don't want you to finish too fast, do we? Besides, I don't think your front curtains are voyeur-resistant, and I'd like to be where we can do anything we want without worrying about being watched.'

He nodded, knowing that he should have been the one to make that comment. 'The bedroom is upstairs,' he said.

Her lips pouted. 'How absolutely ordinary,' she said. 'Beds are much too conventional. What about . . . the basement!'

His heart skipped and a dim suspicion bloomed, only

to fade as the two sisters slipped the knots on their blouses and shook their breasts free of the tissue-thin silk.

'But it's dirty down there,' he said, making a half-hearted attempt to dissuade them.

'We know,' the golden one said, arching an eyebrow. 'We like it that way.'

She walked up close and took him into her palm, milking him as she tugged him forward. 'Come on,' she breathed. 'It'll be fun.'

He could do nothing but follow as she led him through the kitchen toward the cellar. Her sister had already opened the door ahead of them and the light was on. They went down the steps together, the three of them side by side. There wasn't a speck of dust on those stairs, nor anywhere in the basement, but neither of the whores made a comment. They were too busy taking off their clothes. He watched them, and, at the same time, watched the room around him. There was no sign of death in the place, no smell except for Lysol. The tarp over the wall completely hid the nailed-up hands, and the rugs on the floor lay just right over the loosened boards.

His eyes dilated. *Yes*, he thought to himself. This would be even better than upstairs. He could do it to them here, right on top of the other bodies that he had buried. And they would never know. Unless—Unless he told them just before taking them out. His smile might have seemed nice to those who didn't know what it meant.

The first whore, the one who had been dressed in gold, mistook his smile and went down on him again. Her sister lifted his left hand and started to lick and suck at the little pads of meat between his fingers. He didn't mind at all. It was the right hand he used to kill.

He palmed the knife just as a tooth nicked his erection. But what was a little pain compared to the pleasure to come? He glanced down, smiling, and she looked up from her knees to meet his eyes. Her face was glowing, the bare skin shining almost translucently beneath the fluorescent lights, just like his father's face when killing and his mother's face when dying. He watched her slide a hand across her breasts and up her throat, across her lips where their two bodies merged. He could see her tongue moving beneath the drawn skin of her cheeks and could hold himself back no longer. Her eyes widened as his come spurted into her mouth. His own eyes closed, for a second, and when they shuttered open again the knife was out where everyone could see it. Only, he didn't use it.

The woman had released him from her lips and was smiling at him, drooling his thick ejaculate as she grinned up at the knife in his hand. She replaced his cock with two of her fingers, with two fingers and then her whole fist. And she was tugging on something, her face suddenly spiderwebbed with cracks. His eyes screamed, and his mouth screamed, and his body screamed, as her hand went down her throat and pulled her face off from the inside.

Behind that face was another, and, when she pulled that one off, another. He saw women that he had killed – the chubby Texas teen, the Mexican banker's wife – but there were others, too many others that he had never seen, women, and men, and children, and animals, all of them dead. These weren't whores. They weren't even human. But he had a sudden knowledge of who they were, or, rather, what they were. He knew because they were telling him, because he could watch the images flashing on the inside of his retinas like the fast-forwarded frames of some horrid movie.

They wanted him to know, he realized. They wanted him to understand how they had been following him since his childhood, using him for a stalking horse and then helping themselves to his kills, and those of his father before him. He had thought his daddy killed only animals before killing his mother! He should have known better, and now he did as these things unfolded the story for him. The beatings and the sexual abuse had never been random, as they had seemed at the time. The candy had never been an afterthought. His daddy had been nurturing him along, but it had been these creatures that had filled the bottles with hatred. And now they wanted him to believe that he was finished, used up, a worn-out tool whose charm was fading and whose urges were increasingly hard to control.

He stopped screaming and lifted the knife. He would show them who was used up. He would show them what it took. All he wanted in the world was to drive that blade down through the top of the kneeling thing's skull, but she was faster than he was as she bent her head forward and bit off his cock.

The knife slipped from his right hand, and at the same time the second whore/thing dropped her pretence of humanity and began to feed his left hand and arm into the clashing daggers that had suddenly filled her mouth. The new pain was nothing compared to the first, however, and he was still looking down when the kneeling whore spat pieces of him out and opened the cavity of her face to the arterial stream that burst out at his waist. His arm gone, the second creature moved around to snap his spine with her hands, holding him up for a moment to bleed for her sister before dropping him on to the floor like a wet bag of groceries.

He was beyond screaming now, and beyond moving. He could no longer even feel the pain. But he could still see. The first whore/thing got up and walked over to the basement wall where she stripped away the tarp that had covered his trophies. She plucked out the nails with one finger and tossed a pair of dead hands across to her sister, keeping another pair for herself.

The being that had broken his back knelt down beside him with her pair. She kissed and licked them gently, and when they were completely covered with saliva, and with pearl-like strands of something else that had come up out of her throat, she slipped them over her own hands as if fitting on gloves. He watched as the dead fingers came to life and started to move, dancing and twisting like a bowl of eels. They jerked and leaped at the end of their new owner's arms, dragging her forward with their strength.

And then they were on his chest. He did scream again, even though he would have sworn that he had nothing left, and the hands crawled up under his skin like dried white razors. His eyes bulged as they tore into a lung and sliced downward into a kidney, bypassing the heart that thumped alone amid the white heaps of cracked ribs. The first whore had begun ripping up the boards underneath which he had hidden his victims, and the second got up and went to join her, leaving the hands buried inside of his body like dead birds. Only these birds were still moving, and digging swiftly deeper.

The blood that had been streaming out of him in a dozen places began to slow to a trickle, though that probably just meant he was dying. He found that he didn't care any more. In fact, he welcomed it. He watched one of the whores peeling the skin off a dead face and patting it into place over the void of her own features. He heard the two of them laughing and giggling over which piece to try on next, and he was grateful when his mind began to empty.

It wasn't so bad, he thought. *Not really. Bleeding to death doesn't take that long.*

But then, he wasn't quite dead yet. And it wasn't quite over either.

One of the creatures stepped on his cock where it lay like a discarded toy on the floor. He watched as she bent over and picked it up, and he saw a new awareness come into her eyes. He saw her slide the wet piece of meat up the long slope of her thigh and shove it root first into the hole she had been using for a vagina, and he saw the pink flesh seal up around it like the puckering of a wound. A few strokes of a hard-nailed hand and it was erect, harder on the body of a whore than it had ever been on him.

The second hooker came and kicked him over on to his belly, then carefully positioned his head so that he could watch as her sister knelt down behind him and pulled off his pants. He knew what they were planning to do, but that didn't mean he had to co-operate. He squeezed his eyes tightly shut as the thing moved up between his legs, and he was thinking about how a broken back would prevent him from feeling anything below the waist. He figured the bitches had finally outsmarted themselves there, and he almost smiled. They had made a mistake that neither he nor his daddy would ever have made. You didn't give the prey a way out of the pain.

At least that was what he figured for a moment, until the creature kneeling by his shoulders used her fingernails to rip off his eyelids and hold his head in place. Then he had to watch. And he found out that he could still feel some things, like the searing agony of a whore/thing's come spewing into his rectum, like the scraping of dead hands inside his body shell as they sealed off ruptured arteries and veins to keep him alive.

In the end though, when the thing had done with him and he had been nailed to his trophy wall and had his cheeks stuffed with sweets, his thoughts did not dwell on his pain. They were focused on the squirming movements inside his peritoneum as the dead hands curled up tightly and began to encyst. The whore/things had one more use for him, he realized. When the hands had gone inside his body they had been covered with strands of tiny beads that resembled pearls, but which he now knew to be eggs. And those eggs had just been fertilized.

Propellor

PETER JAMES

ROSEMARY CARPENTER HAD the first dream exactly one week before the trip to Switzerland.

In the dream a propellor was spinning towards her, dark and menacing, the blades thrashing through a swirling vortex of cloud, the sound of the engine a deafening, echoing roar. She tried to move but could not. She was paralysed, helpless as it loomed towards her.

Then she woke up. Ted snored beside her. The digital dial of the clock radio said 2.01 a.m. A faint red glow leaked out from it into the darkness. The sheets were clammy with perspiration and the underblanket was rucked up beneath her. Her nightdress was twisted like a tourniquet. She stared at the dark shapes in the room with frightened blue eyes.

When Ted has first mentioned the trip it had sounded great. A four-day sales conference in Montreux in Switzerland and the spouses were invited, all expenses paid. Ted would have to work in the mornings, but the afternoons would be free. They could stay on for the rest of the week, just pay the extra on the room and for their meals. Perfect. Perfect until he said that they would be flying.

She had said nothing, did not want to seem pathetic, did not want to be the only wife not to go. Besides, they couldn't afford a holiday abroad this year, so the trip would be ideal. Ted needed a break. They both needed a break. Ted's parents would take the children. Flying would be all right, she had done it before. Somehow she'd force herself to do it again.

She lay silently in the darkness and tried to put the dream out of her mind. Afraid of flying; it was natural she'd dream about it. Outside, the wind rifled through the dense midsummer foliage of the trees.

Rosemary had the same dream the following night. Except the propeller came closer. When she woke she was twisting and thrashing as she tried to escape from the spinning blades and Ted, poor, tired, drained Ted, grunted, then lapsed back into his droning snore. Her throat was tight and her mouth dry. Tiny pulses beat all over her body. Her ears were filled with a faint roar that might have been the distant motorway or the blood coursing through her veins.

In the current recession Digitech Software (UK) Ltd was making redundancies weekly. Ted was sales manager and worked hard, desperately hard. His recent bouts of temper that made her frightened to discuss anything with him were unlike him. It was his work, not letting up. Six days a week in the office, and most of his Sundays in his den at home, hunched over his personal computer, lower lip clamped beneath his upper teeth, hair flopped over his forehead, making brightly coloured building-block graphs on the screen, muttering to himself about vertical integration and product synergy.

He had stopped playing rugger Saturday afternoons, hardly noticed Tom and Alice, lost his good cheer and his sense of humour, and his skin had become pallid, his face drawn. The strain was killing him.

Rosemary wished she could be more help, wished she had a better-paid job, but she knew she was lucky to keep the one she had, as part-time clerk at the DSS, which enabled her to drop the kids off to school and pick them up again and take time off during their holidays, and she wished they could sell the house, get rid of the crippling mortgage and move back down to something easier to afford, like the tiny two up and two down at 12 Nursery Close where they had lived for the first three years of their marriage and been happy.

But Ted said the new house was important to make a good impression with his clients; and in any case, with the market the way it was they'd never get back what they paid for it. So they struggled on, Rosemary doing overtime, Ted trying to maintain his bonus target levels. It would get better soon, Ted said. The recession was ending, mortgage rates would be coming down again. Another year and they'd be laughing.

She dreamed the same dream again the third night running. The propellor came even closer. The fourth night it came closer still. Rosemary lay shivering at the image of the blade spinning in the darkness, the vortex of air thrashing her brown hair around her face, the sound deafening. Clear, so vivid. Not like any other dream. The dream was telling her something and she knew what it was.

Don't fly.

Ted used aeroplanes like buses. His work took him all over the world. He wasn't afraid of anything and that was one of the things she had first loved about him. He made her feel safe.

A breeze shifted the curtains. A vixen wailed in the woods beyond the garden fence. She had not flown since their honeymoon, when they had travelled to Greece. She had not admitted to Ted then her fear of flying, had not wanted him to think he was marrying a neurotic coward.

But she could still remember clearly how afraid she had felt as they took off from Gatwick airport in the pouring rain, afraid that they would die before they had even had their first night of married life together. She had been in a window seat just in front of one of the engines, and as the plane had climbed she had watched ghostly tendrils of cloud swarm around the cowling until they immersed it, shrouded it from her view as the silver plane drummed and vibrated and hauled itself up out of the rain up through the floor of a snowbound mountain range in the sky and out into the clear sun, and she'd been scared then, scared in the knowledge that soon they would have to descend back down through that cloud, scared of all the things that could go wrong and what it would feel like to know you were crashing, to know you were going to die. To know she was going to be apart from Ted for ever.

Flying was safer than driving, Ted had said when he saw the expression on her face as he told her they would be flying to Montreux. He assured her it was safer than boating or walking or travelling by rickshaw or bouncing along on a pogo stick and she had grinned and felt a little better and put the tickets and the passports safely together, and had gone out, and even though they were broke had bought a new swimsuit in a sale and a new pair of sunglasses, and water-resistant suntan lotion.

Tom and Alice were asleep in their rooms across the landing. Tom was four and Alice two. She thought about dying and being parted from them always and she swallowed, felt a lump in her throat and tried to think of good things, of nice things. When she had bad dreams as a child her mother always told her to imagine nice things.

Montreux was a nice thing. They were going to Montreux on Lake Geneva in Switzerland. Ted had shown her the brochure of the hotel and she had looked at the colour pictures and fallen in love with its baroque exterior, its old-fashioned grandeur, with the huge airy-looking bedroom (which the wording beneath, in three different languages, said was a typical room) with its deep bathtub and plump duvet and shuttered windows, and imagined breakfasting on rolls and croissants and thick jams and rich coffee on the balcony overlooking Lake Geneva.

She went back to sleep with the sensation of bright rays of sunlight through shuttered windows falling on her face and the taste of homemade apricot jam on her lips.

On the fifth night running that Rosemary dreamed of the propellor her scream woke Ted. He snapped on the bed-side lamp, grunting, confused as dazzling light flooded the room for a moment then faded into creamy pools between the shadows of the furniture.

'Wassermarrer?'

Rosemary closed her eyes and tried to think clearly. Her heart pounded inside her chest, a steady *boomf-boomf-boomf* like a boxing glove on a punchball. She swallowed. Her mouth floundered and her voice had to wait until she had caught her breath.

'I'm sorry,' she whispered, her ears popping the way they popped in a climbing aeroplane. Then she opened her eyes and the normality of the room was a comfort. The pink curtains brushed gently against each other with a listless sigh and she felt a breeze on her cheek and smelled the stale cigar smoke on Ted's sour, vinous breath.

'What is it, darling?' Ted picked up his watch and looked at it.

'A dream,' she said. 'I keep having the same dream.'

'About what?'

'Do modern aeroplanes have propellors?' she asked.

'Some.'

'The sort of passenger plane one would go to Switzerland in?'

'It would be a jet. They have turbines.'

'Are turbines like propellors?'

'Yes – sort of.'

'I don't think we should fly,' she said.

'Huh?'

'To Switzerland. I don't think we should fly.'

'For God's sake, darling – flying is—'

'I know. I know how safe it is. I keep having this – it's – it's – like a – premonition, I suppose.'

Ted sat up and sipped some water. His Tom Clancy novel fell on to the floor with a rustle of paper. 'You're frightened of flying – you're probably dreaming of it because you're frightened.'

'It's more than just a dream,' she said.

Ted put his arm around her. 'Love you,' he said and kissed her cheek.

'Love you,' she said, staring at the ceiling. A moth flitted past her face and she heard the beat of its wings.

Ted switched out the lamp and she lay in silence. A creature in the darkness outside shrieked for its life; pitiful squeals. Another shriek, then another, then one lingering terrible one. Then nothing but the *hiss-puff . . . hiss-puff* of Ted sleeping, and the drone as he began to snore.

The next night the propellor came again, closer this time, closer than ever before, and she screamed for Ted to help her and saw him tumble away, helplessly, falling through pink-tinged cloud, and she screamed again and he couldn't hear her, reached out, but could not touch him, trying to back away from the propellor, but could not move, felt it towering above her, below her, so close its vortex was sucking her in, pulling her into the blades that were like giant steel knives.

She screamed, screamed again, screamed again.

'OH JESUS!' Ted bellowed. 'I have a meeting at seven in the morning.' He snapped on the light.

Rosemary sobbed. 'Sorry. I'm sorry. I'm sorry.'

Ted held her gently.

'I can't go,' she said. 'I can't go if we have to fly. Even if we get there safely I'll spend the whole week worrying about flying home.'

'What about driving?' he said.

She nodded. 'Yes. OK. That would be OK.'

'No bad dreams about driving?'

'No.'

'No dreams about being hit by a truck or anything like that?'

She managed a weak smile. 'No.'

'We'll drive. Leave Friday afternoon, drive through the night, we'll get there the same time as the others flying out Saturday morning. How would that be?'

'That's going to seem really foolish.'

'I'll make something up,' Ted said. 'Tell them that I have clients to visit – that I need to take my car.'

'I'm sorry, Ted.'

'You really think something's going to happen to the plane?'

'Yes.' She hesitated. 'I mean – I don't know.'

'You want me to tell everyone at work not to fly?'

She was silent.

'You'd look pretty silly if nothing happened, wouldn't you?'

'Yes.'

'You don't know which plane? The one the group's taking out? Or taking back? Or the one we'd have been taking back?'

She saw the propellor in her mind again and shook her head.

They took a late ferry from Dover and drove in Ted's Ford through the night. They stopped at service stations and drank thick black coffee in tiny cups, and pulled into lay-bys and dozed a couple of times and they arrived in Montreux shortly before midday.

The hotel was like the pictures in the brochure, the

staff were dressed in sombre dark clothing and were courteous and a little old-fashioned, which Rosemary liked, and they were taken to a room on the fourth floor that was big and airy and had a balcony that looked straight on to Lake Geneva.

Kate opened the shutters and went out and leaned on the balustrading and stared at the slack, glassy water and a white ferry, way out in the distance, and the Alps through the heat haze beyond, and she blinked against the brilliant sunlight and looked down at a pontoon where small boats were moored on loose painters, and she heard the slap of water against the shore and smelled baking bread and yacht varnish and lesser snatches of oil and rust, and she felt Ted's arms slide around her, and she knew just from that gesture that he was already relaxing, and she felt good, it had been the right decision to come.

They went down to the lobby to see what was happening and a coach pulled up outside that had brought Ted's colleagues and their wives or husbands from the airport. The plane had arrived safely. She watched them all pouring out of the coach, cheerful, normal people with their cases and yellow duty-free bags. They'd had a good flight, a jolly time, and Rosemary felt foolish. But they still had to fly home. They still had that in front of them. She wondered again if she should warn them, go up to them, tell them, 'Look – I had a dream . . .'

But that would embarrass Ted. And she wasn't certain, now, wasn't certain at all.

They made love that Saturday night and woke on Sunday morning with the sun streaming in and made love again and had breakfast on the balcony wrapped in soft white towels with the name of the hotel embossed on them, ate warm brioches and croissants and homemade apricot jam and drank freshly squeezed orange juice and fresh coffee.

The sales conference ended at midday on Wednesday, and Ted suggested they had a picnic on the lake. They'd hire a rowing boat and go exploring, or maybe just drift around. While Ted and his colleagues went into the conference room for their final session, Rosemary went shopping, to a baker and a charcuterie and a patisserie, and bought crusty bread, ham, salami, tomatoes, and cheese, and *tarte au citron* and a bottle of wine.

The boat was a small blue and white clinker-built rowing boat with a number and the name, Hélène, hand painted on the prow, and it rocked precariously as she stepped in while Ted held it steady.

She watched the wake of bubbles, and sensed the small tugs of acceleration each time Ted pulled the oars. She leaned over and trailed a finger through the water and it was cold, much too cold to swim. Their own hotel and the rest of the hotels along the shore slowly grew smaller, and the lake which had seemed so flat from the shore had undulating waves that seemed to be getting larger the further out they rowed. She felt a prickle of anxiety. Felt very small out here in the tiny boat.

Then she looked at Ted and saw the happiness in his face. In the three afternoons they had spent together out here, his face had tanned, filled out a little, and his shoulders seemed to have broadened a little. He was beginning to look his normal strong self again.

Ted carried on rowing for a good half-hour, towards the mountains on the far side that did not seem to be getting any closer, although the hotel and shoreline of Montreux were now almost invisible through the thickening heat haze.

Ted shipped his oars, and lay back, Rosemary spread the towel she had borrowed from the room on the bottom of the boat, and laid the picnic out on it. She had borrowed their toothmugs for wineglasses, and filled Ted's up halfway for him.

They ate slowly, lazily, the boat rocking about, water slapping against the side, sometimes hearing the hum of a speedboat or a faint shout carried from the distant shores. Neither of them noticed that the haze was thickening into a mist. Not until Rosemary, who was wearing a thin white T-shirt with a picture of Donald Duck on the front, suddenly put her arms around herself and realized she was feeling chilly. A wisp of mist, like cigar smoke, curled past her face; the water had turned a bottle-green colour.

Ted removed his sunglasses and she saw a brief flicker of anxiety as he looked around. They were engulfed by mist, rolling like cloud towards them, swelling up the water that separated them from it, until it engulfed them completely and she was having trouble now in even seeing Ted.

She heard the thudding of her heartbeat; then she realized it wasn't her heartbeat, it was another sound, a drumbeat, *boomf . . . boomf . . . boomf . . .* Then the droning sound. It was faint at first, but getting louder. Ted heard it too, turned his face towards it, his expression stiffening.

It was the droning sound she had heard in her dream.

Getting louder.

Louder.

She tried to say something, but fear was pulling her scalp tight around her head and for a moment she could not connect her brain to her voice. Her mouth opened and shut. She tried to communicate with her eyes, tried to scream at him with her eyes.

The droning was getting louder.

'Row! Please row, Ted.'

He gave her a helpless smile. 'I don't know which way.' His own voice quavered, uncharacteristically, with anxiety.

'Just row! Please row!' she screamed at him.

The boat began to rock harder; water slapped angrily against the sides and droplets of spray struck her face. Something dark loomed through the mist, like the wall of a mountain moving towards them.

'Ted, please row!'

She heard roaring, thrashing, drumming. The water was erupting, boiling, livid white swirls. The dark wall was on top of them. Then an unseen fist slammed her face down into the water. She cartwheeled through bubbles.

Briefly above her she saw the top of the water and the sky beyond. Then the prow of the ferry slid over her like a shadow. She saw the green slime that was attached to its hull, and tendrils of weed trailing beneath like wet hair, heard the *thump-thump-thump* of its engine.

Then saw the propellor.

Like the propellor of an aircraft through cloud. Coming towards her. She turned, tried to move, saw Tom tumbling away from her, tried to scream, but water poured into her mouth. She twisted, tried to back away. It was coming closer. Dark, menacing, swirling, the huge blades spinning, bubbles exploding.

Closer.

Her head bumped along the hard, slimy hull. She tried desperately to push herself away with her hands but the propellor was sucking her in towards it, filling her ears with a deafening, resonating droning.

Closer.

She saw Tom's face, helpless, eyes wide open, reaching out towards her. Then he was torn away in a pink swirling cloud. The water all around her was pink, deepening in colour, turning to crimson. She reached again, tried to kick with her legs, but she couldn't make them work, couldn't feel them any more. She lunged with her arms, but they wouldn't move any more. She was sinking. Sinking down away from the hard, slimy hull, from the thrashing propellor, from the roar, the crazed bubbles.

Sinking clear. Safe. The propellor was getting further away, higher above her; she could see the entire hull of the ferry now, passing by above her; a crimson trail was rising up from her to greet it, like a coloured smoke trail.

It was fading now. The shadow of the hull of the ferry was fading. The ceiling of the lake above her was fading. She couldn't see the propellor any more. The crimson trail plumed upwards. She was safe down here.

She lay under the fresh white sheet, her eyes closed, her face peaceful. She was not dreaming now, had no more nightmares about propellors. She slept a long sleep that would remain undisturbed by dreams or the wind in the night or by fears of flying or dying.

The mortician pulled the sheet over her head and gave

one of the helpless shrugs he had given to so many people over the years. He was glad the woman's husband had not wanted to pull the sheet down any further. The propellor had struck her just below the rib-cage, making a clean cut through the centre of her body, leaving her intact from the chest upwards and pulping the rest of her body.

The frogmen had found the upper half of her torso resting on the bed of the lake near the remains of the boat. Of her lower half, they had only so far found her left foot, and a strip of flesh that looked like it was part of her thigh, and some intestines that were probably hers.

One of Ted's colleagues, whose name right now he could not even remember, put his arm around Ted's shoulder and led him slowly away. 'It would have been quick, Ted,' he said, 'if that's any consolation at all. The gendarme said she'd never even have known what hit her.'

They Take

JOHN BRUNNER

'ARE YOU SURE we're going the right way?' demanded
Ann Bertelli. Strictly she was Annunziata, but in the
trendy circles of Milan and Turin the shorter English
name was far more fashionable, like her sleekly coiffed
fair hair, her wraparound sunglasses, her brief clinging
frock and massy gold bracelets.

At the wheel of their Alfa Twin Spark, whose shiny red
paintwork was dull with dust, her husband Carlo snapped,
'It's the way you told me to take! You've got the map
Anzani sent us!'

'Who in his right mind trusts a lawyer?' Ann retorted.
'In his letter he described Aunt Silvana's estate as "fertile
and productive", but I can't imagine that being true of
any land in this area!'

Late summer sun beat down on the countryside. Either
side of the rough road crops bent their weary heads: beans,
maize, tobacco. In the distance they now and then saw
peasants at work, helped or hindered by balky donkeys
and scrawny oxen. More than once Ann had said this trip
was like travelling back in time – yet it wasn't as though

they were in the deep Mezzogiorno. Indeed, they were still well north of Rome!

Ahead lay a T-junction. Braking, wiping sweat from his forehead with the sleeve of his slub-silk jacket, Carlo demanded, 'Which way now? Right or left?'

And when she delayed an answer, trying to orientate the photocopied sketch-map that was their only guide, he went on savagely, 'When I think that but for your damned aunt we could have spent the rest of our fortnight in Nice—'

'Getting off with that German girl you had your eye on?' murmured Ann.

'Oh my God!' Carlo shifted out of gear and applied the handbrake. 'We're not going to have another fit of jealousy, are we?'

Ann raised her head and glanced around. 'Not right now,' she replied composedly, pointing through the dusty windscreen. 'Later if you like . . . But what about that?'

Fallen from its post, a white on blue sign lay among dry yellow grass, spattered with rust-marks as if it had been used for target practice. But the name Bolsevieto was just legible, and its arrow-shaped end pointed right.

Annoyed at having overlooked it, Carlo spun the car's wheels in dust as he made the turn. From the corner of his mouth he said, 'What's the time?'

'Two hours later than it ought to be.'

'How the hell was I to know there'd be such a jam on the *autostrada*? A crash like that happens only—'

'It would have helped if we'd got away on time! We're only going to look my aunt's place over and you insisted on packing enough for a month in—'

'Oh, shut up! At least we're practically there.'

'There' – Bolsevieto – was a village of a hundred or so houses, plus outlying farms, encircled by a ring of low hills. The central square, where they were to meet Signor Anzani, was easy to find, for it was the only place the road led to. There was a church, of course; there were a few trees, a few shops, and a *bar ristorante* outside which stood iron chairs strung with red and yellow plastic.

And sitting on one of the chairs, looking distinctly bad-tempered, was a glum middle-aged man sweating in a black suit, with an empty glass and a briefcase on the table at his side. Parking the car, jumping out without waiting for Ann, Carlo strode over hand outstretched.

'Signor Anzani? I'm sorry we're late! There was a big crash on the *autostrada* – did you hear?'

The lawyer hoisted himself to his feet, forcing a polite expression that didn't really qualify as a smile.

'Ah, what is another couple of hours when you had to miss the funeral of your wife's aunt more than a week ago? You are Signora Bertelli?' – to Ann as she joined them. 'Charming, charming!' He bent to kiss her hand. But Carlo detected a transient frown of disapproval at her too-short dress.

There were few other people in sight: the waiter at the door of the bar; a blank-faced man of about thirty with a slack mouth and dirty clothes, possibly a village idiot – such creatures did still exist in remote areas like this – two elderly women in black who seemed to be complaining about the price of tomatoes, although their accent was so thick he couldn't tell whether it was the cost in a shop or what they were offered for their garden produce; and, glimpsed at opening shutters, people rising from siesta.

Those apart, there were no living creatures in view save

birds, flies and a couple of large, loose-limbed black dogs that now and then yawned to display their red maws, but showed scant interest in the arrival of strangers.

Yet he felt a sense of being under scrutiny, like an itch. As he and Ann accepted Anzani's offer of a drink he cast his eye around the square in search of its cause. The fronts of the houses – some of them once fine, now losing plaques of stucco, the ornamentation of their porches eroded by wind and weather – offered no clue. The façade of the church, on the other hand . . .

Yes, the church struck him as unusual, more French perhaps than Italian. It bore many carved faces, most of a style he would term demonic, up to its eaves and beyond. He turned to ask Ann's opinion. He himself was an ordinary commercial sort of person and earned his living selling whatever might turn a profit: formerly, food and furniture, at present life insurance. Ann, though, had graduated in the history of art and currently worked for one of the most prestigious galleries in Milan. Occasionally he felt a trifle envious of her broader knowledge.

But she was already riffling papers that the lawyer had produced from his briefcase, saying, 'Carlo darling, you ought to be looking at these. You're much more business-like than I am.'

Sighing, Carlo complied.

Yet there seemed to be no real need to consult him, for shorn of legal jargon her aunt's will said what had been summarized in Anzani's letter: she had become the owner of a run-down house, its contents, and a parcel of land. They had promptly reached an agreement to dispose of the lot, in spite of their frequent quarrelling – and why not? As the proverb put it, *L'amore non e bello se non e litigiello*. An occasional row lent spice to life. But it didn't have to affect genuinely important decisions.

He cut short the pointless conversation by suggesting that they ought to head for the house at once if they were not unduly to delay Signor Anzani. His office was not here in tiny, time-forgotten Bolsevieto, but the nearest town of any size, Matignano, eleven kilometres away.

Glancing gloomily at his watch, the lawyer nodded agreement, drained his glass, and rose.

So, to the second, did one of the dogs. He had been stretched out on the church steps. Now he jumped up, tail wagging, as the door swung open and a priest emerged in a black cassock and a broad-brimmed hat: a thick-set man, heavy boned, heavy jowled, clean shaven but with what Ann and Carlo had learned to call by the English name 'five o'clock shadow' in preference to that absurd American term 'designer stubble'.

By now, Carlo noticed, people had begun to appear on the street again. The opening of shutters at the end of the siesta had harbingered their emergence. Unlike the incurious dogs they stared at the outsiders, making him feel like a specimen under a microscope with a score of observers.

Yes: definitely it would be best to sell Ann's inheritance for whatever they could obtain. Small towns – town? Bolsevieto was at best a village! – got on his nerves.

Hers too, he imagined.

Elderly people, slow moving, crossed themselves on noticing the priest, who responded with a wave as, the dog at his heels, he headed towards Anzani. The two were clearly well known to one another. Each uttered a few phrases in a dialect too broad to follow. Then Anzani addressed the Bertellis in a formal tone.

'As possible future residents of our community, you should be introduced to Father Maru.'

Ann and Carlo exchanged glances on hearing the peculiar name, but forbore to comment. Presumably it was a local pronunciation of Mario, conceivably still influenced by the Latin Marius after all these centuries.

Its bearer, with an expression appropriate for meeting people who had so recently lost a relative, shook their hands, regretted that they had been unable to attend their aunt's funeral, and said he would expect them at Mass next Sunday (*Fat chance!* freethinker Carlo married to a freethinker growled to himself). Then he tried to present his dog, who turned out to be called Ercle. But the animal's only response was another yawn.

To Carlo's surprise, and somewhat to his annoyance also, for he was anxious to avoid more delay, Ann reacted on hearing the dog's name. 'That's unusual!' she exclaimed. 'Isn't it the Etruscan for Hercules?'

'Why, indeed it is!' the priest beamed. 'But I assure you it's not unusual hereabouts. We are, after all, on the terrain of Etruria, are we not? You'll find many survivals of that sort. The very name of our *paese*' – he used the word that means both village and country – 'is half Etruscan: the same root that one finds in Volsci, plus the Latin for old. There are many ancient patronymics here, as well. Have you visited your aunt's grave? No? Well, I have half an hour to spare. If you like I can take you to it now and show you what I mean on the way.'

'I'm sure that would be very interesting,' Carlo said hastily. 'But we shouldn't detain Signor Anzani too long.'

'No, of course not,' Father Maru granted. 'Well, doubtless there will be another chance.'

With visible relief the lawyer stumped towards his car, a sober dark blue Fiat, instructing them to follow.

As Carlo was starting up Ann said thoughtfully, 'I think that priest has an Etruscan name, too.'

'What?' – swinging into the wake of the Fiat.

'Maru. You assumed it was a variant of Marius at first, didn't you? So did I. Now I suspect it's much older.'

'Since when do you know so much about Etruscan?'

'Since last year when we held an exhibition of Etruscan art,' she retorted. 'I wrote the notes for the catalogue, remember?'

Embarrassed at having forgotten, Carlo said, 'So what does Maru mean?'

'I'm not sure – I don't think anybody is – but either priest or magistrate, maybe both. Back in those days there wasn't much distinction between religious and civil office.'

Carlo said nothing further for the time being. Now they were out of the village Anzani, more familiar with the area and perhaps less concerned about damage to his car, was setting a fast pace along a rough and stony track, and he was having trouble keeping up without being blinded by the clouds of dust.

Aunt Silvana's former home was a typical farmhouse of the region, its roof of tiles unaltered in design since Roman times, its walls of hollow bricks covered with flaking stucco and partly masked by a sprawling vine. Chickens were scratching around a disused well in what passed for its front garden; near by a donkey brayed; there was a noticeable odour of goat; sweet peppers and tomatoes were laid out to dry in the sun. An elderly woman clad in black, her face lined, her hands gnarled, several of her teeth missing, awaited them at its door with the timeless patience of one to whom clocks were still a novelty. Emerging from his car, Anzani gave her a curt greeting, and would have gone on to introduce Ann and Carlo but that she interrupted.

'Ah, so you are Signora Silvana's niece. I don't need to be told. There is something about your eyes. One can tell your ancestors hailed from our *paese*.' Her voice, though wheezy, was clear and easy to understand despite a trace of the regional accent they had heard in Bolsevieto. 'And you, *signore*, must be her husband. Welcome! Please call me Giuseppina. I am used to it. Sometimes I almost forget I have another name. Come, let me show you to the room I have prepared.'

Ann and Carlo exchanged glances. They had been planning to return to Bolsevieto, or even Matignano, for the night. Ann turned to the lawyer intending to say as much, but he forestalled her.

'You'll lodge better here than at the *albergo* in Bolsevieto,' he grunted. 'And in a cleaner bed, most like. Besides, the property is an extensive one. You'll need to take your time inspecting it . . . Oh! Before I forget!'

He strode back to his car, leaned in, and reached for something on the back seat. Returning, he held out to Carlo a bottle of Asti Spumante.

'A token to mark your arrival,' he said. 'Well, now I must leave you. There's no phone here, I'm afraid, but you have my number and if you need any more information you can ring me from the bar where we met. *Signora – signore –* Giuseppina *– a rivederci.*'

The abruptness of his departure left them astonished. Not until his car was a hundred metres down the lane did Ann murmur to her husband, 'He could at least have made it champagne.'

Not only was there no phone; there was no electricity, water came from a spring on the hillside – here they were just below the high ground that encircled Bolsevieto – and the outside privy was so noisome Ann declared her intention of hiding behind a bush rather than make use of it. But the huge brass-framed bed was indeed clean, and looked rather comfortable, and despite being cooked over a wood fire the mess of spaghetti, eggs and wild mushrooms that Giuseppina prepared for their supper was tasty as well as filling. Moreover the *grana* cheese she served with it was *stravecchio* – extra mature, of the highest quality. Also there was a salad of tomatoes from the garden dressed with fresh basil and local olive oil. And even though there was no refrigerator, half an hour in the running water from the spring chilled Anzani's wine to acceptable coolness – made it, indeed, quite palatable.

They had expected Giuseppina to eat with them in the *salone*, but she retreated to the kitchen. When they asked why, she shrugged and indicated her sunken lips, implying that it was embarrassing for her to eat in company lacking so many teeth. They nodded understanding but insisted she take a glass of wine along. When she came to clear the table and deliver grapes and figs by way of dessert, she left them with a warm good night.

'Bedtime?' Carlo said as the door closed behind her.

'Well, we're out in the wilds,' Ann sighed. 'No TV, no radio even – unless you want to sit in the car until the battery runs flat. We might as well take the hint. If we get up early we can look over the estate before lunch and be on our way by afternoon.' She glanced around the room, fitfully lit by a paraffin lamp that Giuseppina had set on a handsome but neglected nineteenth-century sideboard. 'We ought to be able to raise a fair price, don't you think? There's a good deal of land.'

Carlo nodded firmly. 'Enough to pay off the mortgage on our apartment, at the least.'

'You're not tempted to sell up and return to nature?' Ann enquired with such mock gravity that for a second he took her seriously and almost choked on his last swig of wine. When he recovered he started to laugh.

'Come on, let's turn in,' he managed at length.

'OK. I just hope that donkey doesn't start braying in the night. And there's bound to be a cockerel, too.' She reached for her handbag, checking abruptly.

'Damn. I meant to save a mouthful of wine to swallow my Pill. I hope that water's safe. Pass me the jug.'

Luckily the night proved tolerably quiet. The only noise that did disturb them was the barking – rather, the baying – of a large dog, perhaps one of those they had seen in the village. But it didn't last for long, and by the time Giuseppina's movements disturbed them at six they had had plenty of rest. Besides, it was a fine morning.

After breakfast Ann kept her promised rendezvous with a bush, as did Carlo, and having arranged with Giuseppina to return for lunch at noon they set off on their tour of exploration armed with the sketch-map Anzani had supplied.

The land had been neglected, but the lawyer had told

the truth after all. Thanks to the spring welling from the hillside it was indeed exceptionally fertile compared with the area they had driven through yesterday. It was also less flat than the surrounding terrain, forming a series of gently undulating hills, some adorned with trees and bushes planted by past owners: chestnuts, olives, mulberries, lemons. For a wild moment Carlo felt tempted by the idea Ann had mooted as a joke, then dismissed it sternly. Certainly it would be possible to survive off a farm like this – one might even live quite well – but he had no wish to be transported back in time, as Ann had put it.

Then, abruptly, everything changed.

In shorts today, Ann had run up the next hill ahead with a laughing accusation about smoking too much – it wasn't true, he'd given up at her request when they got married – and come to a dead stop. Not until he had caught up did she recover from her shock.

'Carlo, I don't believe it!' she whispered. *'Look!'*

Ahead, in a sort of bowl, there stood a tumulus in the form of a wide low cone. The irrelevant thought crossed Carlo's mind that it was exactly the shape of one of Ann's breasts. Though it was covered in scrub, a single glance sufficed to show that it was artificial, for it was ringed by a stone wall, about shoulder height, and it had a door, or rather a doorway: a low stone porch was crudely blocked by wooden planks nailed to a wooden frame and lashed in position with ropes that served for both hinges and latch. All around were signs that this was or had recently been someone's home: a pile of rubbish, another of ashes, a bucket, an axe, a stack of firewood.

'Something like the *nuraghi* we saw on Sardinia the

other year?' Carlo hazarded, shading his eyes against the sun.

'Idiot!' She strode down the slope, leaving him to keep up as best he might. 'We're slam in the middle of an Etruscan necropolis! I bet the sides of these hills have as many burrows as a rabbit-warren! And look at this!' Halting beside the mound, she pointed at a long box-like object, half full of water. Its reddish-brown sides, patched with lichen, bore traces of elaborate moulding.

'What is it?'

'An Etruscan coffin! Lord, it must be worth millions and it's being used as a drinking-trough!'

Darting towards the porch, she attacked the rope that fastened its door.

'Ann, do you think you ought to?'

Over her shoulder she snapped, 'According to the map we're on my land, aren't we? I suppose I have some rights as the new owner!'

The rope fell away. She dragged the door aside and peered in. Reluctant, Carlo followed her example.

Cut into the side of the tumulus there was a large, low-ceilinged room, its roof upheld by square pillars. There were more signs of occupation: a bed, a table, tools, kitchen utensils. In a niche beside the entrance stood four primitive statuettes, presumably very old, garlanded with withered flowers, and these stopped Ann in her tracks with an exclamation under her breath: '*Lares and penates!* And still receiving offerings! In this day and age!'

But what really seized and held her attention were the walls – rather, the paintings on them. Grimy and faded, they were none the less astonishing.

'My God,' she whispered. 'Look! This scene of two

men in hoodwinks, that one with a club and this one with a dog roped to his arm! Only one other like it is known to have survived. It's supposed to represent some sort of trial by ordeal, maybe a precursor of the Roman Games. Presumably the man with the club had to flail about hoping to cripple the dog before it could sink its teeth into him. Carlo, you realize what this means, don't you? I've inherited a fortune! There must be other tombs all around us, so provided they haven't been ransacked—'

'Listen,' Carlo broke in.

A moment, and it came again: a deep baying sound, the cry of a dog such as Father Maru owned.

'I think the occupier may be coming home,' he whispered. 'Let's get out of here.'

They returned to daylight, and his guess proved right. Staring down at them from the crest of the same hill over which they had passed stood a thick-set man with a heavy black beard, cradling on his left arm a broken shotgun, at his right a dog that might have been litter-brother to the priest's. At their appearance he shook the gun closed with a swift and practised motion, and made to raise and point it.

He shouted something they failed to understand, to which the dog added a growl, its hackles bristling.

'We're the – the new owners!' Ann called back. 'I'm Ann Bertelli and this is my husband Carlo!'

Eying them suspiciously under bushy brows, the man advanced. It could now be seen that he had a pouch slung at his side, from under the flap of which protruded the ears of a fresh-killed rabbit. He halted five or six paces away, studying them from head to toe. Especially Ann.

He scrutinized her, the way, she imagined, he would inspect a horse or ox he planned to buy.

He had extraordinary eyes, not just dark, but actually black – as black as though she were looking through them into nowhere.

Eventually he said, his accent thick but his meaning clear enough, 'All right. Just don't come poking around again, hear? This is mine! So unless you want Cerbero to help himself to dinner off your backside . . . In your case' – with a nod at Ann – 'that would be a shame. Now be on your way!'

'Now look here!' Ann began hotly, setting her hands on her hips. Carlo checked her with a touch on her arm.

'Gun,' he said succinctly.

Not to mention dog. She conceded the wisdom of beating a strategic retreat. But she fumed all the way back to the house, describing what she was going to say to Anzani for not having warned them they had a squatter in residence.

Carlo uttered occasional murmurs of agreement.

'Odd!' she said at last as they approached their goal. 'I couldn't help feeling that that fellow looked familiar. As though I've seen him somewhere before.'

Her husband shrugged. 'Probably a local type,' he suggested. 'I imagine there's a lot of inbreeding in communities like Bolsevieto. Everybody's probably everyone else's cousin.'

'Yes, perhaps . . . Now where's Giuseppina? I have a few questions to put to her, as well!'

They found her at her wood-fired hearth stirring a *bollito misto* of kid meat, sausage, and assorted vegetables. 'So you met Tarchuno Vipegno,' she said when she heard Ann out. 'Yes, he has the right to live there.'

'But those are Etruscan tombs! They must be full of priceless archeological relics! If they haven't been plundered, of course.'

'None the less,' Giuseppina said composedly. She turned away from the pot, wiping her hands on her apron. 'There were Vipegnos living here long before my day, let alone yours. They do say: since a hundred generations.'

'Oh, that's ridiculous!' Ann stamped her foot. 'Does he have a wife, does he have a family?'

Giuseppina let her apron fall.

'The Vipegnos don't marry,' she said. 'They take.'

After an ill-tempered meal nothing would satisfy Ann but that they drive to the bar in Bolsevieto and ring Anzani. Carlo's reminders about the siesta fell on deaf ears, and at last he reluctantly gave in.

It was, however, as he had predicted: there was no reply from the lawyer's office, and the bored waiter assured them it was useless to try again before half-past three. Too restless to sit for so long, Ann cast around for distraction. Carlo suggested they might visit her aunt's grave, and she listlessly agreed. They found it without trouble – there were few recent tombstones in the little cemetery – stared at it inanely for a while, and turned back the way they had come. As the priest had mentioned, many of the names above the other graves were unusual and archaic, and the sight of them set Ann complaining again.

'What I don't understand,' she muttered, 'is why the site isn't famous. It doesn't look as though it's ever been properly excavated. Certainly this – this Tarchuno has no business treating it as . . .'

The words tailed off. Carlo glanced a question at her.

'I just realized,' she said after a pause, 'that his name is literally Etruscan.'

'How do you mean?' They were strolling side by side towards the village square and the church again.

'Tarchuno – Tarquinus, as it was in Latin. And Vipegno – that's too like Vibenna for coincidence. There were two brothers called Aulus and Caelius Vibenna who lived during the last years of kingly rule in Rome, supposed to have been friends and allies of Servius Tullius . . . Did you know the Etruscans were the first people to use the modern European style of naming, a given name plus a family name?'

Without waiting for an answer, she plunged on.

'Soon as we get back to Milan, I must get in touch with the people I met while I was writing up those exhibition notes. Heavens, this place ought to be one of the biggest tourist attractions in the area! And couldn't it do with a shot in the arm?' They were in sight of the square now, where the only signs of life consisted of a few buzzing flies and the usual drowsy dogs; the human inhabitants were still in hiding from the heat.

Carlo hesitated. After a pause he said, 'Does this mean you've changed your mind about selling?'

'Not at all! But now we know what comes with the property we'd be fools not to milk it for every lira. And if there are a decent number of saleable relics in the necropolis we might well consider doing up the house and keeping it on for weekends, hm? It's not all that far from Milan, and it wouldn't half impress people.' Ann checked her watch. 'Damn, still another quarter-hour to go. Suppose we take a look at the church.'

And, as though her eyes had been newly opened, she found much to comment on there, too. The sinister carvings Carlo had noticed yesterday – most of them had semicircular recesses, much ornamented, around the faces, not at all like the haloes usually accorded to Christian saints – she referred to as *antefissi* and said they must have developed from the protective icons the Etruscans used to mount on the corners of roofs. The very structure of the church, which to Carlo seemed dull and ordinary, excited her, too. Apparently it was built to an Etruscan pattern with three distinct chambers, or one chamber and two cells, instead of the conventional Christian layout.

'I wish there were a guidebook!' she exclaimed.

'Even if there were,' Carlo sighed, 'we couldn't buy one. There aren't any shops open, and if yesterday is anything to go by there won't be until four o'clock. But it's half-past three and we can try raising Anzani again. I suppose they take a shorter siesta in the big city.'

At the idea of Matignano as a big city she managed to crack a smile, and they headed for the bar arm in arm.

Anzani sounded as though he had not yet fully woken up, but at the sound of Ann's angry voice he briskened.

'Yes, I'm sorry not to have explained about Vipegno,' he cut in. 'It was one of the things I planned to discuss with you. But do remember you were over two hours late, so I scarcely had time to go into detail.'

'I wouldn't have thought an Etruscan necropolis was a mere detail!' she snapped. 'Especially one that's being ruined by a squatter!'

'Ruined? Not in the least.' Anzani had regained his normal professional tone. 'One thing the Vipegnos have always been noted for is the way they guard the site. You sound knowledgeable on this subject. Can you name anywhere else like it that's actually in occupation?'

'Of course not, but . . .' Ann drew a deep breath. 'You said Vipegnos, plural. Giuseppina said something about them having been there for a hundred generations. I never heard anything so ridiculous! Why, that would take us right back to Etruscan times – twenty-five centuries!'

'All I can say,' Anzani answered after a pause, 'is that he holds rights in perpetuity. How far back they date I can't say, but the generally accepted term is "from time immemorial".'

'Oh, this is getting more and more absurd!' Glancing at Carlo, who nodded vigorous agreement; she was holding the phone a little away from her ear so he could eavesdrop. 'What about – what's the term? – eminent domain, isn't that right? Nobody has any business monopolizing part of our national heritage! Especially not on someone else's land!'

'I'm afraid his claims have been challenged over and over,' Anzani sighed. 'And they've always had to be upheld – even against the *Soprintendenza dell' Etruria*, even the *Direzione Generale delle Antichità e Belle Arti*. The reason your late aunt lived in such straitened circumstances was because her father attempted to dispossess Tarchuno Vipegno's predecessor, and it virtually bankrupted him. Of course, if you have a taste for expensive lawsuits—'

Taking the phone, Carlo broke in. 'How would Vipegno meet his legal bills, then?'

'Ah, Signor Bertelli. I can guess what you're thinking – it might be worth trying to exhaust his presumably limited resources, is that right? Drive him to surrender? I can only say I wouldn't advise you to try. Certainly it didn't work in the case of his father, though of course that was before my time.'

'This is getting us nowhere,' Ann sighed. She reclaimed the phone and promised – or rather threatened – to call again.

They had bought some wine in the village, marginally more interesting than Asti Spumate, and sat gloomily after their evening meal – the broth from the lunchtime *bollito* plus mixed broken pasta of the kind that children call *tuono e lampo*, thunder and lightning – sipping a second bottle and debating what to do. Clearly the opinion of another lawyer would be called for; Ann's contacts among Etruscan scholars offered a further line of approach; and in any case it was impossible to imagine a government department being defied by a dirty-nailed peasant.

In the end, this time having remembered to save enough wine to wash down her Pill, Ann announced her intention of turning in. Carlo, though, felt too much on edge, and preferred to sit up a while longer. Shrugging, she headed for the back door, saying that if they were going to keep this as a weekend retreat the first thing they'd have to do something about was that revolting privy.

'Want the lamp?' he called back.

On the threshold, she glanced at the sky. 'No, the moon's up. It's a bit cloudy, but I can see my way.'

'OK. With you in a little while.'

And he delivered himself to the tantalizing contemplation of a billion-lire windfall.

Finally it dawned on him that he hadn't heard Ann come back. Puzzled, he consulted his watch. Fifteen minutes had gone by. Muzzy from the wine, he debated whether to go looking for her. She could scarcely have missed her way, but the ground behind the house was rough and she might have twisted her ankle, or caught her foot in a tree-root. Sighing, he rose, reaching for the oil-lamp and was struck by a better idea. There was a flashlight in the car. Where were the keys . . .? Ah, here in his pocket.

Duly equipped, he set out in search, calling her name softly for fear of waking Giuseppina. Swinging the beam from side to side, he caught sight of marks in the dust among the bushes Ann would have made for.

Footprints. Not his – they were too big – and certainly not hers. Besides, they were paralleled by the paw prints of a dog.

Vipegno? Surely not! But – who else?

Advancing in bafflement, he abruptly noticed something else. There was a wet patch with scuff-marks near by. The footprints leading towards it, approaching the house, were shallow. Those leading away were much deeper.

Made by someone carrying a heavy load.

Carrying Ann—?

Without thinking Carlo began to run.

He lost the prints as soon as dry grass covered the ground, but that didn't matter. He knew where he must go. Shortly, panting, he breasted the final rise overlooking

Vipegno's ancient home, and only then wondered what use he could be, without so much as a stick to wield against the kidnapper's shotgun – not to mention his dog. Oh, there was no doubt he had come to the right place; light could be dimly seen in the porchway, and a moving shadow.

An armed man, a dog . . . and not even a stick. This was ridiculous! Feeling all the agony of a city dweller confronted with primitive rural violence, he cast around for something, anything, to serve as a weapon. Aided by the half-moon, veiled by scudding clouds but shedding useful light, he spotted the woodpile he had earlier noticed by the door. Perhaps there . . .

Switching off the flashlight, he stole towards it, hoping against hope he would not alert the dog. Sweat ran down his dusty face; he felt streaks of the mixture on his skin, foul as mud. There was a branch that looked as if it might be suitable—

The ramshackle door slammed wide. With a gasp Carlo found Vipegno confronting him, Cerbero beside him with lowered head and sharp, bared teeth.

But he had no gun. Instead, he carried objects in both hands: in his right, a cudgel and a rope; in his left, two bags made of cloth.

At a gesture the dog circled around behind Carlo to cut off his retreat.

Nodding approval, his master spoke.

'You've taken a woman of our *gens*. I shall reclaim her if I can so she may bear a *zili*'s heir. That was the custom of my ancestors. It has endured a hundred generations. But by ancient law you—'

Carlo finally found his tongue.

'What have you done with her?'

'Look inside,' Vipegno invited, stepping back so he could approach the doorway. A guttering lamp revealed Ann slumped against one of the square pillars, her eyes closed, her shirt torn from shoulder to waist in testimony to the resistance she had put up.

How could he not have heard her screams? Thoughts of chloroform crossed his mind. He caught sight of pale cloth on the beaten-dirt floor; had that been what Vipegno used?

Then he focused on it: Ann's shorts and panties. They would have been down around her knees so she was unable to flee, then ripped from her legs on arrival . . .

He began to curse under his breath.

'Take this,' Vipegno said, holding out one of the black bags. 'And your chance of rescuing her with it!'

'What?'

'I said take it!' – throwing it at Carlo, who caught it by pure reflex. 'Don't don it yet. First tie this rope to my wrist. I'll have to put it on Cerbero because he won't let anyone else touch him.'

'I—' Carlo's mouth had already been dry. Now as it dawned on him what he was condemned to, it became like a desert.

That picture. The one Ann had explained . . .

'Move! If you don't, I'll let Cerbero attack!'

Cerbero – Cerberus. Of course. The guard-dog at the gate of hell!

Whimpering, Carlo accepted the rope and did his clumsy best to knot it tight. Then Vipegno looped it around his dog's neck.

'Take the club,' he commanded, straightening. 'And put on the hood.'

So saying, he did the same himself, and waited, muttering what might have been a prayer, or an incantation. It was not in any language Carlo recognized.

Wild hope seized him. If the hoodwinks were indeed opaque Vipegno could no longer see him, and he would take a while to release himself from the rope. To run, reach the car, bring help – it would be too late to save Ann from what the devil had in mind for her, but . . .

'Put it on!' Vipegno rasped. 'I may not be able to see you but there are plenty who can!'

Who?

Slowly Carlo turned around. On the slope of the hill behind him were ranged half-seen figures; he could not tell how many were men, how many women. But they numbered at least a score.

Bring help? Oh God! There wasn't going to be any help!

Of a sudden his brain was ice cold. Fixing his and the other man's relative positions as exactly as he could, he picked up the cudgel; Vipegno had let it fall while fastening the rope around Cerbero's neck. It felt reassuringly massive. Perhaps he might smash the dog's snout. Grasping it in his right hand, with his left he drew the bag over his head. At once there was an unmistakable sigh from the onlookers.

Belatedly he began to swing the club, aiming for where he recalled the dog had been – and it met air. Losing his footing and almost his balance, he cried out and tried again. This time he connected with something, but it was not the dog: Vipegno's arm, perhaps, for the blow elicited a grunt of pain. For a fatal instant he dared to remember what hope used to be like.

And the cudgel was gone, snatched from his hand.

Screaming in terror, he ripped off his hood. The dog had seized the stick in his enormous jaws. Now he dropped it and lunged, his blunt muzzle slamming into Carlo's midriff, driving the wind out of him. An instant later he was sprawling on his back with Cerbero standing over him. Drops of slaver fell on his throat, like acid.

'Hah!' Vipegno said with contempt. 'When my father took Giuseppina her brother put up a better show than that! Broke the dog's foreleg before it bit his ankle to the bone. Walked with a limp until his dying day!'

He added something harsh in dialect, and Cerbero responded with a growl.

Hood discarded, he untied the rope and cast both aside. Carlo tried to follow what he was doing, but if he so much as rolled his head the dog snarled again, so he dared move only his eyes. He thought he made out that Vipegno was bringing – leading, dragging, carrying? – Ann into the open and laying her down. Some kind of mantle was spread over them, though he couldn't see by whom. There followed moans.

Vaguely he grew aware that the witnesses had descended from the hillside and were watching intently from close by. Ann had said something about the Etruscan trial by ordeal being a precursor of the Roman Games. Here was the nearest to their vicious audience he had ever dreamed might still exist in modern times . . .

And there was another dog! Beside it stood its owner – and oh God, it was the priest's, here was the priest, and no wonder Ann had thought she recognized him, for were you to shave Tarchuno's beard you'd find Father Maru's double underneath!

He moved too far, and Cerbero administered a warning nip, not even hard enough to break the skin, but fearful. He lay rock-still again, ears tortured by the loathsome sounds of glutted lust.

'You can get up now,' the priest said eventually. Carlo felt as though he might never move again, but managed to, cramp-stiff in every limb.

'Has the world gone mad?' he mumbled as he forced himself upright. 'The bastard's kidnapped my wife, and raped her, and you – *you* – and all these people *watched*!' Words failed him. Fists clenched, he rocked back and forth on his heels, staring towards Ann. She lay with eyes closed, her torso at least obscured by the mantle Carlo had seen being delivered to Vipegno, but her long lovely legs bare to the thighs and bruised and smeared with grime.

'It was done beneath the mantle, as is proper,' said the priest. 'There has been no offence.'

The mere effort of standing had drained Carlo of the ability to wonder what that meant. He could think only of the pathetic broken figure on the ground.

'Help her, damn you!' he moaned.

'Mother, see to the girl,' Maru commanded after a pause. Mother? Carlo jerked his head around.

Of course. Giuseppina. Who else? But she was making no move to comply. She was showing something, a bag – Ann's handbag. She was showing something from it to her son the priest. It was flat, and shiny on one side,

111

and . . . and it was the dispenser pack holding Ann's monthly supply of the Pill.

For one wild second Carlo wanted to laugh. If the purpose of this loathsome ritual was to ensure there would be another generation of Vipegnos, this time it had misfired. Then he was snatched back to the horrors of reality.

Face darkening, Maru flung down the foil pack and ground it under his heel. 'An abomination!' he rasped. 'Now it will all have to be done again!'

Tarchuno was standing by the door of his home, fastening his belt, his expression indecipherable thanks to his dense beard. His brother stormed over to him and muttered in his ear. At once he tensed with rage. He strode towards Ann, cuffing aside Giuseppina and other women approaching to attend her, snatched away the mantle, and spat upon her naked belly with a curse. The sight drove Carlo over the brink. No matter what it cost, that must be avenged!

But he couldn't move. He was held tightly by his arms, and far too weak to break away.

Furious, he turned to see who gripped him, and said after a terrible pause, 'You too?' He almost uttered the words in Latin. Sad-faced, slump-shouldered, this traitor, this Brutus, was Anzani.

'It's no use fighting what you're up against,' he said after a pause. 'They've had too much practice. The Romans couldn't stamp out this tradition, nor the Church, nor the Fascists . . . Sometimes I think the Bolsevietans aren't people any more, not as we think of people. Not individuals, I mean. More like a collective organism. At any rate they behave like one.'

He seemed to be talking for the sake of talking, to distract himself.

'You wondered whether you might exhaust Tarchuno's funds by taking him to law. I told you the father of your wife's late aunt tried that and failed. I didn't tell you why. It was because they act together. He wasn't only suing one man. He was suing the whole community, and it would take a billionaire to match their resources. They've been here a long time, Signor Bertelli. When they speak of a hundred generations they're not exaggerating. Two thousand five hundred years . . . and in all that while they've never lacked a protector, a *zili*. At present they are especially strong, for as you must have realized Giuseppina bore twin boys, so they have a *maru* too.'

'What' – Carlo barely recognized his own voice – 'what if the child is a girl?'

'At least they no longer kill it out of hand. Now they try again with someone else. I'm afraid this won't apply to your wife. They regard her as having evaded her obligation. When her contraceptive has worn off—'

'No! No!' Wrenching himself free, Carlo seized the older man by his lapels. 'It's impossible! The whole idea is crazy! They can't just imprison us here! We have jobs, friends who'll come looking for us, we have—'

'As much chance of resisting as of stopping Etna from eruption,' declared the lawyer. 'To my cost, I know.'

Carlo dropped his hands, searching Anzani's face. 'You . . . ?'

A nod. 'My late wife was one of these people. I made the mistake of coming here last year with our daughter.'

'But—' Carlo hesitated. What he wanted to ask seemed so terrible, he could not frame the words.

'Why has he taken your wife too, so soon after?'

'Uh . . . Yes!'

'Serafina's baby is a girl.'

'They did the same to her? And you – you come here, you do their work, you . . . Oh, God. The world *has* gone mad.'

'It's a very old kind of madness. So old, it may in fact be more like sanity.' Anzani's face was grey in the moonlight.

'Nonsense! Rubbish!' Carlo cried. The lawyer ignored him.

'You see, they will give you a dog.'

'What do you mean?'

'A dog that will make sure you don't go away.'

'This grows madder by the moment!' Carlo set his fists to his temples. 'I'm going to take Ann back to our car, and I'm going to drive her home, and I'm going to rout out a notary to take her sworn deposition that she was raped, and a doctor to verify there's semen in her vagina, and get it typed so it can be proved that it's not mine, and . . . Why do you keep shaking your head? They'd have to kill me to stop us!'

'Your car isn't there,' Anzani said. 'You don't own a car any more.'

'*What?* Goddamn it! I still have the keys in my pocket! See?' He fumbled for, produced and dangled them.

'Do you think that matters to these people? No, you sold it this morning and the new owner collected it soon after you reclaimed your flashlight. By morning it will be in Yugoslavia, or on a ferry to Greece. The proceeds have been deposited in the bank account you've opened in Matignano. Your apartment in Milan is up for sale. You

114

see, when you arrived here you fell in love with Bolsevieto and decided it was the only possible place to live. Letters confirming the fact have already been delivered to your respective employers. They may be surprised at receiving them so promptly, considering the state of the post these days, but at least they will appreciate being notified, though no doubt annoyed at losing your services with so little warning. Still, your holiday has a week to run.'

'No! It's impossible!'

'I assure you it isn't. How often do I have tell you? These people have had two and a half thousand years of practice! And the letters and other documents, including the authority to sell your apartment, will withstand the closest scrutiny. I can assure you of that, too.'

'You? *You* faked them? Why, you bastard!' (An echo of Ann: 'Who in his right mind trusts a lawyer?')

'Your wife seems to be recovering,' Anzani said, ignoring the fist that Carlo raised before his face. 'You'd better go to her.'

'Not until you tell me what drove you to throw in your lot with these monsters, this spawn of hell!'

'Haven't you guessed?' the lawyer whispered. 'I love my daughter. Poisoning your aunt, forging her will – the land was never hers, of course, but the Vipegnos' as it's always been – that was the only way they'd let me have her back, and my grandchild. You see what I mean about them being sane? They are dreadfully, terribly, horrifyingly sane. They obey the most pitiless kind of logic. They belong to an old world that had no room for generosity or kindness. They are what all of us might have remained had there not arisen teachers to reveal a better way . . . Go to your wife. If you can prove you love her in spite of what they've done, even their iron hearts may some day soften. I pray to that end, every morning, every night.'

His voice broke as he turned away, stifling sobs.

'They did it to me as well,' Giuseppina said as she sponged dirt from Ann's bruised legs. 'I'm still here. And I do have two fine sons.'

The reality of the trap had closed on Carlo. The Alfa had indeed disappeared. Photostats of the letters forged by Anzani had been waiting here for him to read.

'Mind you,' the old woman went on – she was not truly old, he realized, just aged – 'no other man would look at me after I'd born children out of wedlock. Men don't understand. The women were kinder. She's lucky: your wife, I mean. You're a modern husband. Things are different nowadays, aren't they? You hear about it, read it in newspapers and magazines. Even married women can take lovers and their husbands think it only fair. Well, so it is. They've always been used to having mistresses. They say that's how it was in the old days. The Romans insulted Etruscan women because they dined with the menfolk and drank wine in company. So they told me when I was a little girl. But they still wouldn't help me find a husband . . . It's the cruelty of the Church, you know.'

Someone – perhaps her son the priest – had provided a bottle of grappa. Carlo had drunk three glasses, not before persuading Ann to sip a little, and that had helped. He thought of the contrast between Giuseppina's view of the Church and Anzani's reference to teachers and kindness. The lawyer had been wrong, totally wrong, to say these people had remained unchanged. They were obviously trying to, yet their mental armour had been breached.

Only not enough. How long would it take? Another two millennia?

Ann stirred as Giuseppina completed her work and bore away the bowl of water and the washcloth. She had shed all the tears she could; her swollen eyes were dry.

'Carlo . . . ?' she whispered.

He darted to kneel at her bedside.

'Carlo, I cheated him, didn't I? I figured out what he had in mind. I remembered what Giuseppina said: Vipegnos don't marry, they take. But he didn't reckon with my being on the Pill, did he? When I realized that, I stopped fighting him off. Wouldn't you rather have me more or less in one piece? He could have beaten me unconscious, scarred me for life! He gave me some kind of drug – he had something in his palm when he put his hand over my mouth to stop me screaming, and even though I didn't swallow when he forced it in I suddenly felt weak and dreamy . . . Carlo?'

'Here!' he whispered, sliding his arm under her head.

'We'll go home in the morning, won't we? And we'll call in the police, and somebody will put a stop to all this, and the Etruscan relics will be put in a museum where they belong.' She was trying to keep her eyes open, but failing, and her voice was growing fainter.

What was he to do? Tell the truth? Say, 'They stole our car, Anzani is in league with them, it's no use prosecuting or suing because they've been around since before money was invented and they know more nasty tricks than the Mafia and the Camorra and Freemasons added together – and anyhow that lot were probably taught by them in the first place!'?

But Ann was asleep.

There had been a tap at the back door, and half-heard speech. Now Giuseppina reappeared. On a leash she held one of the tall lean dogs. Rising to his feet, Carlo stared in sick despair, remembering Anzani's words.

'This is Aplu,' she announced. 'Apollo, you would say. Great-great-grandson of Tin that watched over me and my sons. He will guard you until the child is born and nursed and old enough to live with his father and learn the knowledge he must learn. If he dies beforehand they will send another. He will sleep outside your door. Don't try and pass him. I've put a chamber pot beneath the bed. Now get what rest you can. It's been a busy night.'

Carlo was too stunned to speak. As the door closed, Ann stirred a little and seemed to smile, as though hope had occurred to her in a dream. Convinced that hope was an illusion for them now, Carlo poured more grappa and sat drinking until the oil in the lamp ran out. Dying, the flame smoked its chimney as black as the future.

And the past.

The Last Drop

NICHOLAS ROYLE

HE PUSHED THE man gently back on to the consultation chair and withdrew a gun from the pocket of his white coat. He pointed the muzzle at the man's forehead and squeezed the trigger.

Then he had a better idea.

Dallman sat in his study until he heard Queenie get up and announce she was going to bed. She leaned against the study door, eyelids heavy with gin.

'Are you coming?' she asked, brushing hair out of her eyes.

'I have to finish this,' Dallman said, gesturing at the papers on his desk. They were scrap, old case notes he used for rough work. If she came and read over his shoulder she might realize, but she was unlikely to take the trouble.

She pouted and let fall the hand that was holding her unbuttoned blouse in place. He looked down and caught sight of her petticoat trailing below her skirt.

Dallman felt his ears redden. He knew that he would

never stop wanting her. After she had gone he took a packet of photographs from a desk drawer. Taken a few months ago, they showed her as happy as when they had first met. Laughing and running in a city park on a Sunday afternoon. There was one of himself smiling broadly, his eyes clear and happy.

He later calculated that they were taken around the time she started seeing Kent.

For three months after he began to suspect, he did nothing. The signs became obvious to him. She started going out more often, to see French films and meet old friends in art galleries. 'I suppose you're busy,' she would say and he would collude with her, nodding miserably. He did nothing because she was happy and he didn't want to take that away from her. It made her glow.

Dallman pushed his chair back quietly and reached across the desk for his car keys.

He injected epinephrine into the scalp causing blood vessels to contract, so that when he cut into the shaved section of skin there would not be so much blood that his view was obscured. A retractor held the scalp apart, revealing a tiny rhomboid section of skull.

He took the craniotome, a stainless-steel drill with a bit that disengaged when the bone was penetrated, and pressed it against the skull. There was no nurse available to spray sterile water into the hole as he drilled. But in the circumstances it didn't matter.

He pierced the dura with the scalpel and used an electrical probe, wire-thin, to disable the motor cortex, the part of the brain controlling the voluntary muscles.

★

Dallman parked a couple of streets away and walked to the practice. His card permitted entry twenty-four hours a day. On the third floor he passed his own suite and proceeded to the door bearing Kent's name. In case of emergency, both senior partners had keys to the other's door. Dallman let himself in, still hoping he wouldn't find the evidence he was looking for.

He had seen the name of a restaurant in Queenie's address book when she left it by the phone one evening. La Cucina. It was not a place they had ever eaten in, nor had she mentioned it when he asked her where she went with her friends.

In the top drawer of Kent's desk Dallman found credit card receipts from La Cucina. He crumpled them in his fist and sat down heavily in a leather armchair, sighing. Regrets filled his mind. That Queenie was having an affair. And the she had chosen Kent, his partner for five years, a fine neurosurgeon and a friend.

Dallman leaned forward over the desk and jammed his knuckles into his eyes. But he couldn't stop the tears. They'd been building up since the signs first appeared and he'd been determined to contain them until he knew for certain one way or the other.

Shoulders heaving, his tears fell on to Kent's blotter. He opened his eyes and the office presented blurred forms of its angular furniture. He looked down at the blotter that was soaking up his hurt. Among the doodles he saw small concentrated groups of the letter Q.

He used a local anaesthetic the next time he opened up Kent's skull so that he could talk and his patient would be able to hear. The craniotome was required again to access another part of the brain. He located the occipital lobe and reached for his electrical probe.

'I imagine you know what I'm doing,' he said. 'Take a good look around while you still can.'

With a quick burst of volts, Dallman killed the visual centre of the brain.

Before the anaesthetic wore off he also removed Kent's power of speech, though he hadn't used it for some time, by disabling Broca's Area on the left side of the brain.

He said nothing, to Queenie or to Kent. Maybe it would run its course and she would tire of him. He was no great conversationalist, though it would not have occurred to Dallman to criticize him before in any respect. Although their liaison clearly consisted of more than talk he didn't imagine they ate in silence at La Cucina.

Weeks passed and Queenie continued to spend as many evenings out of the house as in. Dallman would go into their bedroom and smell her clothes – a scarf or petticoat – hoping in vain that her scent would bring him some pleasure.

In his study, work papers were scattered across the desk. He pored obsessively over the photographs taken in the park, as if searching for a way to alter the past.

He took out the auditory centre and a portion of the somatosensory cortex, which received and analysed sensory impulses coming from all parts of the body. He wielded his lethal probe in the fissure between the two hemispheres to block messages to the brain from the trunk, hip, leg, foot, and genitals.

Kent was sustained by a drip-feed and catheterized. A

machine aided his breathing, but his condition was by no means vegetative.

Vegetables didn't think.

Dallman had so far left untouched the prefrontal area of the frontal lobe so that Kent could think about what was happening to him and why. Maybe he would look back on the affair and wish he had not been so foolish for the sake of a few Italian meals, a pile of credit card bills, and whatever secrets he and Queenie had shared. Dallman hoped so.

Revenge came unnaturally to him. Initially, the end of the affair had numbed him. But within hours, paralysis gave way to grief such as he had never known. It fell upon him with the force of a house collapsing. Even when he thought the pain had levelled out, lone bricks detached themselves from the ruins and thumped him in the head.

He had loved Queenie. But just how much he found out when it was too late.

Reluctantly, he burnt out the prefrontal area. If thoughts of Queenie had comforted Kent at all throughout his cranial decimation, they would do so no more.

Dallman reached a point where action had to be taken. Queenie was drinking herself to unhappiness. He couldn't bear to see her go into a decline.

He acquired the practice secretary's signature on a piece of letterhead, then typed a note from Kent to Queenie proposing dinner that evening at La Cucina. He sent it by courier and told the secretary Kent was too busy to take calls.

He waited an hour at La Cucina and discovered later that the car crash had happened half an hour before he arrived at the restaurant. Kent had phoned Queenie and they had put two and two together. He picked her up to drive to La Cucina and confront Dallman. But they never got there.

Kent was badly shaken but unhurt. Queenie was dead.

Dallman regarded the man in the bed. Amidst all the technology and hardware of life-support he seemed barely human. Within his skull, however, were remnants of life: the premotor cortex, controlling muscular coordination, and that tiny part of the somatosensory cortex relating to the nose. The drip and the catheter continued to feed and empty him.

Dallman stared out of the window a few feet away. Dusk obscured the few people out on the streets, but he watched them pass and wondered what it must be like to *be* them. He took Queenie's petticoat from out of his pocket. The last pedestrian passed out of sight and he turned back towards Kent.

He held the petticoat under Kent's nose. Dallman could smell it himself from where he stood. Nothing changed. The drip fed him and the catheter emptied him. Dallman waited. He didn't take his eyes from Kent's.

Just when he thought it was hopeless and was about to take the petticoat away, he saw what he wanted to see.

A tear formed in the corner of Kent's eye, like dew on a rose and swelled until it overflowed and trickled slowly down his cheek. Dallman watched it for a moment, then wrapped it in the petticoat.

Pick Me Up

DAVID J. SCHOW

I FEEL THE way an executioner must feel, a heartbeat before he does the thing that kills. Every time I stick out my thumb, I feel.

I think of the SURGE button on the panel that feeds the electric chair. That special button with the hinged metal lid to prevent anyone from depressing it accidentally. I think of the DROP switch that prompts the intermix of cyanide in the gas chamber. My thumb. I see it cocking the hammer of a Smith and Wesson Model 39, my favourite automatic. They haven't manufactured that one for nearly a decade, now.

I stick my thumb into the rainfall and feel the usual good feelings. A flash of headlights passes me by. My thumb's dripping. Rain does funny things to people. Some, it makes benevolent: *Oh that poor man, stuck out there in the elements.* Others wonder what brand of lunatic would be hitchhiking in the rain in the first place.

Those latter are alive today, generally.

I begrudge the discomfort, but not the coming of the rain. I get more rides in the rain. It's those former people, running their little logic chains about me, and why they should pick me up just this once.

Once is enough.

Keep on rationalizin', sez me.

KABOOM! Lightning scratched across the night sky and I swore I can feel fork tines raking acrost the back of my skull from the inside. Shot past afore I could slam my eyeballs shut. Light strobed the wipers across the windshield of my Truck.

What a show; all for free.

The best things in life are low-cost and high-maintenance. That's a joke.

Excepting my Truck. Tuck and roll *costs*, lifters and glasspacks *cost*. You think riders ever pitch in uncoached? It all comes out of my wallet, which is a Lord Buxton and weren't no cheap billfold, neither. I got it for free when I bought two pair boots – one fancy lizard skin, the other regular black cowboy, which I'm wearing right now. My wallet is safe in my hip pocket.

All props. My Truck is the stage. The show usually goes on.

Ever try to clean blood off Mexican leather? I mean, even that thin hide they use for them one-day, in-and-out, south of the border upholstery jobs? Sweet Jesus! I finally had to dye the stitching black, with boot creme to make everything uniform. I used Meltonian. That ain't cheap. But nothing but the best for my Truck.

Sometimes the only thing that makes any earthly sense to me is gobbling highway stripes as fast as my Truck can feed 'em to me and farting them out rearways. Zip in. Zip out. I'm on the highspeed highwire; stay outta my way because I don't slow down until I feel what Grampaw used to call *the grumble of honest appetite*.

Shoot. Road's picked clean. I eased down the foot-stomper and listened to my tyres sing in the rain.

Even before the highbeams slow and pull left I know this is a single guy, doing the whiteline trance routine in the middle of the night. It's never a woman, not on a night like this. If woman there is, she is always accompanied by a husband of recent vintage, and she always vocally disapproves of giving a lift to a stranger. Domestic disagreements have been the foundation of some of my more exhilarating kills. I get picked up because the woman in the car says *don't pick that guy up, John* in this wrong tone for her man's mood.

Bang, bang, double zero, nobody gets laid. Sorry.

In girl/guy combos the man usually has to be killed first. Easy, because at this time of night the man is usually the driver. He make his honey snooze across the back seat so the hitchhiker won't get any ideas . . . just in case he's a pervert or recently escaped mental case.

OK by me. Girl or guy, alone or together, once those headlights slow down and pull over I know I'm going to reap some action. The ingredients don't matter.

I try not to carry weapons. If the hypos roust me and rummage my pack (and they have, hundreds of times, never mind *my* rights, thanks), they'll find my kit, my clothes, and whatever ID I care to flash them. I know sleight of hand. I can make a deck of playing cards do gymnastics in the palm of my right while juggling three golf balls with my left. I went to dealer's school in Reno and once did a six-month gig on a cruise ship as onboard magician. I was the guy who did tricks while chefs cooked at your tableside.

I can pluck out your larynx and show it to you before you realize I've twitched.

The killing part I learned from the army and jail. Fort Benning and Folsom. That's some nasty business you don't really need to hear about.

Anyhow, my clothes are always clean. And the ID cards – I have twenty, all for different states. I prestidigitate them and don't spend too much vagrant time in the slam unless the local badgemen are hardcases who don't like my hair or my looks.

I move on and they forget about me. Usually.

So the first thing I check on an incoming car are the lights. No flashbar. Then I check to see if it's an unmarked cruiser. You can tell by the tyres or the rear deck. If I can't spot a bubble light, I can read the codex of municipal licence plates.

Not cops. Not this time.

I lean out and shield my eyes from the rain and glare as the cabin light pops on to reveal a single guy. I win again. Late twenties or early thirties. Longish hair. Well built. Good clothes, clean. Careful smile.

I smile right back. Showtime.

This dude looked like trouble waiting to happen, so at the last moment I cranked hard right, floored the foot-stomper and mashed him good. My Truck's ram bumper ate his face and he pinked one of the headlights. Rain rinsed it clear in no time at all.

His stuff was soaked through. His backpack was cheap.

He had twenty-seven bucks and some chicken change. Took nearly all of it just to gas up.

Rainspots hobble my Truck's finish, but raintime means better hunting. When the elements sour, folks will hitch with fewer qualms. When they're not so particular about the character of whomever pulls over to help them along. Storms make it simpler for me to help them along.

So to speak.

Along near eleven I hit the Stop 'N' Go to get me a couple of them microwave burritos. A hypo growler was up front, parked across three spaces. Turns out the place had just been robbed.

Damn, but I do hate that. Them little joints is the only outlets open for night-owls any more. Guy works a dead-dog shift selling smokes and beer to unemployed ground-pounders, and for his trouble he gets a Smith and Wesson stuck up his nose by some pimply faggot with Underalls on his head.

The robber had shot the place up. No kills, though.

Guy working the counter had a nametag that said ROCKO. But nobody works a detail like this using his or her real name. He seemed to take the robbery in stride, like it was all no strain. But I was mad and told him so. Cop glared at me. What good are the cops if they couldn't respond while a robbery-in-progress was still in progress?

I've always had much more use for convenience stores than I've ever had for law enforcers.

Guy working the counter drove a big-block Camaro. Looked like he took care of it OK, and so, it took care of him. Course, if it ever broke down and stranded him of the roadside, at night, in this kind of rain . . . well, things would be different.

I hit the driver in the throat, a good hard chop. The car is going forty; my hand, about seventy.

He gets this expression as though he is terribly disappointed in bad clichés, like the ones about picking up hitchers. Then he tries to kill me. At least, he thinks he does.

The essence of victory is total commitment.

Normal people never expect you to reach over and strike them while the car is moving. My advantage. What the hell do they think seatbelts are *for*, anyway? Five seconds past that thought, things are usually academic.

And here I am.

But this chap wants the old struggle-for-life bit. Bared teeth in the face of imminent demise. The protohuman chucking his façade of civilization. Last-ditch time.

His car jumps the abutment and wraps its grille around a boulder. The storm has caused rockfalls and washouts. He is still trussed up in his seatbelt as we hit. I get a few scratches from his flailing around.

One sharp rap to his upper row of teeth, one more to the bridge of his nose, and he's done. I rifle his junk while blood purples his eyesockets. By the time I find his gun, he looks like the Lone Ranger. Then he stops twitching like a spazz.

The revolver is not my favourite firearm. I prefer automatics, remember? But it was a Smith and Wesson. Now, say that name a few times: Smith and Wesson. Sounds like power, doesn't it? Power. Right there in your hand.

He has some credit cards and a hundred bucks in cash. I strip the car of documents the way I strip him of his very identity. In seconds he is nothing more than a lump of protein. Nobody. He no longer has an identity. I've taken it.

I ditch the corpse and burn the registration. Mr Gun takes a siesta in my pack, which is waterproof. I don't find a box of shells. Six rounds only, snug and dry.

Since I've won the piece I decide to bag a Stop 'N' Go that turns up. It takes two shots: one for the camera and one for the surveillance mirror, to make sure there isn't a rent-a-cop snoozing back there. Sometimes they give rent-a-cop rubber guns. Or real guns with no bullets.

Bang, bang, and Mister Counterman damn near pops his spine making me wealthier. Half the time those floor safes sit open anyway. The rest of the time, the employee knows the combination, and no one faults him for spilling it under the sort of duress a Smith and Wesson in the ear can provide.

Say it: Smith and Wesson.

And remember that always: The safes are there for you to empty.

I take the cash and coin rolls and ignore the money order blanks. Into a small bag goes a six of imported beer and some of those thick-sliced potato chips with the skins still on. Beef jerky and chocolate chip cookies and a quart of lo-fat milk. A flashlight and some fresh batteries. They're dated now so you can tell how new they are. A locked counter spinner holds pocket knives, imitation Swiss army issue. I take the one that does most things.

Never would I have killed the counterman. He is just logging his hours and understands, as I do, that insurance companies conquer all. On the road I would have taken him, his Camaro, everything. But there in his workplace he is safe from the likes of me and will probably never appreciate this or even realize it.

I pay cash for the motel cabin. I take a very hot shower. There are sex movies on the cable TV. I sleep like a babe until past noon the next day.

Tiresome. Folks in general can be so tiresome.

My favourite part of acceleration is the shifting: 1–2–3–4, watch that needle climb. The game is to make it not stutter, like not jiggling the bottle when you're decanting some fine wine, which I've heard you ought not to do. I learned that from a guy I picked up.

Not this guy today. This guy was a talker. Talked from beat one, like he was trying too hard to form some kind of bond with me. The fellowship of the road. Bum pals for life. I killed him and sort of made the second part true right away. My eyes were the last thing he ever saw with his.

He had rattled on, very academician, about what he called the psychology of hitchhiking. How in the Sixties there had been so much trust, and how an entire generation of happy rebels had Yupped out to the point where they wouldn't even give each other rides home because car pools were a status dip. He talked too fast, trying to reassure himself that *I* was OK in terms of *his* manifesto. Dumb shit. Dumb overeducated shit. What he never found time to understand is that hitching a ride is a gamble. A risk consciously taken. Life is a risk. And I am the law of averages. Nothing personal. He died well.

I used this hank of piano wire with wooden grips. I made it myself and hadn't used it in a while. Variety's

the spice. Then I hit the road, 1–2–3–4, no further inter-
rupts, and it was good.

His chatter, though, got me to thinking about small
towns. You know, those desert suburbs full of retirees.
And trust. Living there, you always saw folks like him in
the crosswalks. Usually while you were warming a booth
in some sleepy coffee shop. And you thought to yourself
transient. Cops should come sweep him up. Hustle that
sucker along smartly to the next town. Don't let him
linger and keep him on the move.

Like school. Like the military. Keep moving. I keep
moving, but on my own terms. Nobody tells me when to
sit or git.

Long as the transients keep moving, the flabasses dent-
ing their recliners don't have to bleat about some dude
coming through their doggie door to liberate the flatware.
If transients were organized, if they communicated, why
hell, they could wipe Suburbia USA clean. Dumb people
already have too much leisure time. Give a dude nothing
to do and pretty soon he invents alcoholism and lynching.
And before you know it he's sniping from a freeway over-
pass or wrapping gerbils in duct tape to jam up his butt-
hole.

I'm passionate about self-sufficiency and using my time
wisely. Had to sit jury duty once. One of the questions
they ask you, in criminal cases, is, 'Have you ever been
the victim of a crime?' And my answer was, 'Yeah, every
April 15th the US government rapes me.'

Bye-bye jury duty, and my time is mine once again.

The rain let up enough to make mud everywhere. Bad
for my Truck's finish. Can you believe it, even mud is

corrosive now? I pull to the shoulder in that kind of mud, it'd better be worth it.

I actually passed one or two hitchers up. Boring. Too much like the one I just did. Variety, right?

I was in the mood for love. I could've made a whole day of a woman.

Jesus, I hope I'm not getting a cold.

The good old boys piloting pick-ups always want to talk classic Man Stuff. Forged iron, true grit, honest labour in the heartland. Conquering the weaker sex. All in the crudest detail. They wear baseball caps with stupid patches. They have no taste in cologne.

Not this guy.

Ever notice jeeps? Real ones, not those bogus tin-can rice-rockets. If a woman is driving one, she's always attractive. If it's a man, nine times out of ten it's the sort who should be driving a pick-up truck instead. Rattling loudly on about bar fights and beer and pussy and which team kicked butt. They're ugly and hostile. They slap dumb bumper stickers over good clean chrome.

ASS GRASS OR GAS – NOBODY RIDES FOR FREE
THIS VEHICLE PROTECTED BY SMITH & WESSON
IF YOU'RE RICH I'M SINGLE

Proof that in America there's too much spare time available to people who haven't the dimmest notion of how to utilize it. No potential Magrittes or Nietzsches there.

I can spare them some of their pain.

So I spot the outline in the rain and think, *damn, another truck*, because of my experience of longbed rednecks. The kind that still joke are-you-a-boy-or-a-girl if you sport anything lengthier than a jarhead buzzcut with pink side-walls.

Noise and light from behind the oncoming truck, sudden and jolting. A speeding ambulance cuts a wide berth around the truck and blazes past me. I get splashed in the name of their mission of mercy. On their way to some accident.

The truck is still poking up the hill long after the ambulance fades. It is kept up well. No bumper stickers.

I decide to put out my thumb as it nears. I feel that killing power once again.

Spotted flashbars and for a sec thought it was them hypos from the Stop 'N' Go last night. Instead it was a van-type ambulance. The paramedics rode level with me. I blinked them around in plenty of time, hi-lo with the lights, and nuzzled the shoulder as best I could in the rain.

They cut their siren, out of respect or courtesy it doesn't matter. Good of 'em. They blew past close enough to rake water acrost my windows. I felt my Truck sway. What a joke: Their mission to save lives costs me mine as I tumble ass over teapot down the cliff. Next story.

There's sure something hypnotic, though, about them red and blue flashing lights as they cut the storm. The colours of civilization.

Those boys were on their way to an accident. A real one. I haven't seen any action tonight, and what I do can't rightly be called accidental.

Road's snaky. Makes the flashbar prettier as it loops and dwindles and finally hits the top of the hump and drops out of sight. Still no siren.

Even in this piss-poor visibility I can see the dude they just passed. Up ahead, two hundred yards, give or take. Dunked and drenched, thumb out and dripping. Hitch-hiking in the rain and thinking to himself: *Just my rat luck, an ambulance. Where're they going that they can't give a quick lift at 90 per? Wherever they're going, it's closer to civilization. No Riders. Damn my rat luck.*

Selfish for folks to think that way. Dudes who think that way never needed first aid before. Till now.

I'm still not going too fast because of the ambulance and it's pretty much already decided that I'm gonna pull over.

'Hey, thanks for stopping,' the rider said, shucking loose water like a hound dog.

'Climb on in afore you have to *swim* in,' said the driver.

'Sorry about your seat.'

'Don't mind that. I waterproofed it.'

'Had it waterproofed, huh?'

'No. Did the job myself with that tri-chloroethane spray stuff.' He pronounced the word carefully. He would not be expected to know such big words. 'Saturated it.'

'You did it up right, then. I don't feel so bad.' The rider patted himself down and tried to scare up a dry cigarette.

'No smokin' in my truck,' said the driver. 'If you don't mind.'

'Bad habit anyway.' The rider shrugged and chuckled. 'Like smoking will make you dry on the inside when you're soaked on the outside, or something.'

'What's that?'

The driver didn't get it. The rider let it die. As they

hit the grade he watched the driver shift gears. He was pretty good at it.

'Where you bound?'

'What's that?' Now the rider felt foolish. When the driver had said *bound* he'd thought he'd meant tied up. There was water in his left ear.

The driver enunciated. 'Where do you need to get to?'

'Oh. Well, where are *you* going?'

It was another game of the road. Don't say where you're headed and swat the question back. Then feign delighted surprise when the answer turns out to be *right near* the destination you'd intended all along!

'Up toward Lansdale. Got a friend I haul loads for, back and forth.'

'That'll cut a chunk off my travel time,' said the rider. 'Mind if I stick with you that far?'

'Long as you talk and help keep me awake. Radio reception sucks out here.'

'It's the ozone. The storm.'

'That's what I said.'

The rider sneezed explosively, once, twice. Then came that third hanger-on sneeze you can never quite coax out in rhythm.

'You need a Kleenex?'

The rider nodded and automatically pushed the glove-box button. It was locked.

The driver reached behind his head and produced a tissue from the dark clutter rearward, seemingly out of nowhere. The rider watched the driver's hands with interest. Then he blew his nose.

'Not gonna see town lights for twenty minutes even at dry road speed,' said the driver. 'Nobody out here but us. Animals all hiding. I heard there's this one kind of snake that waits till it rains to hunt. Knows all the other animals are in their burrows hiding from the rain. Doesn't have to forage.'

'Wow.' It wasn't yet time to ask the driver what time he thought it was.

They passed another mile in silence.

'How 'bout that ambulance?'

'Hope they made it OK,' said the rider. 'That must be a crap detail and a half. Rescue in the rain. Think you could spot me another Kleenex?'

'Sure.'

When the rider sneezed again the driver grabbed a fistful of the kid's hair and rammed his forehead into the glovebox button, which did not budge.

Except that the rider hadn't sneezed. It was a fake that nearly covered the lateral chop aimed at the driver's windpipe.

Which the driver inadvertently deflected with his hair grab.

The truck slowed and wandered into the oncoming lane. It lurched as its accelerator got pinned, then picked up speed like it had a purpose.

The two men inside were all over each other. The pilot window starred to a crushed-ice pattern. The rear-view mirror snapped off. The truck executed a question mark trajectory up the far side of the road, then crossed to drop over the edge. It rolled, picked up speed and began to throw off broken and twisted parts.

It was a long time falling.

Take this one down by hand. Something about the hitchhiker's eyes made me want this kill to be from the gut. Immediate. Knuckle-skinning.

Problem is, I'm a touch too cocky and sometimes I get what I ask for. Shoulda just jammed my buck knife into his gobblebox and clicked him off, first thing. What do I think I am, some artist, like a fag chef on TV?

Dammit.

I knew he was going to hit me. Knew it the second he did it, which made me half a second too slow. Figured I'd turn his head cold to my advantage and nail him while he was busy sneezing. You get in the first two hits, you can generally call yourself the winner. But he faked me out and the next thing I saw clearly was headlights across dirt and I thought, *We're bailing*.

Thought I was dreaming about rocking in a bed. Earthquake. Woke up and saw hoses and canvas straps and aluminium tubework. I saw a dude flicking his fingernail against a hypodermic needle, and even though I could see his orange hazard jersey it took me a long while to figure out that I was in the ambulance, horizontal and hurting good. Like having a word right on the tip of your tongue that drives you nuts until you can pin it.

The siren was off. Maybe that helped confuse me.

Felt like my shoulder was dislocated. Could feel it grind and pulse even though I was strapped in firm. I knew that when the paramedic saw my eyes open he'd say *There he is* and ask *How do you feel, Captain*, and tell me *Now don't try to move*. He did all that while I was wondering where the blood on his shirtfront came from.

Then he spoke mystic words like *concussion* and *greenstick fracture* and *compound broken this or that* and I finally swooned. Fainted dead out, wondering how much damage was prevented by my seatbelt versus how much had been caused by it.

The rider had never buckled his. Hitchers almost never do. They don't want their getaway hindered in case their ride turns out to be a psycho or a groper.

When I opened up my eyes again the paramedic said take it easy and mentioned how lucky I was.

I knew I got in a lick or two. Good solid ones. Wasn't as if I never took one down while driving. I know the risks. But like I said, something about this particular rider made me want to cancel him out even before we hit my planned excuse to stop.

Maybe it was the sense that with *this* dude, I'd never get the opportunity to pull over, stop, and do it neat. Not have to mop his brains off the tuck and roll.

Maybe it was because I'd seen his eyes, plenty of times, already looking back at me from my own rear-view mirror. Thought that in a flash as I was using the mirror to knock his teeth through his brain pan.

Part of me died with the realization that my Truck was probably a goner from the moment that guy put his hand on the door handle.

Then another part of me tried to die. I felt something snap slack inside, like a water balloon busting and making my lungs all hot.

When the paramedic moved I saw the rider. He was laying in the rack across from me and there was blood all over his face and he had been watching me the whole time.

And while the paramedic's back was turned, the rider's eyes said to me:

There's a helluva lot two guys like us could do with an ambulance.

A miscalculation, that's what it was. For this man, driving this pick-up, I should have saved the Smith and Wesson. On the other hand, it is probably good that the paramedics have not caught me packing. Questions. After that sort of questioning always comes cell time.

I swear the son of a bitch *knew* I was going to snag him while we were still moving. Damn, but he reacted fast. I'm right-handed. The advantage was his.

No, not Mister Country Pud in his pick-up, not at all.

Funny: Only two vehicles on this road all night, and I get to ride in both of them.

I recall thinking the driver is no problem because I can see his class ring hanging on a thong from the rear-view. As though he has peaked out in high school, given up on making anything of himself, and so stops wearing the ring because it reminds him of that failure, yet doesn't have the heart to toss it, so it winds up on the mirror.

My teeth are folded back and my whole mouth is numb. I recall meeting the dashboard head-on before falling base over apex down the hillside. I don't think I sustained any broken bones. Score one for no seatbelts.

When the driver regains consciousness I catch him looking at me and think, OK. Now the masks are off. He'd handled me like he's used to it. My gag with the tissue didn't detour him nearly enough.

Call me the Kleenex Killer, I think. Hah. What shall we call you, my truck-driving comrade?

He spasms. Some kind of convulsion, subtle. As the paramedic turns I spot a haemostat on the van's rubberized floor. I reach down to retrieve it, feeling my muscles work. Some kind of painkiller is amping me.

The ambulance driver says something and the paramedic steps forward. That's when I catch the pick-up driver's eye again. His expression tells me that, if I want him to, he can arrange another little seizure as a perfect distraction.

I can put out the paramedic's eye with the haemostat. Jam it into his brain. A hard enough swing will bury it in his carotid. It doesn't have to be sharp. 1–2–3–4.

The paramedic comes back to check on me. Taps up a vein to give me an injection. More jungle juice. It'll help me and the pick-up driver get our thing done.

'We're doing you a big favour,' says the paramedic.

As the plunger goes down I see the orange bubbles in the syringe. I smell the gasoline. The pick-up driver, tied securely down, begins to make noises.

But the needle empties and I know I'll never get my fist up in time.

The Frankenstein Syndrome

R. CHETWYND-HAYES

MORRIS SMITH WAS that terrifying phenomenon –
which is fortunately thin on the ground – a genius.

But one person recognized him for what he was, Mary-
Jane Jenkins, his girlfriend. And when she tried to
acquaint her family of the undoubted truth, she was – as
tradition will have it – laughed to scorn.

For Morris – like many of his kind – gave every sign
of being remarkably stupid. It took him an extraordinary
long time to answer simple questions; he blinked at people
he had known all his life, and seemed to have great difficulty in remembering their names. Simple mathematics
were beyond his comprehension, although he acquired the
art of reading and writing by the age of five, and could
memorize entire books – *Pilgrim's Progress*, for example –
by the age of eight, but was absent-minded.

It took Mary-Jane eighteen months to discover in what
field Morris's genius flourished.

'Why,' she asked, 'have you chosen to become a butcher's assistant?'

His reply came without hesitation.

'Because I want to know and understand the various parts that make up the animal body.'

For a while she did not speak, and he, as usual, walked with lowered head, hands sunk deep into his trouser pockets, maintaining a disconcerting silence. Presently she said a trifle impatiently: 'I don't know what I see in you.'

Now he nodded slowly: 'Neither do I.'

'Unless it be you are a challenge. And I can never resist a challenge.'

'That must be it. Do you want to know why I am interested in animal body-parts?'

'If you will condescend to tell me.'

'You won't laugh?'

'I never laugh at anything you care to tell me, unless you intend me to do so. Which so far you never have.'

He kicked an abandoned cigarette carton into the gutter before speaking again.

'I am interested in creating life.'

Mary-Jane did not laugh, but she frowned, shook her head from side to side, then took his left hand into her right.

'Would you care to explain what you mean by creating life?'

It was now his turn to frown.

'I should have thought it was simple enough. I want to create life. Make, invent, manufacture if you will, an entirely new life form.'

'But that's impossible – isn't it?'

'Of course it's not impossible. The process is complete

in my brain, but so far I haven't been able to sort of bring it out into the open. Put it down on paper, get down to actually making something that moves. Lives. I've called the entire business the Frankenstein Syndrome.'

Mary-Jane released his hand and drew a little to their left so that there was a space between them. She gave him a quick glance from between long lashes. Her voice when she spoke was a few octaves above a whisper.

'I've always known that under your shyness . . . Well, I mean you have an exceptional brain which only needed a sort of kick-start to come up with something really . . . But creating life! What gave you the idea? One of those old Frankenstein films?'

'Of course not. No, it was when I found a dead dog in a field.'

'A dead dog?'

'Yes, it had been lying in the sunlight for some time I should imagine. It was all swollen up, its belly was enormous. Then I kicked it. The belly I mean, and it burst open and a mass of writhing yellow maggots flowed out. The stench was awful.'

Mary-Jane swallowed and turned rather pale.

'Yes, I should think it would be. But how did that horrible sight give you the idea of creating life?'

'Don't you understand? And they call me stupid. The dog was dead, but from its dead body there had come forth life. That's a rather beautiful thought, isn't it? Maybe in time, after much experimental work – the thought came to me in a flash – that ugly wriggling life could be directed into a definite channel, then one would have a new life form. I applied to Mr Carter the butcher for the job of his assistant and as I only asked for a nominal wage, he gave it to me. He will tell you I picked up the art of butchering in a very short time and he's really amazed.'

'I expect he is.'

'But I'll soon be leaving him. My new life form will have little in common with any animal or creature on this planet. I will start from scratch. The humble maggot, then build up from there.'

Mary-Jane thought long and deeply, then released a long drawn-out sigh.

'If only your genius had taken another channel.'

He sighed also. 'One cannot decide in what direction one is to be gifted. Thanks to you and the gods I found out in time how to make use of my gift. Without your faith in me I might well have finished up in a lunatic asylum.'

Mary-Jane did not comment but emitted another deep sigh.

Morris Smith vacated his parents' house – rather to their relief – and thanks to a respectable legacy left to him by his maternal grandmother bought a tiny cottage that was situated a mile from the village. Mary-Jane was all for moving in with him, but he put paid to that idea by stating she would be an intolerable distraction, but he had no objection to her visiting once a day to prepare him at least one solid meal and maybe do a little light housework so long as she did not disturb any of his equipment. But that would be unlikely as he had turned the small back room into his laboratory and into this foul-smelling den she had no intention of entering.

However, she managed to keep him more or less clean and tidy, for she insisted he take a bath at her house every

Tuesday evening when her parents had departed for their weekly bridge club session, wash and shave once a day, and have his hair trimmed once a fortnight. His laundry went into her mother's washing machine, even though the lady objected to the yellowish and evil-smelling stains that fouled his shirts and the front of his trousers.

Some little hints as to the progress made in his life-creating experiments were hesitantly given over their shared meal, although they failed to reignite Mary-Jane's curiosity.

'Got them down to quite a few little ones and one big one. But the one big 'un exploded into some fairly smallish ones. However, the added sperm seems to have given them active life. They jump quite high.'

Now Mary-Jane expressed rather fearsome curiosity.

'Jump!'

'Jump I said, jump I mean. But I have to keep my mouth shut. I may have swallowed one or two. Be interesting to see what happens. But don't listen to me. Rambling.'

She turned the conversation into more mundane channels.

'You're looking very tired. There's big bags under your eyes.'

'Of course I'm tired. In these middle stages I cannot relax for a moment. Some have to be culled. I did not allow for this unexpected growth. But never mind.'

And he would then invariably get up and shut himself in the laboratory, slamming home some heavy bolts he had recently installed.

The days passed and despite Mary-Jane's nourishing casseroles Morris grew noticeably thinner, also he seemed to spend more and more time asleep, sprawled out on the double bed with gaping mouth from which emerged harsh snoring sounds and the occasional spluttering speech.

'They aim for the mouth. Can't be certain . . . can't be certain.'

One day Mary-Jane found she was unable to endure this almost obscene muttering, so she grabbed him by the shoulders and shook him into consciousness.

'Morris, this has got to stop. If you continue like this either your sanity or body will suffer. Perhaps both.'

At first she was not certain if he heard or understood what she was saying and was about to start more drastic means of restoring him to full awareness, when he said quite distinctly: 'I cannot stop. Not now.' He sat up and raised a shaking hand: 'Listen. The father of them all is getting restless. I must go to him. Wants din-dins.'

Mary-Jane listened and heard a soft slithering sound that culminated with a heavy thump on the door. She drew back and pressed her shoulders against the wall.

'In the name of sanity, Morris, what have you got in there?'

A bubbling chuckle emerged from his throat and his right hand pawed her breast. He spoke with some difficulty, quite possibly not fully understanding what he was saying.

'Something you should stay away from. Don't let it attach itself to . . . anything that protrudes.' A louder thud made the door shake and Morris pushed her away. With a supreme effort he rose up from his bed and staggered towards the door, leaning against it, patting the quivering panels and speaking as though to a backward and erring child.

'Hush. Let peace come to my creation. I've laboured for more than seven days and now I should rest. So should you, my undulating child.'

'Mad,' Mary-Jane whispered, but not so softly that Morris did not hear her. He waved a reproving finger while gently kicking the door.

'Not I. Can a god go mad by merely gazing upon his creation? If so then surely our creator must be raving after watching the antics of the human species. But . . . I warn you – get out before I open this door. Maybe if you see what I've made, just maybe you won't be so very sane.'

Mary-Jane had never been so frightened in her life, but she had the courage that comes to a person when they know a loved one is in deadly danger. She had never had occasion to measure her courage before, walk boldly through the mists of fear, face the unknown with wide-open eyes.

Standing there watching Morris patting door panels, whispering to something that slithered, jumped, and bumped, she told herself that the unknown could not be so terrifying as imagination suggested.

Morris could have found a comatose snake; possibly a large species of grass snake that had but recently fed, but now was fully active again. But grass snakes did not jump – or did they?

And was Morris so far deranged that he was mistaking a harmless reptile for a monster of his own creation?

For an immeasurable period of time they stood looking at each other, no one speaking, but listening to the continued slithering that came from behind the closed door. Then it happened.

Without warning the door trembled from a mighty

crash. Mary-Jane cried out even while she tried to imagine what could have made such a sound.

A sledgehammer? But that would have shattered the door. A man's shoulder? The sound came again only this time it was a little louder. A definition came to mind. Something pliable – something with a heavy object on one end.

'The head has hardened.' Morris spoke more to himself than the terrified girl. 'Now it will be able to unlock its jaw. I will have to put it down and start all over again. Maybe not. But I mustn't run the risk of it getting loose. Feed and breed. Always goes for the protruding parts.'

It was some time before Mary-Jane was able to speak and when she did every word dripped fear; her eyes glazed as her hands clutched one to the other, then she shook them and placed them under her armpits.

'I'm cold. My hands are freezing as though all the warmth has been drained from me.'

'Don't think about it,' Morris told her. 'Don't try to imagine what it's like. And get out. Get out before I open the door. Apart from anything else there may be a few loose jumpers. The father will sleep after I've fed him. And the little jumpers – if the worst must happen – I can feed on them.'

It was then that Mary-Jane tasted that emotion which is generated in that wild country that is situated beyond fear. It is not the uncontrollable cold terror-storm that we call panic; but rather a searching blast of horror-wind that suspends life for a few seconds and gives us a view of what might come.

She had a glimpse of the interior of her lover's brain and it was a limb-freezing vision. A twilight country that flowed as a red-tinted plain until it reached the black slopes of fire-crested mountains. *They* slithered, reared hideous heads, then sank down into liquid shadow that nestled between mist-coated rocks, and Mary-Jane sensed their presence rather than saw them.

The room quivered and suddenly flickered into stark reality; she saw Morris lurching towards the door – the one that still trembled under a softly bumping onslaught, and she watched his hand go out and grip the black plastic handle. Then after an unimaginable period of time, during which she could see his mouth opening and closing, ejecting unheard words, his eyes flashed a warning, even as he turned the handle, and with an explosion of movement the door flew back – crashed against the left wall . . . and his body all but filled the opening . . . Yet she had a glimpse of an upright smooth white column of flesh that was crowned by a pink pulsating face which was a horrible parody of Morris's own.

Then the door closed with a resounding crash that seemed to make the house shudder and Mary-Jane was crouched on the floor ejecting vomit from a heaving stomach, cold as never before in her life, particularly in the hands and feet.

Merciful oblivion extinguished the illusion of space-time and for a while Mary-Jane slept in that limbo that has never known the agony of awareness.

Then she awoke.

The first thing she noticed was the bed had disappeared.

She climbed to her feet, sank on to a hard-back chair and stared at the empty place where the bed used to be.

Morris must have moved it.

The question was: Where had he moved it to?

There was only one answer.

While she was unconscious Morris Smith had with deliberate intent, opened *that* door, pushed, pulled, and otherwise moved one four-foot-six divan into that room he called a laboratory. The place where something that looked like a flesh-coloured snake reared up to one third of its length and sucked the warmth from any living object that just happened to be in the vicinity.

God, Morris Smith, plus a little help from the devil had created life. No, God had no interest in this project. It might even be below the devil's consideration. If there was a new life form behind that door, Morris Smith alone was responsible. He was the undoubted genius.

Mary-Jane knelt behind the door and put her left ear against one panel.

There was sound.

A loud sucking interposed by low groans.

The sucking suggested a grotesque baby with thick blubbery lips taking nourishment from a large feeding bottle. Yes . . . yes . . . thick pink lips clamped to a feeding bottle. And sucking . . . and the bottle groaned.

Mary-Jane jumped to her feet and pounded the door with clenched fists, and experienced fearful surprise when it slid back without so much as a squeak, to reveal that room which she could now view with a clear eye – take everything in: an enamel top table under the window was covered with what looked like decayed meat. A glass tank was filled to the brim with wriggling yellow, green, and pink maggots. Scraps of raw flesh littered the floor and there was a plenitude of flesh-coloured worms that seemed to wriggle in her direction the very moment she placed a foot in the room.

A little worm – or maybe a special kind of green maggot – left the floor and jumped on Mary-Jane's right breast. Before she could move, it fastened a toothless mouth on her flesh and began to suck. Mary-Jane screamed and brushed the hideous thing off, only to find that three more were clustered around her left breast and two more were trying to get into her mouth.

Fortunately they were easy to dislodge, but it was in a state of near collapse that she approached the bed and tried to take note of what was happening there.

Morris wore a Marks and Spencer's red vest. Just a red vest. He was naked from the waist down. For a young man he had pretty legs. The thought slid across Mary-Jane's mind. White and smooth. And between them there was a third white and smooth leg and it jerked back and forward. Jerked back and forth. And this third leg was very long; it undulated across the floor and seemed to be circling the room, even making pulsating bulges across the doorway. Coyly blushing in places, its otherwise lovely white skin could have graced a beautiful woman's shoulder.

Life must live. Existence must exist. Newly created life must feed.

Mary-Jane gazed upon the flesh-snake (good word) and now came to realize that its head was nestling down between Morris's legs, feeding as the young are intended to do. She then turned her attention to her loved one, the genius, the creator, and gradually she began to understand. She allowed obscene knowledge to take shape in her brain until, after emitting an ear-splitting shriek, she grabbed the round warm-flesh thing and pulled with all her might. Morris screamed as she had never known a man could scream, and there was a lot of stretching, but presently the flesh-snake came away with a muted popping sound. The pink grotesque face parted its thick lips and spat at Mary-Jane.

Morris lay prostrate, with not a sign of life, and there was a lot of blood and torn gristle between his legs. Such is the power of love that Mary-Jane did not concern herself with what squirmed on the floor. Standing over the motionless young man, she pressed her lips to his gaping mouth and tried to give him the kiss of life.

She felt the movement in his stomach and would possibly have pulled her mouth free, only there wasn't time. In fact no time at all.

She felt the rubbery lips fasten on the tip of her tongue, then became painfully aware that the pressure was tightening. A terrible pain raced up her tongue, spread into the jaws, froze her neck muscles – and she pulled back, not caring that her tongue stretched, lengthened like a piece of rubber. So did the flesh-snake that had its tail coiled in Morris's stomach.

A duet scream. A long, quivering length of tongue. But the flesh-snake soon regained its normal circumference, so that the tongue came out by its roots.

Groaning, moaning, dribbling blood, Morris would soon die – and so would Mary-Jane, but not before the maggot creatures that came from every corner had eaten from her, and later feasted on the still figure that half reclined upon the bed.

Morris had indeed created a new life form and it wriggled, writhed, undulated, seethed, and emerged out on to the landing, then slithered down the stairs.

Much later, when the sun had set, the mighty big one and all the little ones, the bits and pieces, came out into the moonlight and spread out in every direction.

The new life form was preparing to be fruitful. To multiply.

To take over the earth.

High-Flying, Adored

DANIEL FOX

THE GODS LOVE the high places. The gods and us, the semi-divine, their acolytes and servants: even in our mortal aspects we too feel the thrill of standing high above the earth, of looking down.

Humankind is too afraid of falling.

I saw my lover first in black and white, a picture in the *Chronicle*. He was smiling, posing with a stonecutter's mallet and chisel beside a leering gargoyle; the article explained that he was a master mason, recently arrived to take charge of restoration work at the cathedral.

The following week I visited the Close in my ongoing search for suitable locations for photo-shoots. An elderly man showed me around, debating cheerfully the rival calls of God and Mammon; we agreed that the lights and cameras of my work, the designer-bodies of my models would be inappropriate to the cathedral itself or the hallowed ground it stood on, but that all other buildings in the Close should be open to me.

I was quite content with that, and thanked him sincerely

as he shook my hand and left me in the cloisters. I wandered around for a few minutes by myself, the negotiator in me displaced by the artist as I gazed at the weathered limestone archways and the harsh chiaroscuro of sun and shadow.

At length I was drawn by the sounds of voices from behind a tarpaulin screen hung on scaffolding, the sounds of metal on stone. I was curious, and curiosity has never seemed a sin to me. It has the drive, the force that I have always associated with virtue; all action is to be commended, and only passivity is wrong.

So I lifted a flap of the tarpaulin, and walked through.

There were half a dozen people working in that screened-off corner of the quad, men and women both. There were designs being traced carefully on to blocks of new-cut stone, there were earlier tracings being chipped away more carefully still, the first nervous sketches towards a final sculpture.

Closer at hand, the man who was to become my lover stood with a bare-chested boy, instructing him on how to mix cement and sand into a mortar.

I listened, and learned; and tonight I have used that knowledge acquired seemingly by chance. Tonight I have mixed cement under my lover's eyes, I have shown him that nothing is ever wasted.

The man spoke to me, when he was finished with the boy. He was friendly and accommodating, pleased with my interest in his work; after a few minutes he invited me up to the cathedral roof, to see the damage wrought by wind and rain.

In that high place he stood with his hand on a savage and malignant face concealing a gutterspout, strong fingers digging at flakes of dark and rotting stone; he looked down to the green graveyard below us and the ancient buildings of the Close, he looked across to where the metal skeleton of a new tower block was rising above the city, and I could see no fear in him.

Even then, even so early I remember thinking that I could love such a man, a man so unafraid to fall.

Tonight, he is afraid. Tonight his body stank of terror, when first he overhung the abyss. I reassured him calmly, kindly; I told him he had no reason to doubt my ropes, my knots, myself. *I will not let you fall*, I said to him. But still his eyes rolled white in his skull, still he screamed his fear and still his body stank, until I covered it.

In the dark my lover came to me, in the queue outside a club at midnight. Neither of us was surprised, I think, to find the other there. I used my membership privileges to sign him in; then we drank, and danced, and tried to talk above the pounding music. At last frustration took us out into the cool street again, tired and sticky with sweat, our ears ringing in the sudden silence. There we could talk, and did: on the walk to the high-rise where I lived, on the long ride up in the slow lift. I had the penthouse flat; we kicked our shoes off in the hall, left a trail of clothes from there to the bedroom and fell on to the duvet closely tangled, quite naked, enough of talking.

As then, so now. Now too I have had enough of talking. My lover is secure in his ropes, in his certainties; there is nothing more needing to be said. He hangs silently above the drop, no longer frightened of a fall that will not come. Perhaps he whimpers a little still, deep in his throat; but perhaps not. Perhaps it's only the wind singing in the girders. Windsong is potent and ever-present at this height, in this emptiness.

And with my own work done, if roughly and clumsily done, I feel no call to speak myself. I sit with my feet dangling, the street lit yellow far below me; I look at what I have achieved, and am content. My eyes turn up, higher than flight or fancy; I gaze skyward, starward, looking for godsign among the constellations. And find none, only a paling towards the east where the sun will rise soon. The gods speak when they will; we their messengers can only wait, only watch and listen and be ready.

In the dark my lover left me. In the dark, when I was sleeping. I had talked long and late that night, had drunk the better part of a bottle of whisky and told him what I knew of the gods and of myself, how I had served them.

When I woke, the flat was empty. He had gone, he had packed what clothes he kept there and was gone, leaving only a brief and confused note that showed how little he had listened, how much less he had understood.

His understanding must be better now. What cannot be explained has been demonstrated to him. I have brought him up to this high place and shown him all the kingdoms of the earth; and soon now, soon he will see me depart into them.

He must remain, of course. Though his body is no longer flesh, he cannot follow me on the paths that I shall take. He can do nothing but crouch where I have set him, and see me on my way.

In the dark, my lover left me; and in the dark I took him back. I left a message for him to meet me at a pub we knew; and when he came – as I knew he would come, his sense of honour would compel him – I was waiting for him. Not in the pub, though. I was on the scaffolding above the street, where they are building that new tower block. The pavement was closed to pedestrians, but I knew my man. Coming to the pub from his lodgings, he would walk in the gutter rather than cross the street twice.

And so he did; and so I caught him. I dropped a noose over his head, drew it swiftly tight and hauled his kicking body up, with the line passed over a scaffolding pole in lieu of block and tackle.

There were no challenges, no questions from the street. I drew him in and let him fall, half-strangled; then I tied him hand and foot, and rested for a while before carrying him up stairs and ladders to the top of the unfinished building.

If there was a watchman on the site, he left us undisturbed, even after my lover started screaming. I had all night to do my work; and I did it as carefully, as well as I could.

There are no walls as yet on these upper levels, only rough concrete floors and iron girders rising like the bars of a cage. I cut the clothes from my lover's body, cutting him also, a little, when he struggled; then I dragged him to within a yard of the floor's ending, and cautioned him to lie still.

That's when the fear first hit him, when he learned to be like other men, afraid of a fall.

I had brought up my materials earlier. Now I mixed cement and sand and water, working them well with a trowel, as he had shown me. When that was ready, I set my lover where I wanted him. I forced his shivering legs to bend, using all my strength against his reluctance: I placed him and roped him, crouched at one corner of that topmost floor, facing out across the city with his back to a rising girder. His wrists were tied to his ankles, his knees rose up almost to his chin, and his voice sobbed and screeched uselessly into the wind.

I fetched a bucketful of the stiff mortar.

He saw my intention then, or a part of it. His foot flinched away, as best it could in its bonds; but I coated it none the less, it and its twin. As I worked my way higher so he fought the harder, screaming and threshing against the ropes. Much of the mortar was lost, falling away towards the gaudy lights below us. But I had time and more cement, more sand and water; and I was very patient. Every tall building should have its guardian, its watch.

And now my lover is a gargoyle, one of my own creation. He squats in his grey and hardening skin, wild eyes staring out at the pale sky. Blood trickles from his open mouth, where I have cut out his tongue; rainwater was ever a dishonour to our breed.

We have been spotted, finally. Dawn comes late at this time of year, and work on a building site starts early; they are aware of us now. There are police cars on the ground, lights and sirens; in the air a helicopter, circling.

I have pulled up the ladders giving access to this floor, and the police are watchful, wary, keeping their distance. No doubt they think my lover a hostage against my freedom; no doubt they think me caged within these girders.

They are fools. Soon now, soon I will take upon myself my true form, my other aspect. I have taken my clothes off already, in preparation. The sun will be stronger in a little while; and then my skin will darken. Iron claws will tip my fingers and my feet; there will be leathern wings upon my back, and this human mask will fall away. Then shall they see my face, and know the truth of us; then shall they understand what race it is they have been mocking through the centuries with their demons and gargoyles and grotesques.

Then shall I leave my lover to mock us no more in his unbelief. They will not dare to move him then, when they see what hand has wrought this change upon him.

Then shall I spread my wings, and fly.

Soon, now. Soon.

A Night With Claudette

BERNARD DONOGHUE

CHARLIE SAT IN the chair by the window with a dressing-gown draped around his frame while Claudette lay naked upon the bed. The air was heavily scented with her perfume.

They had been married now for twenty years but this was the first time he had seen her in days.

Charlie had decided to use the quiet stillness of the night to take a long, lingering look at his wife's voluptuous body. He lit a cigarette, tossed the spent match into the ashtray on the bedside table, and decided to start with her hair. Claudette's hair was a stunning golden blonde, the long, soft curls tumbled around her shoulders with her every movement, framing the delicate features of her face while reflecting the soft lights of a restaurant or the bright rays of a summer sun. Her hair graced the pillow now, softly cushioning her cheek, and he smiled as he remembered how often he had felt it brush against his own face during many nights of unashamed passion.

He flicked some ash from the cigarette before inhaling deeply from it. There was no denying it, her hair was certainly beautiful, probably her most instantly attractive feature. With the possible exception of her breasts, of course. But he would come to those later.

Charlie's eyes ran slowly along her jawline, seeing the smooth skin of her face and throat. Her sensuous mouth was open slightly and the light of the waning moon which poured in through the window glanced seductively upon the soft swellings of her lips. And how much pleasure he had received from those lips!

Charlie looked then at her hands, the slim-fingered hands which were curved slightly in her relaxation. As usual her nails were impeccably varnished in a deep pink and her left hand was adorned with a broad golden band on its third finger. Claudette's hands were beautiful. And she was good with them. When he was holding her hand she could communicate her needs through her gentle grip. He could tell, for instance, when it was time to leave a party and have some private fun somewhere – usually here in the bedroom, though she would often ask him to stop the car in some quiet lay-by for a little while.

Her legs were certainly an appealing feature. They were drawn up so that her knees were towards him as he stubbed out his cigarette. Her legs were long and slender, but not so thin that the tone of the muscles could be seen; they had a good feminine fullness about them. Her thighs in particular were just as a woman's should be: soft, smooth and warm, always so sensuously warm, an indication of the pleasures which lay ahead to an eager, roving hand.

He stroked his chin now, feeling the new growth of stubble which he would shave off in the morning, as his eyes alighted on what he considered to be her best features of all.

Claudette's bare breasts were nothing less than perfect. They were gorgeously soft and heavy, so full, so good to look at, and so exciting to touch and caress. And although she would never dress in a cheap way, she would always do so in such a way as to maximize the subtle message of her latent passion and she would often wear long-chained necklaces outside her blouses to emphasize the seductive slopes.

Unfortunately, it was this very exudation of sexuality which had caused the downfall of their marriage. It had been, without a doubt, the most traumatic time of his life when he came home early one day and found her in bed with . . .

Well, let's face it, they weren't exactly just *lying* there, her and . . . Roger. Roger the bloody lodger.

Charlie held his head in his hands. The painful memories flooded back, drowning the sweet reverie of his thoughts. He had said and done many things that night, some of which he deeply regretted. The thing was, he totally forgave her now; he was ready, even willing, to forget that the whole episode had never occurred. But it could never be; the rot had set in and it was simply too late. Tonight would be the last time he would see her.

He rose from the chair and walked over to the wardrobe, hoisting from its interior the large, empty suitcase. He laid it by the bed and opened it up.

Bending over the bed slightly, he stroked her cheek gently, whispering, 'I'm sorry, darling, but it's over now.' Then he placed his hand upon her breast, cupping it very gently in the palm one last time.

Although the years had certainly been kind to her, even here in the pale, silvery moonlight, he could see that there were some changes about her: her skin had lost its youthfully charged glow and its suppleness, her hair had lost some of its lustre, her breasts felt cold . . .

Regretfully, he picked it up, placed it into the suitcase and then put the other one alongside it. Next he carried the stiffened torso and fitted it snuggly into place. After he had packed the bent legs, the arms and the head, he stuffed the hands and feet into the remaining spaces before picking up the pillow and brushing the shaven hair off it. The golden curls, he noticed, decorating the body in the suitcase as they had decorated her head in life.

As he brought down the lid a waft of air escaped, filling his nostrils with the pungent smell of death and decay. He reopened the case and liberally sprayed the contents with the perfume bottle from the dressing-table until the stench was masked once more. Tomorrow, he promised himself, he would give her a decent burial in the woods. Unless, of course, he felt like seeing her just one more time . . .

Casey, Where He Lies

STEPHEN GALLAGHER

IT WAS IN my car and it was late, and I was coming back from I don't know where . . . I was alone, I remember that much. I think I was on the motorway. I'd let the radio hunt up some local station and I was playing it, loud. It was the late-night all-CD show; give me digital technology and a clear FM signal and a good fast road at midnight, and I'll show you a movement of heaven. And because it was a new company vehicle and not one of the clapped-out old roadsters that have littered my car-owning career, there was little competition from road noise.

Enjoy it, kiddo, I thought to myself. *You've earned it.*

Me, in a company car. And a big one, too. After seven years in A&R I'd managed to hand in my leather bomber jacket and now I felt that I'd finally made an arrival. I reckoned I deserved it, and I was going to enjoy it. I'd set the cruise control and I was leaning back and I was eyeing the mirror every now and again because I'd set the control on the wrong side of legal. The band on the air was one of our own, a defunct but well-loved set of rockers from the late Seventies named Alice the Goon. They'd recently broken up after their drummer's fatal heart attack; the big lesson here, kids, is never to snort cocaine when the jacuzzi's on maximum. By now the survivors were all in tax exile but their followers were still around, a little bit greyer and a lot more affluent and a ready market for the CD rerelease of the Alice back catalogue. *Goats and Monkeys* had been out for a week, and the advance orders had already sent us into a second pressing.

A copy had been on my desk for a lot longer than that, but of course I'd yet to listen to it. I'd played the album to death when it had originally come out on vinyl and I suppose there was little temptation in it now. Some things in your life, you just say goodbye to them and that's that. But here it was, and I was well in the mood, and so I cranked it up high; never the most subtle band in the world, they tested the limits of the in-car system and made the door panels shake. And then . . .

Well, first let me try to explain. Do you remember how there was once a vogue for including little bits of studio crap and background at the beginning or end of a track? It probably started with a simple *ah-one-two-three* every now and again and then got out of hand. Alice the Goon had gone in for that kind of thing along with everyone else. The idea was to let the punters glimpse the secret world on the other side of the mike. There was something here as the track ended . . . somebody slow handclapping, somebody saying something that I'd never yet been able to make out.

But I found that I could make it out now. And it came as such a surprise that I almost forgot that I was driving, until a blast on a big truck's airhorn warned me that I was wandering out of my lane.

Casey? I was thinking, disbelievingly.

His name was Francis Case, but he'd been Casey to everyone for as long as I could remember. Casey and I had been at school together. When we'd gone to the same redbrick university we'd shared a room in the Residences and I'd managed to get him a job on the Entertainments Committee. My job there was to book acts and to help work out the concert schedule for each forthcoming term. Casey's was to drive the van down to the station and pick up the cans for the weekly film programme. But to hear him talk in the bar, you'd think he was a personal friend of Paul McCartney; big on dreams but limited in his achievements, that was Casey all the way.

But it wasn't me that got him the job with the record company. That was something that he'd managed on his own. He became a song plugger, mainly working the radio stations; he took DJs to lunch wherever they'd let him, he handed out hats and T-shirts and promotional junk which mostly finished up in the bedroom of the secretaries' children, he called each Head of Music by his first name while the Head of Music was clearly making no effort to remember his. At absolute rock bottom, he'd wait in the foyer for hours in the hope of catching someone of influence on his or her way out. All to get airplay. And mostly for nothing.

I bumped into him in town one night. Part of my job – in fact the main part of my job then – involved a restless hopping from club to club wherever new talent was playing. On an average night this could mean five, six different venues, usually with no more than ten or fifteen minutes spent at each. Sometimes I'd go miles out of London and know within that same first fifteen minutes whether my journey had been wasted. More often than not, it had. Some bands, a very few, were just an insult to a paying audience. The vast majority were proficient enough, but in essence had nothing to say. Only a tiny percentage showed that instant glimmer that even inexperience and lack of practice can't disguise, and then I'd be in instant competition with all the other A&R people on the same circuit.

The night I ran into Casey was bang in the middle of the rise of punk. Remember those days? I was checking out the Snots and had found them to be about as promising as their name suggested. The club was hot and dark and shoulder-to-shoulder with toilet-brush haircuts and sweaty binliners; I was squeezing my way through towards the exit and suddenly there was Casey, beaming and pumping my hand like a long-lost brother.

I looked him over. I could hardly believe it. The last time I'd seen him he'd been in Hush Puppies and one of those Marks and Spencer's sweatshirts, about as unhip as it's possible to get without actually wearing a tie. But now . . . now he was in a black leather jacket with lots of silver studs and no sleeves, tight jeans with black suede pointy shoes, and his hair was gelled up into spikes. The problem was, he still looked as if he belonged in Hush Puppies and a chain-store pullover.

'Hey, man,' he said. 'How've you been doing?'

And I thought, *Man*? Casey's calling me *Hey, man*? Back at school, in the days when everyone else had been into David Bowie, Casey had just been on the point of discovering the Carpenters.

But I said, 'I was just leaving. I only wish I'd seen you earlier.'

Casey was nodding, although it was hard to be heard over the background. 'I know what you mean,' he said. 'Are the Snots a radical outfit, or what?'

'You *like* them?' I said, unable to conceal my surprise, and Casey seemed to falter but then recovered.

He tugged someone out from behind him and said, 'Did I ever introduce you to Mariella? We're going around together. She's a big fan of Alice the Goon.'

'Hi, Mariella,' I said.

Mariella was hanging on to Casey's elbow and had been half-hidden by him; now she waved as he swung her into view. 'Hi,' she said.

She seemed awfully young for Casey, but that wasn't the most surprising part of it. She had black hair down in a long fringe that covered her eyes, like a sheepdog's; this with purple lipstick and a short black skirt over fishnet tights, so that she looked like something out of the audience for *The Rocky Horror Show*. She was grinning a shy person's grin and I noticed that she had probably the most perfect teeth I'd ever seen.

Casey said, 'I was telling her how Alice the Goon's one of the acts on our books. She's been stuck to me like a tick ever since.'

'Well,' I said over the racket with what I hoped was a diplomatic smile, 'who could complain about that?'

Casey didn't care. Casey was obviously in some kind of heaven. 'Want a drink?' he said.

'I've got to pee and go,' I told him, and then I nodded to Mariella. 'Nice to meet you.'

And as I was moving away, I heard her saying, 'Why do they need to send two A&R people to the same concert?'

So, that was his line. I made my way through the crowd toward the toilets, which I knew were going to be a cesspit and they were. The floor tiles were awash, the doors had been wrenched off the cubicles, each of the toilet rolls had been pulled out and unravelled. All of this was lit by a single naked bulb that fortunately was recessed behind strong wire, or else it probably would have gone as well.

As I was standing there, I was thinking that Mariella had to be the least likely girlfriend for Casey that I ever could have imagined. In his fantasies, perhaps, but in reality it was about as likely as a date between Cher and the Pope. That remark about two A&R people made it clear; he'd been hyping himself up to impress her and doing a little editorial work on his CV.

Well, I thought, good luck to him. What I knew of Casey's life so far had been marked by great enthusiasm but little to show for it, and no noticeable mastery of bullshit at all. He was an innocent in his way, which was how I'd managed to put up with him for so long.

At this point I heard the door swing open behind me and I looked back, even though I hadn't finished; I'd learned that you can never be too careful in these places. They'd a no-alcohol bar, but people smuggled in the hard stuff in hipflasks. Others didn't need drink, already having sufficient personality disorders of their own. Casey came in, taking a deep breath after the oxygen deprivation of the concert space outside, but then the smell hit him and he was immediately sorry.

'Fuck me,' he said as the door swung shut and cut out the noise behind him. 'What do they *do* in here?'

'Don't knock it,' I said. 'Six million flies can't be wrong. Who got *you* dressed tonight?'

'I reckoned I was due for a change of image,' he said, a tad self-consciously.

'Yeah,' I said, 'and I've seen the reason why.'

Casey said with detectable anxiety, 'You're not going to mess it up for me, are you?'

'Me?' I said, moving past him to rinse my hands. The washbasin looked more like a toilet than most toilets. 'Nah. Your secret's safe in these hands, Normalman.'

Casey leaned on the wall by the rubber-johnny machine.

'There's something else I wanted to ask you,' he said.

'Somehow this time, I get a feeling the answer's going to be no.'

'You haven't even heard the question yet!'

'No, but the lead-in's ominous enough.'

I turned to the roller-towel, which by some oversight was still working, and started pulling out enough blue linen to dry my hands. Casey said, 'Find out when Alice the Goon have a studio date and get us in there.'

I looked at him. 'Now, how exactly am I supposed to do that?'

'I don't know. Use your influence.'

'I haven't any.'

'You're in and out of the building all the time,' he said, and there was a note of pleading in his voice. 'You know people. That's more than I do. At least say you'll try.' There was a pause, during which I gave up on the roller towel; the stuff coming out seemed no cleaner than the stuff it was replacing. Casey said, 'Please. She actually *likes* me.'

'If she likes you, then it shouldn't make the slightest difference whether you can get her into the studio or not.'

'But I don't want to risk finding that out.'

What could I say?

I said I'd try.

Casey went away happy, diving into the crowd in a hurry to find Mariella before somebody else did, and I hopped a taxi to the next club and promptly forgot all about the promise.

I'll be honest, there was no point in doing anything else. As one of the foot soldiers of the company I didn't have the contacts and I didn't have the influence; all that I could achieve would be to make a fool of myself and, at the worst, even do myself some damage. You don't just 'sit in' on a session with a long-established outfit like Alice the Goon; even your lowliest garage band feels the presence of strangers, and at the level of Alice you operate your security on a basis of natural paranoia. On her looks and her youth and with the help of someone better connected than me, Mariella might just have made it into the session on her own. But Mariella and Casey together? Never. My intention was to let it ride for a few days and then I'd send him a message, I'd tried and it was no go, sorry and all that. The chances were that Mariella would have dumped him by then, anyway.

Some mention of the band on an internal memo about three weeks later made me remember to call him. I didn't have his current home number but I called up the Head of Promotions to ask if he could have one of his pluggers get in touch when he next stopped by.

As soon as he heard Casey's name, he said, 'Him? He got sent up the road nearly a fortnight ago.'

Not understanding, I said, 'Sent up the road to where?'

'I mean he was sacked. On the spot.'

'For what?'

'For trying to blarney his way into the vault under the impression that he could get out some studio master tapes and play them for his girlfriend. And I can tell you, as far as I'm concerned he'll be no great loss.'

I hate to admit it. But I was actually relieved. For one thing it meant that I didn't have to deal with Casey and make up excuses. For another, it meant that I wouldn't have to speak to him at all.

And I never did. Ever again.

The morning after my late drive home, I got to my desk and I sorted through all my unread memos and stuff waiting to be dealt with and finally, in a drawer, found my in-house copy of the *Goats and Monkeys* CD reissue. I put it on the player and then found the track, and quickly ran through it to the end.

The last crashing chord. Somebody clapped.

And in the fade I could swear that I heard Casey say, *Brilliant. Fucking brilliant.*

I pushed the sound up and backtracked and let it play again. The tail-end of the chord came out so loud that it nearly shook the pictures off the walls and brought my secretary to look in anxiously through the door. Casey – I was becoming more certain that it was Casey even though the volume made it harder, not easier, to tell – did his piece and then, right there on the cusp of the fade, I heard a girlish *Yeah!*

I'd only heard Mariella speak the once, and that had been in a noisy club with my head buzzing with the high volume and negligible talent of the Snots. On the evidence, I couldn't have chosen for certain between the sound of her and Barbara Stanwyck. But somehow, as with Casey, I was just as certain.

My secretary was looking puzzled. I call her my secretary, although I actually share her with three other people. I said, 'Do me a favour, Joan. See if you can get hold of Tony Meek for me.'

She seemed doubtful. 'Are you sure he's still with us?'

'Last I heard, he'd gone to EMI. But see if you can track him down anyway.'

The call came through about half an hour later. Tony Meek, formerly our head of promotions, was now an independent press agent and I found myself talking to him on his car phone. I said, 'Can you remember when you were working here, you fired a song plugger for trying to get his hands on some master tapes?'

It wasn't the best line in the world. 'No . . .' I heard him say, and then; 'Wait a minute, yes I do. We're talking about the world's only punk trainspotter, right?'

'That sounds pretty much like him.'

'Frank Case?'

'Casey.'

'You'd better make this quick, the Dartford Tunnel's coming up.'

'Is there any chance he could have interfered with the masters?'

'None at all. He didn't get past the desk.'

'Are you sure?'

'Can you imagine what would have happened if he had? Why, what's gone wrong?'

I almost told him . . . but then I remembered that

178

Tony Meek wasn't with the company any more, and that something like this could just conceivably be considered as a leak.

So I said, 'Nothing . . . his name just came up in some other context, that's all.'

'Hold on a minute,' Meek said suddenly, 'isn't he the one who . . . '

But his voice was lost as the Dartford Tunnel swallowed up both his car and the signal.

I checked with the personnel department and I checked with the people out at the vaults in Cricklewood, and they pretty much confirmed what Tony Meek had said; Casey had turned up one night with Mariella in tow and had dropped a few names in an attempt to get access to the vault, and the night man had told him to bugger off and then had reported him the next morning. It must have been quite a humiliation. He was stupid to try it at all, of course; those big studio master tapes are irreplaceable and are only ever handled under stringent conditions in the presence of one of the company's technical supervisors. But I suppose that having failed in his promise to get Mariella into a recording session, getting her into the presence of holy relics must have seemed like the next best, if somewhat desperate, option. What a hold she must have had on him. And how weak a hold he must have felt he had on her.

I suppose she'd dumped him after that, and that's why he killed her.

There could only be one explanation. The voice I'd heard couldn't have been his. *Goats and Monkeys* was a fifteen-year-old recording and we'd both been spotty schoolboys when it had been cut. Mariella had probably been in frilly skirts and still playing with dolls. If the two of them hadn't somehow messed up the master, then there was no way that their voices could be present on the CD reissue. What I'd heard was just a latent sound that had been there all along, but which had been waiting for new technology to bring it out.

When I got home that evening, there were cars in the driveway. My heart sank. We had guests, and I'd forgotten. I put on my happy-face and went in and tried to be bright over the pre-dinner drinks, but I could see Barry looking daggers at me whenever he popped through from the kitchen because I'd been late in the first place. This was the house we had in Acton, the one with the big picture window looking out on to the garden that Barry had set with coloured lights so that it came on like a fantasy landscape after dark. The guests that night were an agency Art Director and his boyfriend, neither of whom I knew, and the McDowells from two doors down, whom mercifully I did. I poured drinks and we made small talk and I struggled to conceal the fact that my mind wasn't entirely on it. Barry wanted to impress the Art Director, I know, but he was fussing around so much that he was probably irritating everybody.

After the meal and when we'd all moved away from the table, I took the opportunity to disappear and go out to the garage. I didn't plan to be more than a few minutes, certainly not long enough to be missed. A lot of my old boxes were in there, all the stuff that had no place in the house but which I couldn't bring myself to throw away. There couldn't have been much less than a thousand LP records, a lifetime's collection. Probably half of them had been paid for. The others were all promo copies, stamped as such with a gold NOT FOR RESALE overprinting somewhere on the sleeve. Many of these were unplayed. For some reason, I seemed to have lost my interest in album collecting from the day I could get them for nothing. The later issues were uncatalogued. But the early stuff was all in strict order, and I found my vinyl copy of *Goats and Monkeys* in just a couple of minutes.

'What do you think you're doing?' Barry whispered savagely from the doorway.

I looked up at him. 'Just picking some music,' I said.

'We've *got* music,' he said. 'Now, get in the bloody house and sparkle!'

I followed him back into the house with the record under my arm. The fresh air of the garden hadn't done me any good and I was feeling lightheaded and a little unbalanced. As I was putting the album on to the turntable, the Art Director's boyfriend was saying, 'You know, I've got hundreds of records and tapes and I haven't played a single one of them since the day I bought my first compact disc.'

'Well,' I said, more for something to say than because it was anything I believed, 'the trendy thing now is a swing back to vinyl. Some say it gives a warmer sound. But I can live without the surface noise and scratches, myself.'

And then I went and dropped the stylus on to the disc and it made that terrible noise and nearly blew the wax out of everybody's ears, and I knew without even looking at Barry that there was nothing I could do to redeem myself for the evening in his eyes. So I just went on ahead and played the track.

I played it too loud, of course. Conversation stopped and everyone was looking faintly embarrassed but I just hovered before the Sony, and it must have looked as if I was some kind of guard dog all furry and friendly on the outside and yet hyped up to bare its teeth at anyone who made to reach for the volume control. I paced up and down on the rug swinging my arms, and I waited for the end of the track.

I waited. And then it came. I must have heard it a hundred times or more in the course of my life, but only now that I knew what to listen for did it register with any clarity.

Brilliant. Fucking brilliant.

And from the one who sounded like Mariella: *Yeah . . .*

I swung on everyone and stared at them. They were looking a little bit scared of me but that didn't register, not right then; instead I just said, with an urgency that I heard like that in the voice of a stranger, 'There. That part there. Has anybody here ever managed to make it out?'

Everybody seemed uneasy. The Art Director's boyfriend said, 'I've never even heard the record before.'

And the McDowells both said together, 'Isn't it Mott the Hoople?'

'I'll play it again,' I said.

'No you fucking well won't,' said Barry under his breath as he pushed between me and the deck and took the disc off none too gently, ramming it back into its paper sleeve and then thrusting the sleeve into my hands.

I sat heavily in a chair, and was pretty well out of it for what little was left of the evening.

And when the last of the guests had gone, I became aware of Barry standing in front of me. He was calm, he was quiet.

'Well, thanks,' he said.

And that was the last I saw of him that night.

I sat up for quite a while longer in the silent house with what was left of the dinner-party debris all around me. I'd pulled the album out of its sleeve again and had both lying there on my knees. I didn't feel like sleeping. I wasn't much aware of anything around me, either.

About a week after they'd been turned away from the vaults, Casey had gone around to Mariella's place. I later found out that she was even younger than she looked; she was a student and she lived in a fourth-floor room in a mixed block off Gower Street. Casey found her at home, but she wouldn't let him in; and as they talked through the door for a while some of the other girls on the landing sent for House Security, and while House Security was girding its loins to respond Casey kicked down the door and went in anyway. He beat her with the flex of a kettle and then picked her up and, with great difficulty, manoeuvred her over the safety bar at the window and then climbed up with her. They went down the four floors together, holding hands. He held hers, anyway. She might not have been dead when they set off, but she certainly was after they landed.

At the inquest, one of the other girls reported what Casey had been saying. He'd been hammering on the door and shouting, *I can fix it. I can still fix it.*

But they hadn't known what he'd meant.

Poor Casey.

I put the disc back on to the turntable and this time I played it all the way through, only not so loud. In the stillness of the house I could hear it as clearly as I needed to. As I sat and listened, I studied the back of the sleeve. I'd had this particular record for so long and it had moved house with me so many times that you could see a circular impression like a brass rubbing over where the edge of the disc and the centre hole usually lay. The sleeve notes and acknowledgements were in a handwritten art-school scrawl over a collage of black and white session photographs – you know the kind of thing, a longhair in headphones bent over piano keyboards with his eyes dreamily shut, a closeup of a wastebin stuffed with empty Southern Comfort bottles, somebody famous fast asleep with his feet on a chair . . . The biggest shot in the collage was a wide angle from inside the control room looking out through the glass into the studio across the mixing board. The final track was one of those endless everybody-sing pieces like 'Hey Jude'; Alice the Goon had modestly called theirs 'Anthem for the World' and I can tell you, even way back I'd thought that it went on, rather. The photograph featured the band plus every ligger and camp follower and hanger-on that could be gathered behind a microphone, all determined to show that they were *it* and they were having a good time. The longer I listened, the more I found myself staring at this image. And in particular, at a little area of shadows over against the back wall of the studio.

It was obviously two people, way back and out of focus. The rubbed arc went right across them, taking out even more of the detail. They'd always been there, I was sure of that. Now I'm not saying that it was Casey and Mariella, because there would never be any way of telling *who* they were; the definition simply wasn't there. They were hardly more than smudges in the grain, but what kept drawing my attention back was the apparent attitude of the figures. They'd never seemed quite to belong, if you know what I mean. The only way to describe it is to say that it looked as if they'd been propped there, like in those Old West photographs of shot criminals whose open coffins were hoisted upright in the sunshine for the cameras.

I suppose if you look at anything for long enough, your imagination will make something of it . . . but then when 'Anthem for the World' came up, there, in amongst the others, was a voice that had always irritated me from the first time I'd heard the track in my teens. She was piping along and she could barely hold a tune, and I'd often wondered why they hadn't thought to lose her in the mix. Somebody's girlfriend, I'd always assumed. And then on the fade, amidst the whistles and the party noises, I heard something else that I'd begun to listen for. All those years, I was thinking. All those years of hearing that voice, and never knowing. *Wonderful*, Casey was saying, *You're an absolute star.* It wasn't even a surprise to me that I recognized him now.

I suppose in a way, he was right. Stars burn for ever, don't they?

Or at least, when they die, their light burns on without them in some distant place.

The Visitor

PETER CROWTHER

SOLDIERS' FIELD WASN'T really anything to do with soldiers, at least not these days. And Beatty seriously doubted that it ever was.

No, these days Soldiers' Field was to do with shit. Dog shit. And lots of it. Beatty wrinkled her nose at the thought of all those turds scattered about the grass and dotting the small concrete apron around the wooden benches to her right, in front of a red-brick wall which bore the sloppily scrawled legend SARAH CAPPELL SUCKS COCKS. The wall also boasted a hurriedly prepared spray-painted rendition of a large distorted penis and balls poised before a cartoony mouth, and marked the end of the field.

Beatty pulled her cardigan tightly around her, pocket-enclosed hands crossing her stomach. Was it 'Soldiers'' or was it 'Soldier's'? Beatty could never figure out where to put the apostrophe. But then, who really cared? OK, so dad had said that, now she was in the third year, she'd have to work harder if she was going to pass any of her GCSE exams. But then he had said the same thing when she'd moved up into the second year. And anyway, her brother Alan still couldn't tell the time without a lot of prompting, and he was ten – and he couldn't tell his left from his right. But mum always said it was just a mental block and that he'd suddenly figure it out for himself one day, and, anyway, 'You shouldn't keep picking on him like that!'

The sky was noticeably darkening now, and a wind had come up, blowing across the grass and bending the almost leafless trees towards the ground. Over where Ned was sniffing, a large bundle toppled over from its upright position and rolled towards him. Ned barked and hopped back, obviously surprised. 'Don't be stupid, Ned,' Beatty called into the wind. The bag almost righted itself and, just for a second, it looked as though it was going to unfurl completely and envelop the hapless dog. But that couldn't be, because that would mean that the bag had to move against the wind. It looked awfully solid for an old sack, Beatty thought. Ned growled and the bag tumbled away with a fresh gust, though Beatty thought there was hardly enough force to send it scurrying towards the large hedgerow the way it did. Once at the hedge, the bag fell away, through the privet, and out of sight.

Beatty watched the hedge intently, waiting for some sign of movement. Maybe someone was in the bag. Maybe it was one of those pee-doe-file men that dad said hung around the toilets across from where she lived. Dad said they talk to you really nicely and then show you mucky pictures. She'd asked what the pictures were about but dad had just said to never mind, and 'Just make sure you don't talk to anybody when you're out.' She was always told to be in before it was dark and yet they never bothered if her being out in the dark suited them. Like 'just nipping' to the corner shop for a tin of peas, or 'just bobbing' down to the park with Ned. Anyway, she knew what the pictures were about. She'd seen Helen Carter's brother's books that he'd brought back from London. Big black men with cocks nearly down to their ankles, being ridden around somebody's front room by spotty girls with big tits, dressed like nurses or policewomen.

Beatty wondered if *her* tits would ever grow. She shrugged her shoulders inside her coat and felt the reassuring tingle through her jumper and vest. Thirteen years old and still nothing much there at all. Helen Carter's tits were really coming on now – in fact, even the brown bits around Helen's nipples were much bigger than her own, she thought, with dismay. Especially when Helen spat on her finger and rubbed the spittle around and around them. And she knew, too, that Helen rubbed them with her mum's Body Shop cream, some kind of thick paste made from cabbages or carrots or something. They smelt really funny, sort of like a cross between perfume and Lifeguard soap. Maybe Helen got her brother Richard to rub them for her. She wouldn't be surprised. Her dad always said that the Carters were a 'funny bunch'. She watched Ned crouch down in the darkness at the end of the field and heard him growling softly at the hedge.

Beatty couldn't see anything. Behind the hedge was a large wall, and behind the wall the Dunstarns began, 'Street', 'Close', 'Drive', 'Lane', 'Avenue', and who knew what else. Cobbled streets of terraced boxes, stretching out the length of Allbeck and down the long hill into the industrial estate at Allbeck Park – a park which was as

much about grass as Soldiers' Field was about soldiers –
and into the outskirts of Leeds.

'Come *on*, Ned,' she shouted impatiently. She could
now only just make out the outline of the Labrador, way
across the grass. He had turned his attention back to
where the bag had been, and was excitedly – or anxiously
– nuzzling the grass, as though he was foraging for something. She could hear him sniffing: strange that she could
make out the sounds so clearly. She turned around and
looked back along the crescent path to either side. Beatty
had only strayed a few feet off the path but, suddenly,
she felt dangerously exposed. It was like she'd felt when
she was out of her depth in the swimming baths when she
was still learning to swim. She had an intense desire to
walk backwards to the path, all the time keeping her full
attention on Ned and that hedge. And the disappeared
bag – wherever it was. Ned was still growling, head thrust
down as though he was worrying something. Shit most
likely, Beatty thought. Probably an interesting collection
of runny off-white lumps, the kind which always
reminded her of the butterscotch topping stuff which
mum put on plates of mashed-up banana, and gave to her
and Alan for occasional special Sunday teas. Suddenly,
she wished she could see what it was because it looked as
though Ned was eating it, throwing his head back in the
way he always did when he was grinding up biscuits and
particularly difficult pieces of bone.

It was totally dark, now. Black. The blackest black of
the night because the streetlights still hadn't been turned
on. But, no, that wasn't right. The lights *were* on. She'd
just seen that they were on when she'd turned around to
look back at the path. She couldn't look back again,

because then that would leave her front unprotected. At least her back was safe because nothing would come up behind her with all the lights on. But had she been mistaken? Was it just the lights in the windows of the houses on Allbeck Drive that she had seen? Maybe, even now, as she was thinking about the lights, something was gliding and rustling its way across the path beneath the cover of the darkness and the trees, rustling its way towards her back. Her totally unprotected back.

She removed her hands from her cardigan pockets and strained her eyes into the blackness. There was Ned. She could see his crouched form over in front of the hedge. His was the blacker shape against the other blackness behind it. She squinted. Her eyes were playing tricks now. She could have sworn that she'd seen Ned rise up, like he was standing on his back legs, but when she concentrated she saw that he was still sniffing. She could hear him. 'Come on, Ned,' she called. No way was she going to walk over there to get him. Her school shoes would get covered in shit – 'Barkers' eggs', was what Alan called it and mum would throw a wobbly. And anyway, she didn't like the way the hedge was rustling even though the wind had momentarily dropped.

Ned gave out a loud cough which sounded like a cross between a bark and the anguished whooping noises which Alan had made last winter when he got that really bad flu. Then she felt him. In one agonizing instant, one pulse-stopping tiny fraction of a second, she felt the familiar nuzzling of Ned against her legs. She couldn't look down. For an instant, she couldn't move. She just kept watching the crouching shape that she had *thought* was her dog, watching as it reared itself up again and then shambled

191

off, merging with the thicker shade behind it. At her feet, Ned whimpered. But it was without any trace of affection. It was a 'Let's get away from here' sort of noise. And when she looked down, she saw that only a little bit of his snout – the bit on his left – was still in place. The rest of his mouth was completely exposed, teeth and gums bared to the night, with the top of his muzzle covered in runny sores which seemed to pulsate by themselves. Somewhere, she could hear a car horn 'parrp', and there was a brief squeal of tyres followed by an engine revving. Then the silence returned. That was the worst bit, because the silence meant that there was nothing to distract her . . . nothing to stop her returning her full attention to Ned's wrecked face, bathed, as it was, in the glow of the long flourescent red sausage – it had to be a sausage, hadn't it? Surely it couldn't be anything else – that he was holding clamped hard against his teeth. Was it really moving, or was it a trick of its own glimmering shine? Certainly the shine and the madness it illuminated in his eyes seemed to say it all: Why did I do this? they said.

Thinking back on it all later that night, tucked up securely in her bed, it was some time before Beatty could remember how she and Ned had got back home. So much had happened back at the house that the simple incidentals had temporarily faded from her memory.

She pulled the sheets tighter beneath her chin and looked around the room. It was still dark, despite the soft glow of the little night-light which dad had dug up from the loft following her terror at the thought of being in the bedroom, alone in the blackness. Strangely though, the light failed to dispel her fears. Even the bright shine around her room door, from the big bulb in the hallway, proved to be insubstantial. The worst of it was that she couldn't explain to her parents why she felt so scared. She could hardly bear even to think of it herself. Certainly she could not tell her father that Ned had eaten something which glowed red and smelled even worse than the dog's mouth usually smelled, even after he'd had a long bum-licking session (or was that just her mind playing tricks?), something that looked awfully like the spray-painted drawing of a cock which adorned the wall at the edge of Soldiers' Field. She also couldn't tell him that the thing was wriggling in Ned's mouth, like it had a mind of its own, or that there had been stuff coming out of the little hole in the end, and that wherever it had touched Ned's muzzle it hissed and steamed, making the dog's skin and fur drip on to the grass in thick runny globs. Helen Carter said that such stuff was called spunk, but she had also said that it was supposed to be a white colour, like milk, whereas the stuff coming out of the thing in Ned's mouth glowed red, like steel being smelted. She'd screamed at Ned to drop it. Drop it! Drop it! But the dog, whining all the time, had growled at her as she had made to step towards him: he'd never done it before. Beatty had not known whether to cry or laugh. Laugh at the sheer ridiculousness of the whole thing. Laugh at the fact that she was standing on the side of Soldiers' Field while her dog munched on a radioactive cock. Well, what else could it be?

And then, in one strange instant, the thing fell from Ned's mouth. Beatty had watched it, almost as though it was falling in slow motion, as it landed with a soft plop on the grass. She was sure that Ned was as surprised as she was. She couldn't understand it: one second Ned was gripping it with all of his might and the next he just let go. She was sure that, if Ned could actually have spoken – and could actually have made his mind work amidst the barrage of pain from his melted face – he would not have been able to explain why he did it. In much the same way, Beatty would have had trouble explaining why she stooped down and delicately lifted the thing up, between her thumb and index finger, and dropped it into the fluffy depths of her cardigan pocket. She could still hear Ned's insistent, almost pleading whine. Could still see, especially when she closed her eyes, the dog start to stagger, his back legs collapsing to one side, as he slipped away from this world. It was for that reason – plus the fact that her heart pounded with the knowledge of what lay in the drawer of her bedside table – that sleep would be a long time coming.

Downstairs, over the steady drone of the television, Beatty could hear her parents talking. Her father's voice occasionally increased in volume sufficiently for her to be able to hear the actual words, and then drifted away again as he was soothed by Beatty's mother.

Outside, the trees waved in the wind, grown stronger since she had arrived back home, casting playful skeletal shadows on the other side of her curtains. Every few minutes a car or something would go by and cause a greater darkness to blot out the shape of the branches, passing first from the one side to the other, and then the other way. It was strange that the shadows seemed so slow and lazy, and that she never even heard an engine. Perhaps she *was* tired after all. How strange a room is in the dark. Maybe it needs the light to settle it, just like some humans do. Perhaps without that light, a room becomes restless, too. That would account for the little sounds. Nothing much, really, just little creaks and rattles, rustles and whispers. Beatty thought she heard the drawer open, almost believed she could feel rather than hear the skin-cracking grin of something savouring freedom, pulling back its mangled red foreskin and exposing a glinting orange eye as it waddled its way on to the top of her bedside table, to which her back was turned. But then the downstairs toilet flushed and she realized it must have been either mum or dad pulling the chain. Strange, though, that the cistern was taking so long to fill up.

Why had she snuggled down facing the window? The shadows were annoying her, making her drowsy. And the knowledge that the thing was in the drawer behind her, itself hastily snuggled amongst Care Bear paraphernalia and rainbow-coloured Kleenex tissues, caused a warm tingling between her legs, almost like when she got cystitis and felt like she wanted to pee all the time. But she didn't feel like she wanted to pee now.

Beatty only realized that she had been asleep when she actually woke up. She opened her eyes wide and stared at the curtain. It was light outside, and she could hear the familiar comforting drone of the radio from downstairs which mixed perfectly with the faint earthy aroma of frying bacon. Funny how a sound and a smell could be so perfectly matched.

Morning had sneaked up on the world while she had been asleep – dreaming, she suddenly remembered. What had the dream been about? Her earlier thought about sounds and smells fitting together reminded her. A man had called to see her in her room though she didn't know how he could have got in. Somehow, it didn't really seem all that important. While she watched, the man had gently opened her bedside table drawer and removed the thing. Peering wide-eyed over the tightly held bedclothes, Beatty had seen the thing – it definitely *was* a cock – wriggle in the man's proffered hand, wriggle like it was looking for something. It made strange little sucking noises and gave off a thick heavy odour which, despite what she had thought after returning from Soldiers' Field, was not at all unpleasant. Rather, it was oddly exciting, and very thick and pungent, like the smell of the massed purple flowers which towered above the boggy marshland down by the river. The way the thing moved was like it was blind, searching by means of other senses. Searching? What was it searching for? Beatty closed her eyes and tried to remember what the man had looked like. The sunlight through the curtains made it difficult to recreate the night-time scene in her room, but, hazily, the dream came back to her.

He was tall, dressed curiously in a strange mishmash of styles and colours. She could make out the hues and textures of gently and hypnotically moving fabrics, undulating like fields of corn under a soft breeze. It seemed as though the man's head almost touched the ceiling. She remembered thinking that there was no way a man so big could crouch himself down to the size of an old bag, at least not unless all of his bones were broken. Somehow, this realization made her feel much worse; and already her pulse was pounding, heart thumping. Surely he could hear her. Maybe the thing could hear her heart! Certainly, it seemed to be growing more agitated, and Beatty could see the faintest reflection on the end of it where no reflection existed only a moment ago. It looked wet.

The dream became clearer. With a slow, languid movement, the man stepped softly back from beside Beatty's bed and pushed the door closed. Replaying the dream like a video, Beatty watched the door drift slowly towards its frame, silently, without the usual creak which always accompanied it when *she* tried to do it stealthily. The light from the landing faded until, as the door closed with a soft click, it disappeared altogether. The room became suddenly black. Then she felt the man move nearer again. She couldn't actually see anything, but she knew he was moving nearer. Then a car did go past – she could hear the engine this time and, just for a brief second, she saw his face.

It was finely boned, old and wizened, long and tired looking. He looked more like a skeleton of a man than a man himself. The skin was pulled tight across bulbous cheekbones and a long thin nose. His lips were also thin: in fact, they didn't really look like lips at all, but just a slit in the middle of his face. Behind the slit, she saw the promise – threat? – of teeth, glinting in the brief light as though they were actually moving around in the man's gums. But that couldn't be so. Just as it couldn't be so that she could feel a soft cooling intermittent spray from the thing in the man's hand. The sound it was making made her feel strange in her stomach. No, not her stomach: it was lower down. Whether she swallowed hard in her dream or here, now, recalling the dream, Beatty didn't know. Because the final part was unfolding in her memory. It was only now, as the light was beginning to fade again, and the man was pulling back the cover of her bed, exposing her body and the small frilly blue nightshirt that had ridden up around her waist, that she caught sight of the horns. And smelled the smell. She remembered closing her eyes and spreading herself wide and listening, as the little slurping noises became more muffled. The feeling below her stomach went away completely, and she just felt wet. Extremely, deliciously wet.

Beatty turned quickly, eyes open again, and stared at the table. Nothing looked any different, but she knew that the thing had gone even without opening the drawer.

Kneeling up in bed, she leaned close to the bedside table and listened. There was no noise, but then why should there be? Even if the thing was still in there – and she was sure that it was not – there was no reason for it to be making any sounds. Holding her breath so that she could concentrate her full attention on the thing that either was or was not in the drawer, Beatty turned her head to one side. That was when she saw the mess on the sheet.

It was clearly blood. The reddest red she had ever seen. It fascinated and horrified her at the same time. Her periods! She had started her periods during the night! So that was what the dream was all about. Beatty jumped from the bed and looked between her legs. She had started all right. She held her legs apart with both hands and, bending over as far as she could, stared at the congealed blood around her vagina and the pink trails and smudges on her inner thighs.

'Beatty . . . Alan . . . ' Her mother's voice boomed up the stairs. 'Come on now, or you'll be late.' The kitchen door clicked shut and the momentarily freed blandness of the songs which always featured on Radio Two was again contained within the hissing of frying bacon.

Breakfast proved to be the usual traumatic experience of spilt milk and forgotten schoolbooks. But in addition to all that there was Alan's crying – genuine for a change – and her father's presence at the table. Beatty's father had usually left for work by the time she arrived downstairs in the kitchen, but today was a special day. Today, there was no Ned wandering around sniffing at people's plates, and getting under everyone's feet. Alan just sat and sobbed. It hardly seemed the right time for Beatty to tell everyone that she had started her periods, but, of course, she had to say something. After all, her mother would see all the mess when she went in to make up Beatty's bed. Maybe she should just say nothing. Pretend that she hadn't noticed. But that just wasn't believable. The sheet looked like someone had been impaled. The thought made Beatty wince and she knocked the spoon out of her cereal bowl and it clattered to the floor loudly.

Beatty's mother spun around from the stove, clutching her hand to her chest. When she saw what had happened she merely shook her head. 'Be careful, Beatty,' she said in quiet tired exasperation.

'Sorry, Mum,' Beatty said softly. 'Mum?'

'What is it now, love?'

'I've started my periods. The sheets are in a terrible state.' It seemed like a rather blunt way of informing her parents, but there seemed no other way than just coming right out with it. Beatty's father looked up from his bowl of Alpen, chewing, and grimaced. 'Beatty!' he said, his mouth full. 'Not at the table, please. And not in front of your brother.'

Alan did not even seem to hear.

Her mother turned down the gas under the frying pan

and came over to Beatty's chair, smiling. 'I don't know: it doesn't rain but it pours. How do you feel?' she asked, stroking her daughter's head.

Beatty considered for a moment before replying. 'Fine,' she said, at last. 'I think.'

'Any pains?'

Beatty shook her head.

'Well, you might get some tummy-ache later,' her mother said. 'It might be a good idea to take some aspirins with a cup of tea.' She moved over to the cupboard above the oven and removed a smoky coloured glass bottle. Almost as if in response, Beatty's stomach gave a loud rumbling noise and she doubled over with a groan. It felt like her entire insides were being torn apart.

The telephone rang out in the hall, and Beatty's father jumped up from the table. 'That'll be the vet,' he said. Suddenly, Beatty's momentous news was forgotten, and Alan started crying again.

The walk to school was strange for Beatty, for a number of reasons. Firstly because Ned always used to walk slowly down the path and then stand wagging his tail, his head cocked on one side, as she turned into Allbeck Drive. It felt funny to think that Ned would never see her off to school again. But just 'funny', not sad. In fact that in itself was funny, the way she had not really been upset at Ned's death. Maybe the tears would come later.

Secondly, she just felt altogether strange. Like she had just got out of bed after a long bout of flu or something. Everything looked unfamiliar and new, almost alien. But then, when she concentrated on something, it suddenly seemed natural again. She couldn't explain it, even to herself, so she didn't even bother to try to tell her parents.

But the funniest thing of all was when she was walking past the park. It looked normal enough, but yet she sensed that it wasn't. She stopped at the corner of Weaton Crescent and just stared over at the wide expanse of grassland, while the lollipop lady stood waving her sign in the middle of the road. 'Are you going to school today or what?' the lady shouted over to her. Beatty didn't answer, at least not straight away. Her attention was concentrated on a large bag-shaped object that seemed to blowing along the bottom of the hedgerows.

At school, the pain grew worse. Much worse. Beatty started to sweat uncontrollably. She had taken off her jumper and loosened the catch on her skirt, but nothing seemed to help. Even sitting on the toilet didn't ease the stabbing dull ache. Helen Carter told her that it would be crippling all day, and that Beatty should go home. But Beatty did not want to go home.

She didn't want to be in the house at all today. In the house on her own. It was mum's day out with Auntie Margaret – her auntie had told her mum that they could postpone wandering around the shops in Leeds until another day, what with Ned . . . with Ned dying and everything. But her mum would hear nothing of the sort. She knew, she said, how her sister looked forward to these trips to town, particularly since Uncle Eddie had died. And anyway, getting out would do her more good than moping around the house all day.

The scenes at home before Beatty had left for school had been terrible. Moving Ned's basket out by the dustbin; clearing out all the packets of biscuits and tins of dog food . . . it had seemed to go on for ever. And it was funny, but it seemed that, wherever she looked, Beatty could see the usual tell-tale wisps of matted dog hairs stuck to the sofa and the chairs, or wound together like spiralled clouds beneath the table in the kitchen.

A sudden sharp pain interrupted Beatty's train of thought, and she let out a high-pitched squeal. Mrs Crawford turned around from the blackboard and stared myopically over her glasses. 'Beatty? Would you like to be excused, dear?'

Beatty could not answer. Deep down inside her stomach she felt as though something was writhing around, twisting and turning frantically. Yes, that was it. It was a frantic movement. Almost impatient. The phrase 'like a bull in a china shop' sprang into her mind, and she didn't like it. A low rumbling fart-like sound echoed from her lower abdomen, and some of the other children sniggered. Angela Fraser screwed up her face, as though smelling something extremely unpleasant. 'Oh, gross,' she whispered loudly. Beatty didn't hear her, nor did she hear Mrs Crawford suggest more emphatically this time that she really should leave the class. All Beatty could hear, from far down in her body, was the sound of something moving around inside her. Something growing. Something with a mind all of its own. 'Oh, God, help me,' she moaned. Another violent movement and a faint far-off sound from inside her blouse, like someone biting into a slice of melon, brought Beatty to her feet screaming.

Sitting on the toilet seemed to do the trick this time and, after a couple of gurgling noises which failed to produce anything there was a considerable amount of 'action' as her father always put it. Within a few minutes,

Beatty felt much better. It was only when she had pulled up her pants and was getting ready to flush the toilet that she grew worried. Looking down into the bowl, in that brief second before pulling the cistern lever, Beatty saw things which in no way resembled poopsies – it was the word she always used to describe her own excrement, being decidedly more ladylike than 'shit' or 'turds'.

Rather, the blood-flashed coiled greyness heaped in the toilet pan looked considerably more important. In the swirling anxious water which prepared to sweep them away for ever, they looked like things that she really shouldn't be leaving behind. It just goes to show how much an upset can really affect you, she thought.

The ache and the cold sweats and dizziness grew stronger and more frequent as the day went on, with Beatty spending less and less time in any of her classes. After lunch – most of which she left, and the rest threw up almost immediately in one of the ground-floor toilet sinks – she went to the sick room and just stretched out on the narrow cot. Mrs Carroll said that she should go home and even offered to take her in her car, but Beatty didn't want to go home. By this time she had been for four more of the unusual poopsies, each more novel and more colourful than the one before it. Now she could feel something definitely growing. Maybe it was a cancer. At least they could cure some cancers, she thought. But, deep down, she didn't really think that it was anything that anyone could cure. She could feel it uncoiling, filling up newly vacated space inside her, flexing and straining, moving around, still impatient.

By the time school finished, Beatty was almost gone. She could feel herself growing stronger but, almost as though she was nodding off to sleep, she kept losing her grasp on what was happening around her. It was as though she was getting smaller within her own body. And then, on the way home, hardly able to control her own feet, the complex machinery of memories, hopes and experiences that was once Beatrice Carrier, ceased to exist. Like the dot on television, after the last programme of the day, she simply dwindled away, briefly into a white shadow of what she had been, softly questioning, reluctantly accepting . . . and then, nothing. But the figure marched on. Renewed, vigorous . . . reborn. Going home.

What was left of her daughter had been in the house almost two hours before Victoria Carrier returned from a fairly sombre shopping spree with her sister.

Two hours was a long time. A long time for developing and growing. And too long to remain without sustenance. Luckily, the girl's small sibling had come home only an hour after the shell of Beatty had entered the house. As a feast, the child left a lot to be desired, but as a snack he proved more than adequate.

The thing that was now Beatty was almost whole. Perceptions were growing and increasing by the second. The twin screens of reality – the child, screaming his reluctance to lose them, had called them eyes – were merging, coming into focus. She stared at the flapping tatters of skin on the small leg that she now lifted to her mouth. Tasty. She opened her mouth wider to allow the membrane to prepare the food. The thing now occupied her entire throat and peered through between her teeth to the world beyond. When it saw the leg, held delicately outside this small cave in which it now found itself, it sprayed its juice in a fine shower. The skin immediately began to sizzle and smoke, bubbling into small blobs which then burst with tiny pops.

She was tearing a piece off the leg with her teeth – which were fairly blunt and almost useless – when the woman entered the room and screamed. Victoria Carrier screamed at the blood and the mess and the entrails. She screamed at the sight of her daughter, her head bulging, hair almost completely gone, eyes hanging from their sockets like a gruesome Hallowe'en mask, bare belly bursting from her ripped blouse and school skirt, with a pool of grey and bloody lumpy wetness around the patch of floor on which she was sitting. Then, as she turned away from the sight of Beatty with a huge chunk of fresh meat in her mouth, she saw the small pile of bones on the floor beside the bed, some gnawed clean, some still fleshy, some still enclosed in pieces of fabric that Mrs Carrier recognized as being Allbeck Juniors' school uniform.

She was still screaming, shaking her head, when, turning back to face Beatty, she saw – and heard! – her daughter's face split open across the middle. The split went through the mouth and around each cheek towards the ears: there was not much blood, a part of her noted almost absently. Then there was a frantic shuffling and heaving about Beatty's body and, suddenly, the top half of the head lifted, borne upwards by some huge glistening thing, a dull but pulsating orangy-red in colour, that seemed to be pulling itself out of the rest of the torso. It was about then that Victoria Carrier mentally checked out. When the thing, now freed from Beatty's head – and for all the world resembling some ridiculous-looking three-foot-tall penis – wavered in front of her face, pulled back a long frilly foreskin and threw up what seemed like a bucket of hot red paint all over her.

It was the smell that made her smile. An earthy, primal smell . . . a mixture of age and newness. As she writhed and moaned on the floor, the smoke and spray from the exploding pustules on her face drifting in front of her eyes, she felt herself getting wet. In a last gesture of assistance, she lifted her bottom from the carpet.

In front of her, the thing had pulled itself completely out of the useless, empty carcass of her daughter, and now wobbled above her. Settling down between her spreadeagled shuddering legs, it noted, lifting the hem of the blue and grey checked skirt, that this time there would be much more room.

Book End

TONY J. FORDER

RAY GARNER PEERED at the words on the glowing screen. The grin he wore slit his face from ear to ear and made him look ten years younger than his admitted-to forty-nine. He depressed three keys, the space bar, then another three keys.

THE END

There were no finer words in the English language, he thought with a great deal of satisfaction, especially after eighteen months' solid work.

The writer leaned back in his chair, sucked in a lungful of air and let out a long sigh of triumph and relief.

THE END

And it truly was, in more ways than one. Ray had written twenty best-selling novels and almost a hundred and fifty short stories during a career which spanned a quarter of a century. But those final two words would be his last. He was retiring, selling his house in Malibu and returning to spend the final few months of his life back home in England. Of all his novels this latest one had taken the longest time to write, was significantly thicker than any of his other works, and was – in his humble opinion – the finest book he'd ever put his name to.

Ray poured himself a tall glass of mineral water and made a toast, congratulating himself on a fine career. As he drank he scratched the ugly birthmark on the back of his neck. It was about the size and shape of a peanut, and though it never irritated him he had often touched it for luck early on in his career. Now it was an unshakeable habit. When he had drained the glass, Ray rubbed his bleary eyes and checked the Rolex on his wrist. It was nine thirty in the morning, daylight now filtering through the drawn curtains of his study. Once again he had lost track of time and had worked solidly through the night.

He was past being tired, though; the rush of adrenalin that always saw him through the final stages of his work still coursed through his system. Later he would feel drained, too weak to stand, and his body would finally grind to a halt.

But that was later.

Ray left his study and went to collect the mail. In the kitchen he sifted through a large pile of letters, packages and circulars. The last item caught his eye.

VANITY PUBLISHING Co., it read. The company offered a service to authors whose work had been rejected by recognized publishers. For a substantial fee they would edit, proof-read, print and bind any manuscript. Ray didn't need their services, of course; the contract for this novel had been signed long ago. But for reasons he was not aware of, his curiosity was pricked by the single sheet of glossy paper.

For some considerable time now, Ray had been pondering his retirement, how he ought to bow out. A career such as his deserved something special. The fact that he would openly acknowledge the novel as his last would ensure record sales, no doubt. But money was not a problem. He wanted to do something a bit different this time, something worthy of his work, something to be remembered by.

Still clutching the circular, an idea wormed its way into his mind, nestled there comfortably and refused to go away. When Ray had finished working it through, refining and polishing it the way he did with all his ideas, he chuckled to himself. The notion was a vain one, certainly, but there was nothing to stop him seeing it through.

A rotund and jovial man, the bespectacled Ray Garner lived for writing. He had done nothing else since first learning the fine art and delicacy of structuring words and sentences into stories that could at once beguile, terrify, sadden, and bring pleasure, merely on a whim. From a very early age he set out to devote his life to it.

When he was thirteen years old his parents had died in a car accident. He moved across the Atlantic from England, to live with his only surviving relative – an uncle in California – and there he found a wealth of markets for his early work. He sold short stories to magazines while still at school, had his first novel published shortly after his eighteenth birthday and, once he had made enough money to move away from home, Ray bought an apartment, shut himself away from the world, and buried himself in his work. Though fame and riches had come his way, Ray had no close friends, no woman in his life, no social urges whatsoever. He was a recluse. And he loved every minute of it.

Now, however, it was all about to end. Doctors had

diagnosed cancer. It was not benign. Just one of those things. Ray had initially decided to finish his work in progress and return to the Cotswolds to die. But now he had another idea. Once he'd made up his mind, there was no stopping Ray from putting any wild notion into action.

He moved back into his comfortable study, snatched up the telephone and called his agent. 'Gary Thompson, please,' he said into the mouth-piece. 'Yes, it's Ray Garner. Thanks.' An annoying musical tone assaulted his ears for thirty seconds or so before his agent came on the line.

'Ray! Good to hear from you. How's the new book?'

Ray detected strain in the man's voice, perhaps a little panic; the book was six months overdue, and he'd already received a substantial advance.

'Don't fret, Gary. It's done. Just finished a few minutes ago.'

'Oh, great, man.' Ray heard the relief oozing down the telephone line. 'Is it a winner?'

'What a thing to ask. Anyhow, Gary, I've also got some news for you. It's my last book. It's the biggest and best, but also my last.'

Silence filled the line.

'Gary?'

'Ray, tell me you're not serious.'

'But I am. Hell, what's the big deal. You've had ten per cent of me since your old man died. Now it's time to go.'

'I guess you've thought this through carefully?'

'Of course.'

'And I suppose there's no point in trying to dissuade you?'

'None whatsoever. Listen, I'll get over to see you soon, but in the mean time I need a favour. A big one.'

'Anything, Ray. You know that.'

Here goes, Ray thought, crossing his fingers.

'I need you to ask the publishers to allow me to do a limited edition of the book. I want to get it printed, bound, everything.'

The agent whistled; an annoying habit that Ray disliked intensely. Young Master Thompson had none of the refined grace and decorum with which his father had honed the business. 'I don't know, Ray,' he said. 'They paid a lot of dough up front for the sole rights.'

Ray breathed hard. It was make or break time, and he held all the right cards. 'Put it this way, Gary,' he said softly. 'I *want* this. Now, when you tell them that it's going to be my last book they'll cream their collective jeans thinking about the sales. That's one of two carrots to dangle. The other is that if they don't agree I'll send their money back and cancel the deal.'

'You got it,' Thompson said quickly. He would use all of his persuasive powers to ensure it. He was already toying with the office calculator, trying to work out his cut of the expected sales.

'Fine,' Ray said, smiling. The fledgeling might lack style, but he knew a thing or two about harvesting cash. 'I'll send you a copy disc. But my limited edition goes out first.' He said goodbye and put the phone down. So far so good. Now for the tricky part.

From the outside, the premises leased by Vanity Publishing Co. was pretty uninspiring. The low, squat-looking building was in a state of disrepair, and for one moment,

Ray even thought it might be abandoned. But as he moved closer to the rotting wooden door, he heard the unmistakeable sound of machinery in operation.

The noise inside was almost overwhelming. In the dim light he saw a single press pumping out leaflets similar to the one he had received. The sound was just beginning to grate on his nerves when the press came to a sudden halt, and a wiry, elderly man stepped out from behind it.

'Mornin',' he said, offering a wide grin and wiping his hands on a rag. 'What can I do for you?'

'Good morning,' Ray said. 'Are you in charge here?'

'Sure am.' The man stepped forward, hand outstretched. 'Arnie Boyle at your service.'

They shook, and Ray felt slick grease spread across his palm. 'I got one of your leaflets,' he said. 'Thought I'd check it out.'

Arnie nodded. 'I hope I can be of service to you. What exactly are you after?'

'I'd like a manuscript printed in book form. No more than fifty copies.'

The old man's crooked grin slanted across his face once more. 'No problem there,' he said.

'But I want it to be rather special,' Ray went on. 'I have one or two ideas.'

Arnie leaned back against the press, crossed his arms and said, 'Shoot.'

'OK. I'm not too sure about the cover, but I definitely want the print to be in blood-red ink.'

Arnie raised an eyebrow, then frowned. He peered closely at Ray. 'Don't I know you?' he said, chewing on his bottom lip. 'Sure. You're Ray Garner, the writer.'

With a gentle shrug, Ray acknowledged the observation.

'So why on earth do you want *my* services?'

'Do you have somewhere we can sit and talk?' Ray asked. He was weary now; the euphoria of completing the novel had finally worn away.

'Sure thing,' said Arnie Boyle, a frown of concern on his gaunt face. 'Follow me.'

They walked across to a narrow office. There was room for just a desk, a single filing cabinet and two chairs. When they were both seated, Ray gathered himself and explained his idea to the old man, who nodded thoughtfully. Somehow the explanation went on, and before he could stop himself, the writer had told Arnie about the cancer that was eating away at him.

Shaking his head gently, Arnie said, 'That's a damned shame. You're a fine writer. I kind of like thrillers more than I like horror, but your stuff is on a par with the best.'

'Thanks,' Ray said, wishing he hadn't allowed his secret to slip out. But the old man had a way about him; something comfortable, something soothing.

They were silent for a moment, then Arnie stood and began to pace the office floor. 'You know,' he said, rubbing a cleanly shaven chin, 'if you really want to go out in style, I have an idea for you if you'd like to hear it.'

Ray smiled and spread his hands. 'I'm open to suggestions.'

Arnie's gaze narrowed. He seemed to peer right through Ray for a second or two. Finally he nodded once and told the writer what was on his mind. When he was done, Ray simply sat and stared at him for quite some time.

Then he chuckled.

Eventually he nodded.

Arnie nodded too, and went to work.

When Gary Thompson received his copy of Ray Garner's special edition through the post, he was initially stunned by the extremely poor quality of the packaging. The cover was a gossamer-thin dull patchwork that looked and felt as clammy as a sweaty palm. The paper was jagged along the edges, and whoever had printed it had used dark red ink. It was horrible. Horrible to touch, horrible to look at. On the first page was a handwritten note. It read:

> Dear Gary,
>
> I hope you like your copy of the new book. I wanted you, other acquaintances, and some of my most loyal fans who have written to me down the years, to have something personal to remember me by. This seemed like a good idea at the time.
>
> Take care of yourself.
>
> Ray.

The agent picked the book up again, turning it over in his hands. He studied it more closely, shaking his head at the appalling workmanship. It was a nice thought from Ray, but whoever had printed and bound the book had made a real dog's dinner of it, and the binding glue stank like a dead animal lying in the midday sun.

Then an anomaly caught his eye, and he squinted, peering closer still at the back cover. He tried to brush away a speck of dirt, but it wouldn't shift. It looked to be an imperfection woven into the material.

Just like an ugly birthmark.
And about the size and shape of a peanut.

Week Woman

KIM NEWMAN

For Janet

'YOU MUST BE Mad?'

The girl looked up from her green-jacketed Virago modern classic, and smiled a plain, unembarrassed smile at him.

'I'm Peter Mysliwiec.'

He sat opposite her. They were at a table in Mildred's in Greek Street. Everyone else in the small room was a woman. That didn't bother him. Karen was always telling him how tolerant he was. A hostile waitress – almost spherical and with a US Marines haircut – took his order, and brought him a small espresso. He bought Mad a coffee too.

They had never met before, but next week they would be married.

In the last month, he'd been forced to readjust most of his life. This was hardly stranger than the discovery that not only was he not British, as he'd always been told by his deceased parents, but that he was two years older than he'd thought, born not in London in 1947 but Warsaw in 1945.

Mad was late twenties/early thirties, and pretty obviously butch. Peter mentally rebuked himself for stereotyping people, but he was a *commercial* artist and often traded in stereotypes. Mad wore dungarees over an off-pink sweatshirt, shoulder-straps fastened with badges for causes he didn't recognize. Her hair was cropped not quite as close as the waitress's, and dyed an early-Bowie orange. She had a faint moustache, bright eyes, and the first hints of a chubbiness she'd have to exercise as rigorously as Karen to avoid in the next few years.

'Well,' she said, 'isn't this strange?'

Peter was worn ragged. Maybe his parents had been wrong to lie their son's way into British nationality. After all the letters and interviews, it was hard to imagine Poland as any more of a police state than the United Kingdom.

'I've never been married before,' Peter admitted, feebly.

'Me neither. Obviously.'

Mad was the ex-girlfriend of someone Karen knew at the agency. Peter knew almost nothing about her. Karen, inextricably still married to the Dreaded Stanley, was the kind of agent who could get anything given a week or so. A roll of discontinued wallpaper, a particular back issue of *National Geographic*, an aviation expert with photographs of a Sopwith Camel, a marriageable lesbian.

'What do you do?' Mad asked, politely.

'I'm an artist. Book covers, mostly. Ads, sometimes. A movie poster, once in a blue one. And you?'

'Different things. I'm sort of changeable.'

'Um.'

They didn't really have much more to say, but he felt it important to meet the girl. He'd seen the Gerard Depardieu film about the couple in the arranged marriage who were persecuted by US immigration agents, but Karen had ascertained that someone with his history of residency and skin colouring would be unlikely to suffer much. 'Remember,' she had said, 'you're a white, middle-class, house-owning, male heterosexual. In the lottery of life, you've won already.'

Peter got his chequebook out.

'I suppose we should, um, do the business? We agreed on five hundred pounds?'

Mad's face didn't change.

'—leine or —line?'

'Madeleine, e before i and no c in sight.'

He asked her surname, and she told him. Peter wrote out a cheque to Madeleine Waters, and gave it to her.

'No one's ever paid for me before,' she said. Peter wondered if she had something in her eye.

'Here are the details,' he said, giving her a sheet of paper on which Karen's male secretary had typed the address of the Register Office and the time of the wedding.

She pressed the cheque between the pages of her book and stuffed it into her shoulderbag. Then, she stood up to leave. She wore Doc Martens.

'See you in church,' she said, leaving him to finish his espresso.

A week later, Peter was outside the Register Office in Camden. Karen was to be the witness, and Tony Weldon, his accountant, was the best man. He'd worn a suit, but there was no dress code for a sham wedding. Karen wore a suit too, and was reminding him about the deadline for the Bloomsbury cover. She'd bought him a boutonnière, and fixed it to his lapel.

'Is this her?' Tony asked. Peter looked. A girl was walking down from the tube station, combat boots clunking, hands in the pockets of fatigue pants, green braces over a nondescript T-shirt. When she was close enough for them to make out her face, he knew it wasn't Madeleine.

'I hope she won't be late,' Karen clucked. 'Jeannie said she wasn't always reliable.'

'You're talking about the woman Peter's going to marry,' Tony said in mock-outrage. Karen humphed elegantly at him.

She squeezed Peter's arm, and got close to him. She'd been a pillar of the proverbial during the harassment.

'Nice day for a white wedding,' Tony hummed.

'Most important day of your life,' Karen said, unable to resist it.

'What was yours like?' Tony asked.

'Very romantic,' Karen deadpanned, 'with the moonlight gleaming on the Dreaded Stanley's brass knuckles.'

Peter grinned. He would get used to the jokes. Karen had already started calling him 'adulterer' in bed.

'This *must* be her,' Tony said as a taxi stopped directly outside.

'Thank Christ for that,' Karen said. Then her jaw dropped.

The door opened and a flurry of white gauze blossomed out of the cab, with a girl inside it.

'Would someone pay the driver?' a voice said from

220

under layers of veil. Astonished, Tony fished out the necessaries.

Madeleine wore a bridal gown, tight in the bodice and sleeves, vast and puffy below the waist, exploding into lacy flounces at the wrist. In her white gloves, she held a posy of white flowers. Under her veils, Peter could make out the rough lines of the face he remembered, but she was either wearing a wig or had had her hair extensively restyled because she seemed to have a Grace Kellyish blonde permanent.

'Jesus Fuck,' breathed Karen.

Behind them, as Tony helped Madeline negotiate her way to the kerb, the Register Office doors opened, and an official poked out his head.

'Mysliwiec–Waters?'

Madeleine took his arm, and guided him into the building. Karen, astonished, was left beyond the banging doors.

When the registrar told him he could kiss the bride, Peter lifted the veil and thought he had the wrong woman.

Then, he saw it was the same Madeleine. The planes of her face were subtly altered, but that could be because she was wearing make-up and the different hair gave her head a whole new shape. The eyes were the same. Just.

He kissed her mildly, and she responded with startling enthusiasm, warm tongue invading his mouth. Peter wondered how Karen would take this.

This, he supposed, was why her friends called Madeleine 'Mad'.

They had arranged to go out for a meal at a pizza place

afterwards. Tony was supposed to be Madeleine's date, but the new Mrs Mysliwiec wasn't to be separated from her husband.

Karen hadn't recovered from the shock.

Madeleine was chattering inconsequentially, drinking the champagne Tony had arranged as a joke, and never letting go of his arm. In her white thunderstorm, the bride was attracting quite a lot of attention. Peter imagined this was how the young Miss Havisham must have looked.

The restaurant, bribed beforehand by Tony, were playing nothing but romance through their speakers. Frank's 'Wee Small Hours', Bing's 'True Love', Julie's 'Laura', Dean's 'That's Amore'.

Funnily enough, Peter did feel as if the moon had just hit his eye like a big pizza pie.

'It's a shame we don't have time for a honeymoon,' Madeleine said, 'but we can catch up later. Paris, perhaps. Or Rome.'

Peter toyed with his garlic bread.

Peggy's 'The Folks Who Live on the Hill', the Crickets' 'Love is Strange', Nat's 'Just You, Just Me', Ella's 'The Tender Trap'.

Peter imagined the jaws of the tender trap meeting around his crushed shin.

'I'm so glad it was white,' Madeleine said, gripping harder. 'It's more special.'

Karen looked as if she were about to scream at her Hawaiian Extra-Spicy, but instead just said, 'Miss Waters, please take your hands off my boyfriend.'

Madeleine smiled enchantingly, and tutted at Karen.

'You're forgetting yourself, Karen dearest. It's Mrs Mysliwiec, now.'

Then Karen screamed.

A week later, the nightmares were fading.

At first, he couldn't close his eyes without being drawn back to the knock-down, drag-out cat-fight in the pizza place. Karen had screamed and screamed, Madeleine had cried and cried. There'd been no way of explaining it to the proprietor, or the police.

Eventually, they had all escaped. Somewhere, one of the women had attacked him, leaving now-faded rake-marks on his cheek.

Alone in his double bed in the Highbury flat, he quickly got conscious. His heart hammering, he realized he'd been dreaming again, the bridal-gowned Madeleine assaulting him like a harpy, Freddy Krueger fingers sprouting from her lace gloves.

As he shook himself out of the fug of sleep, he heard noises. Someone was in his kitchen, humming. The radio was on to a station he'd normally avoid. Bobby Darin was talking about things.

'Karen?'

He thought she'd not been there last night. She still kept her place in Muswell Hill. Mainly to annoy the Dreaded Stanley, but also because – hey – she was an independent woman. This was the Nineties.

Tying a robe over his pyjama bottoms, he staggered out of the bedroom. Since his marriage, things had been getting fuzzy. He thought he'd been drinking with Tony last night.

In his tiny kitchen, a woman was cooking breakfast. Bacon

sizzled in the pan next to a pair of sunny-side-up eggs.

'Darling,' she chirruped, 'you shouldn't have got up. I was going to bring you a tray in bed. You work so hard, you deserve your rest. You need to be looked after.'

The smell brought him fully awake.

She wore a blue house-dress, with a checkered pinafore. Her hair was worn in a Doris Day helmet, and most of her face was smile.

'Mad? Madeleine?'

She angled her head to one side, eyes shining. Her cheeks had rosy patches like a rag-doll's, and her pinafore was so starched it crackled.

'Petey's Maddie,' she said. 'OJ, hon?'

She poured a measure of freshly squeezed orange juice into a tumbler, and handed it to him.

'We'll soon cure you of those unhealthy bachelor habits. Do you realize how deprived your fridge is? And you have no oregano. Men never have any oregano.'

Peter's head began to hurt again.

'Look at this kitchen surface,' she said, drawing a finger through a layer of dusty grime. 'Never mind, it'll be clean in a jiffy. Clean right through to the squeak, a shine your mother could be proud of.'

Giving in, Peter sipped his juice. It shocked his tongue, and settled his stomach. A cooked breakfast – something he'd not had since school – seemed weirdly appropriate.

Karen came over for dinner, and Maddie cooked for the three of them. She was the perfect hostess, preparing everything from the hors-d'oeuvres through the meat course to the cheeseboard and sorbets, finally delivering coffee the like of which Peter had never suspected could be produced from his old cafetière.

Karen was determined to be calm this time. She hadn't been able to get in touch with Jeannie, and was taking a methodical, careful, tactful approach to the insanity spilling into their lives. She had started to use phrases like 'multiple personality' and 'schizoid compulsive'.

'Peter's so grateful for all you've done for him,' Maddie told Karen. 'Especially since the trouble with the nationality people.'

Peter had told Karen everything. Maddie didn't, at least, expect him to share a bed with her. In fact, one of the disturbing things was that she only seemed to need the occasional cat-nap in front of an afternoon soap opera. Otherwise, she was constantly busy, cooking, tidying, arranging, fussing, vacuuming, rearranging, humming, shopping, fluttering . . .

He thought the woman – his wife, he corrected himself – had a problem with her short-term memory. Like a goldfish, she had an identity – several, in fact – but no moment-to-moment consciousness. She lived in an eternal present, unchanging and perfect.

Karen said it was like being smothered by Nanette Newman.

The evening wore on, and Peter's knots tightened. How would Maddie react when Karen and he went to bed? The kitchen she'd made her home was fully equipped with weapons. Some time last year, Karen had bought him a set of Sabatier steak knives, with wicked, serrated edges.

In the event, Maddie ignored them, humming and clattering as she washed up, refusing all offers of assistance, and telling them to enjoy themselves while she worked.

'My poor little brain isn't up to business,' she told Karen, 'so you talk figures and deadlines and schedules with Petey while my elves and I clean up.' She had permanent smile lines – like scars – etched in under her rosy patches.

Stunned, Karen allowed him to take her to bed and pull most of her clothes off. Maddie had the radio on again. Connie Francis's 'Lipstick On Your Collar', Julie London's 'Cry Me a River', the Ink Spots' 'Don't Get Around Much Any More', Hank Williams' 'Why Don't You Love Me Like You Used to Do?', Del Shannon's 'Hats Off to Larry'. The noise of plates and cups and crockery being cleaned accompanied the songs, and seemed to fill the bedroom.

Neither of them were up to it and they lay together, hugging. Maddie hummed along to 'Stand By Your Man'. Karen shook her head, gave up and got out of bed. She dressed in the dark, and left the flat.

Peter lay in bed, listening to washing-up.

A week later, while Peter was at his easel finishing up a rough for a Pan thriller, a blast of noise came from his CD.

He turned around, shaking. The broken doll he had been sketching fell off its stand.

WASP's 'Fuck Like a Beast'.

Madeleine was naked in the mid-afternoon, but for insectile dark glasses and a pair of high-heeled black patent-leather pumps. Her face was more oval, lines better defined. Long, tangled hair – darker than last week – hung around her shoulders and breasts. Her body was off a Nineties Mickey Spillane cover, and not what he had expected under the pinnies and dresses she'd been wearing.

The Dominoes' 'Sixty Minute Man'.

She came for him, fingers like hooks ripping his shirt and trousers apart. They didn't make it to the bedroom for hours, and then they didn't make it to sleep for nearly a day.

A week later, Peter woke up, still drained from the night before, to find Madeleine had locked herself in the bathroom and was sobbing.

He had to break in, wrenching his shoulder, and found her curled up between the sink and toilet bowl, clutching her stomach, a scattering of open and emptied pill bottles around her, a sweated-in T-shirt ridden up around her belly, stringy hair wrapped around her neck like a noose.

He slapped her semi-conscious and walked her around the flat until the drowsiness wore off. Then he made her drink salt water until she spewed into a bucket. Undissolved pills clustered like frogspawn in her mainly clear vomitus.

She wouldn't say anything coherent, but rambled dark and self-hating drivel at him. From somewhere, she found an Eisenstürzende Neubauten cassette and played 'Der Tod ist ein Dandy' over and over, banging her head against the floor in time to the pounding rhythms until she was covered in blood from superficial cuts.

He phoned Karen but got an answering-machine message saying she was out of the country for a week.

Madeleine started in on Bauhaus's 'Bela Lugosi's Dead'. Where did she get these records from?

There was a noise in the kitchen and he got there in

time to wrestle the steak knife away from her. She inflicted a shallow cut through his shirt.

A week later, exhausted and bruised, he found she'd got up early and left the flat. He used the time to tidy a little, washing some of the long-neglected crockery and scraping at the stains on the carpet. The flat was musty and he opened all the windows to air it out.

He was beginning to recognize the cycle. It lasted almost precisely a week. Peter wondered if there was such a thing as a serial multiple personality.

Perhaps she might not come home?

At six fifteen precisely, she let herself in, and put her briefcase down on the sofa. She was wearing one of Karen's suits, severe but sexy, cut tight on the hips and high on the thighs, with prominent shoulders and a don't-fuck-with-me-jack tie.

'I had to screw them until they bled, but Futura are coming through with your market-value price for the next covers. They specified more maggots for the Hutson job.'

She stuck a cigarette in her mouth, and flipped a silver lighter open, sucking flame through the tobacco tube then exhaling a cloud.

'This place is a tip, Peter, I expect to come home to better than this.'

She pulled her tie off with an expert gesture, and began unbuttoning her blouse.

'I've set us up with a table at Alistair Little's for eight with the commissioning guy from HarperCollins. Try to make a good impression. There might be a dekalogy in it.'

She slipped her skirt over her legs, and stepped out of it. She wore no underwear.

'And I fired your accountant. Weldon's been robbing you blind for years. There's no room for that kind of wimpery in the business. Like your "friend" Karen. She's sweet and lovely, but sweet and lovely just doesn't cut it any more.'

She gave him fifteen minutes to bring her to orgasm, then criticized his broken-doll covers until the minicab came.

A week later, she wanted a baby. She talked of nothing else, and even bought baby clothes in pink and blue, made a start on redecorating the spare room as a nursery, and worked out on the calendar which were the best days to try. By the time the days came around, she had changed her mind . . .

A week later, she stole his credit cards and ran up nearly a six-figure bill on compulsive purchases. She bought more furniture than could fit into the flat, a car neither of them could drive, a complete wardrobe of flashy clothes not in his size, enough food to give Godzilla a three-day belly-ache. And she discovered gambling.

A week later, she went into what he thought of as her *Annie Hall* phase, becoming at once terminally absent-minded and cuttingly witty. Of them all, this was the one he liked the most. When she was funny, they were better in bed. She would pull faces, and remind him of his mother's old theme tune, 'if the wind changes, it'll stick like that'. That didn't seem such an awful fate just now. The wind changed, but . . .

A week later, she brought home a Siamese kitten and lavished her entire attention on it twenty-four hours a day, reading books on cat-care and attending to Mitten's every need. She treated Peter as if he were an intruder in her idyll with the pet. When Mitten put its claws through a half-finished Jeffrey Archer cover, Madeleine spent an hour cooing over it and spitting at him that her precious better not get blood-poisoning from the lead in the paint or else . . .

A week later . . .

A week later . . .

. . . and a week and a week and a week . . .

A week later, he got out of the flat while she was gorging herself on chocolates in front of Anne Diamond on the television. She was bulimic in this cycle, and would stuff herself until she was sick. That left him to look after Mitten, who was fast becoming as startled and neurotic as he was. Madeleine had been anorexic a few turns back, between her poetic consumptive week and her Australian soap opera phase.

They met in Capucetto's. He could see Karen was shocked by the change in him. He'd clearly made up the two extra years, and was galloping into his biological future.

'I've seen Jeanne,' she said.

'And . . .'

'Your lesbian waited all afternoon and went home.'

'What?'

'Her name was Madeleine *Keele*.'

'Then who is she? Our Madeleine?'

'Your Madeleine, you mean. Ask her.'

'She doesn't know. Karen, it's even weirder than you think. She doesn't just change her personality. Her hair changes, the shape of her face sometimes, her body . . .'

'You've been sleeping with her?'

He had to tell. 'Some of her.'

'Fuck you, Peter,' Karen said. 'You can either live with it, or get a divorce and be deported to Warsaw. I don't care any more.'

She left him to pay for the coffee and cheesecake.

A week later, he got back from a meeting at the new agency to find the flat filled with a burned stink. Mitten was in the microwave. Smoke filled the kitchen.

'Madeleine?'

There was one Sabatier missing from the magnetic rack. The world turned around again and Peter was filled with cold caution. He took a matching knife down and gripped it.

It had been inevitable. Sooner or later, Madeleine would turn dangerous.

He explored, cautiously.

The front room was anally perfect, cushions just so on the drum-tight sofa-bed, his framed Graham Greene Penguin covers neatly aligned on the walls, all the magazines tidied away and stacked up. The television was on, and one of a stack of videotapes was playing.

On the screen was a blotchy image of a razorblade sinking into a girl's eyeball, ketchupy gore welling up around the halved olive as a synthesized drone rose in a shriek.

Peter held out his knife as if it could protect him from the picture.

There was a stack of cassette boxes on top of the television, neatly squared, photocopied covers yelling titles. *The Cincinatti Flamethrower Holocaust, They Eat Your Eyes, Black and Decker Orgy, Rapist Cult.*

He shut off the video but the slasher music still came from his sound system.

He stepped into the bedroom and found it perfectly tidy. Except for the headless doll on the bedspread, its torso sawed open and stuffed with red rags. It was his much-used prop, even more abused than usual.

She came quietly out of his closet and got his arm up behind him, forcing him down on the floor. She wore a black leotard and an IRA ski-mask, and her body was hard and skilled as she battered him against the carpet. He lost his knife with the first slam and yelped as she hauled him up.

She threw him on to the bed, then let him go and took the time to peel off her mask, shaking out her wing of night-black hair. He knew she was going to kill him. She put the Sabatier to his throat, and smiled. First, she was going to torture him. For a long time.

Pain had been constant for all his life. He wouldn't have believed pain could be prolonged so long without the subject dying.

Madeleine worked efficiently, tirelessly, dispassionately. She hurt him. With her hands and household implements, she hurt him. She had been methodical about it, skinning the insulation from wires and using low-wattage electricity, wetting him down with water from the bathroom sink between each jolt.

As she worked, she played two singles over and over, Little Jimmy Osmond's 'Long-Haired Lover From Liverpool' and Aled Jones' 'The Snowman'.

Even pain became boring after a while.

Finally, she was ready to end it. She picked up one of his steak knives, and pulled back for a neat thrust.

Before he died, he wanted to hear Brahms, the 'Ode to Joy', Chuck Berry, Eric Satie. Not Little Fucking Aled Osmond's Long-Haired Snowman From Jones.

Madeleine's elbow kinked and she paused. Throughout it all, her face had been a paper blank. Now, he saw an expression . . .

Could it have been a full week?

Night had come and gone several times. There had been periods of sleep and rest between the busy-work. She had been taking care to keep him alive.

He had never seen her change before.

Her hair might be bleaching. Her skin might be tanning. She might be wriggling inside uncomfortable clothes.

She dropped the Sabatier and stood away from the bed. Knowing this chance might never come again, he picked up the knife with nailless fingers and worked it into her unresisting throat.

A week later, Madeleine was still on his bed, in a circle of dried blood. He'd taken out the knife, cleaned it, and clanged it to its rack in the kitchen. There were flies in the bedroom, and her skin was already yellow in patches and starting to give, suggesting the skeleton beneath useless meat.

He had stayed in the flat with her, recovering slowly. He'd used up all the iodine and bandages in the bathroom cabinet. He daren't go out. And he didn't even like to leave the bedroom.

Madeleine must not be left alone.

She was the broken doll now. He'd made many sketches of her, and the bedroom was carpeted with them. He would draw her slack, empty face as it was, and then try to superimpose one of her personalities on it.

Madeleine, Maddie, Mad.

He had to stay with her for more than a week. He had to. It must be a week now. Something was moving under her face.

Peter waited for the next change.

Necrophiliac

PHILIP J. COCKBURN

I MAKE LOVE . . . to the dead.

People think the practice loathsome and repulsive, but they've never experienced the exhilaration of cold flesh against theirs, of cold lips and cold, cold thighs. It's exciting, invigorating. Like winter's chill. Life in the midst of death.

I'm judged perverse, insane even. But what do they know of love? They who blithely sing of heartbreak then practise what they sing; they who betray loved ones with adulterous liaisons; they who kill in the name of love?

Hypocrites!

Is my kind of love any worse? I love the dead, but never hurt; I love the dead, but never betray; love the dead, but never kill.

If crime I commit it is that of love.

Considering the dogma of afterlife might not the dead be pleasured? Might not their souls sing in harmony as their flesh is loved? If love is a birthright why deny the dead? They, too, walked the earth. Once.

So who are the real perverts? Who loathsome and repulsive?

Granted, I, too, am pleasured. But my need is cold; my feelings are cold; my love is . . . cold. Perhaps my heart pumps ice instead of blood. Perhaps my soul exudes the psychic-cold emotions of death. But even cold emotions are better than none at all. Compared with sociopaths I am a kitten; compared with psychotics I'm harmless.

Removing soil from graves is like peeling off clothes layer by tantalizing layer; discarded in heaps like silken finery, dresses and coats: necrotic foreplay to cold, silent love. It tingles my flesh with anticipation as I dig towards their coffins, nuptual beds of pleasure.

Many women have received me; in the dark, in the grave. Murmurs of love soon drowned in night's music: owls, bats and nightjars. Heady atmospheres of damp earth are quickly cancelled by my ardour.

Now Ella awaits, patient as death, with three feet of pebble-dashed clothes between us. A mere three feet, my love, before we lie together, kiss together, love together. The wait will be worth it. I promise.

Three days ago a newspaper divulged: Lady Ella Forthnum; thirty-seven; widowed; recently affianced; died following brief debilitating illness; interment near ancestral home; private funeral though flowers welcome. Of her fiancé little was said; presumed retired to be alone with his grief. Foul play was not suspected.

I saw her in church, terribly pale in an open coffin. Some kind of anaemia, I supposed. She was very attractive: light make-up, smooth complexion, small breasts, youthful, slim. The hands crossing her chest held a single red rose. Leaning forward I stole a glance at the black-edged card: Mine for eternity . . . John.

That's when she whispered.

I'm aware how old churches distort sound, that it might have been a vagrant draught amongst the rafters or meandering around the wainscoting. But this was different. It was Ella. Faint but unmistakeable; a whispered invitation spiced with desire.

I would not disappoint her.

She was buried the following day with traditional ceremony. The weather was fine though chilly. Discreetly, I watched from a quartet of autumn-stained trees near the church, heart hammering a copulatory rhythm.

Ella must have sensed it for she whispered encouragement, goading me to greater sensuality. To demand thus in death implied a truly erotic life. I could only consider John's loss as my gain. He can keep her spirit for eternity, but her flesh would be mine..

Her earthy clothes are loose. Like fingers my shovel strips them away, inch by inch. Musky odours assail me with pungent promise. She knows I'm here; waits with deathly patience as soil is removed. Two more feet yet her presence is already palpable. Soon we shall embrace, kiss, make love. But until then her coy silence is enough.

I never found the dead desirable before my accident. Now, they lure me, sirenlike, to graveyard bedchambers; arouse me in a way the living cannot; receive my cold, cold emotions with a sensuality the living never could.

Their mouths open as my tongue intrudes, lips cold and dry against mine, my saliva lubrication enough for both. With my thumbs pressing and rolling the corners of their mouths lips develop spontaneity as we kiss.

Twice I've found mortician's work beneath funeral dresses where organs had been removed, examined, replaced, stitched without care. These wounds my questing fingers explore, my lips kiss, my tongue caresses. I know my lovers more intimately than ever they were known in life.

It shall be no less for you, dear Ella. Our embraces shall move towards the ecstasy of love and we shall truly know one another. I shall love you like you've never been loved before. And in return you shall release me from dreams that boil my soul.

Nightmares!

Visions of flesh pierced by steel; ribs crushed by plastic; bones snapped by metal; flesh flayed by glass. *My* flesh! *My* bones! Blood everywhere. Mingled with vomit and urine. Lips torn, nose crushed, one eye skewered. Grinding metal, shattering glass, fearful screams. *My* screams! A woman's head rips through the windscreen in a shower of glass, flies towards me, a gargoyle of fear. Her eyes bulge with expectancy, her mouth a sonic 'O' of dread. Until that head collides with mine. Then all is dark; blacker than the deepest space.

Six months in hospital followed. Six months of operations, skin grafts, plastic surgery. The final touch a glass eye. Good as new. Capable of normal life. Or so the doctors claimed.

Normal.

Except for the nightmares.

And . . . my legacy!

I was told later, in pedantic terms that avoided words like 'died', or 'dead', that my heart had stopped for one and a half minutes. While this was not uncommon they wondered if I'd discuss it with their psychologist.

I declined.

They were interested in long tunnels, white light, peaceful gardens, saintly personages, friends and relatives who'd gone before.

What I'd encountered was a pocket limbo suspended in eternity. Huge, empty, cold beyond measure. A millennium passed before realizing I was not alone. Someone or something floated beside me, its atmosphere atuned to the cold. It was lewd, sensual, erotic; explored me with icy fingers; caressed with dead hands; kissed with lips so cold they burned.

Had it snared my soul at the point of death? Dragged me here as companion for eternity? Only its hands answered; sensual, exploring, arousing.

I knew it was female; physical in every sense. I could touch her, feel her, have her; souls entwined like flesh; real as real could be. How, I didn't know, didn't question. The wings of ecstasy had carried me to heaven. Or perhaps to hell. Yet hell was never thus. Nor was my climax insubstantial, crashing through me like rhythmic tsunamis.

She must have been a succubus. Certainly she was alive, genuine, maddening. Erotic beyond imagining; sensual beyond endurance. I would have willingly remained for eternity. To be hers. Always.

But doctors' hands, chemicals, machines, pulled me away, back to the living.

For thirteen nights scenes of broken bones, twisted limbs, mangled flesh, gave way to memory of her. I slept in peace reliving our tryst. But each night the images

239

weakened until nothing but a memory remained. I felt lost and alone, unable to live without her; she of that dark, cold limbo. Even after she'd faded I remembered her touch. I would never forget the exciting coldness of her hands, her lips, her . . . all.

My nightmares resumed and I knew only one thing to dispel them: recapture her essence. Or as close as possible, for I could never hope to gain the *real* her.

But where to find it?

I'd find it in the night. In the dark. In the grave.

Tonight it's Ella's turn to exorcise the blood and wreckage. One more foot of soil before my soul is chilled to life; revived by cold, cold charms. Then surcease for another thirteen nights. Already, my body trembles with expectancy.

And when our love is fulfilled I shall claim her wedding finger as a token of our love. Preserve it with care to remember her by. Keep it with the others. In return I shall give her something more profound than John's red rose.

Ah! Wood! Her bed at last!

My heart quickens in response to short, rapid breaths. My brow prickles with sweat, chilled by October night air. Chilled ready for her.

Trembling hands smooth clear her coffin, feel the outlines of name plate and crucifix. How quaintly paradoxical. Who shall read it six feet beneath the earth? They need only see her tombstone. Was it Ella's or John's idea to inscribe her name below the cross? No matter. Nor am I interested in religious affiliations. I embrace them all. Literally.

Screws are no problem. I come prepared. Always. One

by one they loosen. As each falls free my pulse increases. Breaths grow tremulous as my body burns with the fires of dry ice. My one eye sees well enough in starlight, being used to the small hours.

The grave is too narrow to stand while opening the coffin. So I gouge a channel in the soil along one side. I attach three stringed hooks to the lid's rim before climbing from the grave via a rope tied to a stout marble cross. Standing on the edge opposite the hooks gives me more control. As I slowly pull gravity slides the lid into the channel. With the lid wedged firm it won't fall on top of us.

Quickly, I lower myself back into the grave, straddle the coffin and gaze upon her face. Oh, Ella, how lovely you are! Even in death you seem but asleep. Only your rose has faded. I reach to stroke her cheek, find it amazingly supple. As are her lips.

There's not much room, but if I tear out the silk padding and turn her on to her side . . . There. Tight, but we're slim enough to lie facing each other.

I caress her back while holding her chin in my other hand, tilt her head to receive my lips. Chaste at first, leaving passion room to grow. The hand at her back moves up to her neck, then round to her chin. I position my thumbs. Turning her head I raise mine to deliver my first passionate kiss. Her lips, cold and unusually soft, move to the rolling pressure of my thumbs. It's almost as if she responds.

One hand pinches open her jaw while the other drops to her blouse. As I undo the buttons my tongue penetrates her mouth, so soft, so cold, so moist. Never have I savoured such sweetness. Her breasts, too, are magnificent; firm yet pliable, nipples like spring buds.

Slowly I remove her clothes. Then mine. I turn her on to her back, arrange her body to receive me. I kiss her breasts before mounting her. Against mine her body is cold. Electric cold. Nipples burn my chest like icicles; thighs like soft, frozen snow; belly a glacial cushion.

I insert myself while kissing her neck, commence a steady rhythm. My lips move caressingly to her shoulder. In the process my neck brushes her mouth. It peels back her bottom lip as though in a kiss.

My climax is powerful, ripples of tingling pleasure coursing my body. Ella's lips twitch in response to the extraordinarily pleasant pulses in my neck. It slowly diminishes, numbing my throat.

Oh, Ella! You're wringing my soul. Draining it.

I feel so weak, I must rest a while. Your coffin a bed, your body my mattress. Feel strange. So weak. Getting weaker. What have you done to me, Ella? None of my lovers took so much. I shall soon pass out.

Despite the weakness I raise my head, gaze at her eyes. They're open! So piercing. So beautifully cold. Her smile exposes teeth. Curious teeth. Long teeth. Smeared with blood. *My* blood. Too weak to hold, my head falls back to her shoulder.

She resumes. Nuzzling softly, kissing gently, drinking greedily.

I knew, then, what John was, what he meant by 'Mine for eternity'. Knew why Ella's coffin bore a crucifix; knew what I would become.

Shall we both, I wonder, have her for eternity? Or could I, perhaps, find my succubus?

Before passing out I smile at the irony of my situation, for either way, my lovers shall soon receive me from the *other* side of the grave.

Return of the Shroud

NORMAN PARTRIDGE

PROFESSOR JACOB HEARTHSTONE listened to Dr Taoka's words, mentally translating them with a slight bit of difficulty. Though the Japanese language was second nature to Hearthstone, he still had trouble deciphering terms not used in everyday conversation, and such was the case with the surgeon's medical jargon. But Hearthstone realized that words were not the important thing here. Anyone familiar with the niceties of Japanese culture could ignore the words, concentrate only on Taoka's body language, and easily recognize the true intent of the surgeon's visit.

Dr Taoka was here to beg forgiveness.

Hearthstone closed his eyes and let Taoka's quiet words engulf him. Cloaked in the surgeon's explanations were effusive excuses beyond number. The professor sighed mightily, and Taoka began to speak faster.

The true hell of it was that the surgeon's explanations made perfect sense. After all, Dr Taoka had come to Hearthstone with high recommendations and an excellent reputation among the most conservative elements of the

Tokyo medical community. But Hearthstone, unfettered from the chains of logic and reason during his bride's long illness, had an increasingly difficult time processing information that should have made perfect sense.

The old man fought his suspicions, watching the surgeon's lips twist as he stumbled over a particularly difficult explanation. Dr Taoka was not a butcher, he told himself. The surgeon could not be an avenging murderer. He was exactly who, and what, he claimed to be.

And yet . . .

Taoka was skilled in the use of blades. Hearthstone had watched him from the gallery above the surgery, had seen him take the scalpel from the towel-covered tray, the tray that, covered, existed in shadow. With his own eyes Hearthstone had watched the surgeon put blade to flesh – the flesh of Hearthstone's bride – and he had noted the familiar intensity that burned in the man's eyes.

If man he was.

Hearthstone fought against his powerful memory, but a memory that catalogued even the most minor impression could not be damned. Everything came flooding back. The blade. Taoka's eyes. The cotton mask that had covered the surgeon's mouth. Hearthstone had watched the thin material puff out with exhalation; he'd seen it draw back with Taoka's next breath.

The mask had drawn tight against a lurid grin. Of that, Hearthstone was certain. And at that moment, standing alone in the gallery, the sibilant hint of a Beethoven sonata issuing from stereo speakers below, Hearthstone had remembered another blade and another woman.

And the same grin.

At that moment, the surgeon made the first deep incision.

At that moment, screaming violins sliced the silence.

And now the surgeon spoke of infection and fever. The diagnosis was poor. Hopeless, really, but Taoka was trying desperately not to say that.

Trying desperately, Hearthstone thought, not to smile.

'Thank you, Dr Taoka,' the old man said, his Japanese impeccable, his accent perfect. 'This is awful news, of course, and I find myself terribly saddened by it. But I would like you to put the best face on your report. A happy face, if you please.'

'Professor Hearthstone . . . I'm afraid that I don't understand.'

Hearthstone bent forward. 'Sir, I would appreciate it very much if you would smile for me.'

Dr Taoka was confused. Perhaps this was an American custom with which he was unfamiliar. He made to protest, but as his mind searched for a tactic that would not offend, his lips twisted unbidden into a perplexed grin.

Hearthstone thanked the surgeon and promptly shot him dead.

The first time they met, long before Hearthstone had ever seen Japan, the professor asked, 'Are you demon or angel?'

'I am . . . the Shroud.' The answer came in a purring whisper. 'I come for those who are evil. Those who are evil must suffer, then die.'

Hearthstone shivered, embarrassed to be frightened by such base melodrama. Silly to have come here, to headquarters, alone. The stranger had been waiting for him, had slipped from the shadows and whispered that he was an avenger, a ghost.

Don't surrender to the fear, Hearthstone warned himself. Keep the madman talking until someone comes to check on you. Listen to his insane babbling, and kill him when the odds are in your favour.

Hearthstone turned to the window. Below, the San Francisco streets swam with fog, but it was a low fog. Across the street, it hung far below a theatre marquee bathed in the white glow of overhead lamps, a stark illumination that transformed the reaching grey tendrils into cottony puffs that resembled the cloudy floor of some Hollywood heaven.

Black letters on the marquee. *Frankenstein* double-billed with *Dracula*.

Ah, true melodrama. Hearthstone chuckled at that. 'Sir, if it's evil you've come for, I believe you've come to the wrong place. Messieurs Lugosi and Karloff are across the street.'

Silence.

'A small joke,' Hearthstone began, his throat constricting involuntarily as the stranger advanced, quiet as the evening fog. And then words spilled unbidden from the professor's thin lips, driven by a pure, instinctive terror that he had never experienced previously. 'A small joke . . . from a small, unimportant man. I deal only in narcotics, synthesized through methods I discovered while employed by some of our more adventurous captains of industry. Mere entertainments for the bored and the jaded, those who find no solace in the pleasures approved by modern society . . . I'm sure you understand. Perhaps you, sir . . . Perhaps you would like—'

Laughter echoed from the velvet draperies that hung about the window. The inhuman sound forced Hearthstone to shrink away from the room's lone source of light.

'Please understand,' Hearthstone begged, stumbling toward his desk, his eyes searching the room, 'I am not a rich man, but if it's money you want . . .'

Mellow shadows pooled on the pine floor as the Shroud – now silhouetted in the grey glow of the window – moved forward. Planks complained as if punished by a heavy tread, but the self-proclaimed avenger was drifting toward Hearthstone like the wispy shadow of something floating outside on the night fog. The thing – Hearthstone's instinctive fear told him that this could not be a man – came closer, its harsh laughter rising.

'A shadowshow for you, Professor. Without fee . . .'

Another sound. The swish of a cape on the hardwood floor. 'Mr Lugosi,' the voice whispered, suddenly tinged with a familiar accent.

Red eyes burned in the darkness. Hearthstone reached out, fingers scrabbling across the stained blotter, and flicked on the desk lamp. The bulb flared, then exploded, and the brief instant of brightness momentarily blinded the professor.

The scent of ozone flooded the stuffy room. Hearthstone caught the sizzle of lightning and the slightest glimpse of a scarred neck spiked with twin bolts. 'Mr Karloff,' the voice enthused.

No longer the sound of a sweeping cape. Now heavy boots beat a slow rhythm across the pine floorboards.

Spots swam before Hearthstone's eyes. He rubbed at them, blinking away tears. The spots danced, rotated, all but a single black globe that stared him down and made him sob.

'Anyone,' the voice whispered.

A black slit spread across the ebony circle and split into a grin.

'Anywhere . . .'

Puddled against the wall.

'Any time . . .'

Slipped toward the window.

'Good night, Jacob Hearthstone,' said the Shroud. 'And remember – next comes suffering.'

'Damn,' Professor Hearthstone said. 'Double damn.'

He stared at Taoka's face. The surgeon's corpse didn't grin. Rather it frowned, its thin lips blemished by a gout of blood that was already drying. And though the room was flooded with light, as were all the rooms within the professor's compound, Hearthstone searched desperately for a single shadow.

None near Taoka's bloody mouth. None in the corners of the room. None behind the satin draperies, nor beneath the lacquered desk, nor behind the rice-paper doors of the closet.

His bride had often asked him, 'Why do we need all this light? You've already killed him, haven't you?'

Always he corrected her without drawing attention to the correction, and always he pretended that yes, indeed, he was certain that he had killed the thing. '*It* was a demon, and I am too much the cynic to believe that this world is cursed with the presence of only one demon. There may be others far more powerful than the Shroud.'

No, he would not remember. The path of memory was dangerous. Possibly fatal.

Hearthstone clapped his hands. Pulled himself into the present moment.

He stared at the dead surgeon. At the caked blood on his lips. At the corners of the room.

At the complete absence of shadows.

In the lore of San Francisco's Chinatown, the incident was known as the Night of the Axes. It was Professor Hearthstone's finest moment. He had maintained a low profile for several months, partially due to worry over the strange nocturnal visit that had occurred at his headquarters, partially because his next move required careful planning.

Hearthstone had long coveted the secrecy that a Chinatown operation would afford his particular concerns. The police steered clear of the foreign population, and the professor felt that his business would go undetected if he could conduct it from a section of the city that was little known or understood.

The only problem with Hearthstone's scheme was that there were others who already controlled the area. Namely the Wong Ching Benevolent Society, an organization known as much for its wealth as its ruthless behaviour.

But within that equation lay the answer to the professor's dilemma. If Chinatown understood wealth, then its occupants would understand him. And if the Wong Chings understood ruthless behaviour, then ruthless behaviour would be the order of the day.

Hearthstone recruited a pack of hale and hearty Irishmen from one of the city's more notorious waterfront bars and appointed a recently busted policeman named Thomas Clancy as their leader. Equipped with firefighting garb and axes, the Irishmen descended upon a restaurant called Sun Lim's, which happened to serve as headquarters to the Wong Chings. When their axe blades grew dull and the tiled floors were well oiled with Chinese blood, the merry Irish mob torched the building. They watched the flames dance, drinking strange oriental liquor and singing a merry tune of their native land.

> Then get ye a dozen stout fellows,
> And let them all stagger and go,
> And dig a great hole in the meadow,
> And in it put rosin the bow.

The incident was reported in the local press as an accidental fire. Even in those days, the mayor feared civil unrest if the truth was widely reported. But the mayor needn't have worried, for the true story was known by all in Chinatown. The tale terrified even the bravest members of the teaming populace. The word *riot* was not spoken, was not even thought.

This pleased Professor Hearthstone. He immediately launched the second phase of his operation, flooding the community with money and gifts to demonstrate the largess of the new regime.

In the shabby apartments and cellars of Chinatown, people began to speak happily of the collapse of the Wong Ching Benevolent Society.

In a lavish suite overlooking Grant Avenue, Professor Hearthstone set about learning the Chinese language.

And in the gutted ruins of Sun Lim's Restaurant, a dark thing laughed.

'You should not have let him pass, Mr Machii.'

The yakuza lieutenant, his shaved head lowered, stared at the kitchen floor. Hearthstone knew that the man would not comment until instructed to do so.

Another bumbler, Hearthstone thought. Not like in the old days, when the yakuza were the world's best. No, those days were long gone. Today, too many yakuza were simple punks drawn from the bosozoku gangs. And they didn't leave their bosozuku past behind, still caring more about motorcycles and hotrods and dirty magazines than matters of economics or honour.

'Dr Taoka made the mistake of allowing his loyalties to fall into question,' Hearthstone continued. 'I'm afraid that such questions must be dealt with in a harsh manner. We must act swiftly, even if our suspicions are tenuous at best. As we say in America, we must shoot first and ask questions later.' Hearthstone suppressed a smile. '*Bang bang bang*. Understand?'

An almost imperceptible nod from the yakuza; even a bosozoku could understand such a simple message. Hearthstone watched the man's bristly eyebrows shift as he studied the floor – Hearthstone's shoes, his own shoes, the elegant dish that lay on the floor between them, the raw, teriyaki-drenched filet mignon that filled the dish.

Was he afraid? Or was he thinking, measuring the distance, weighing the time that it would take to strike?

No. That was imagination.

'You will not make this mistake again, will you, Mr Machii?'

The yakuza lieutenant bowed.

Hearthstone brightened, his mind focusing. Of course. A test. That was the sane man's measure of loyalty. 'And you will do something to restore my faith in your abilities, will you not?'

Machii did not hesitate. Still avoiding Hearthstone's eyes, he turned to the kitchen counter and positioned a marble cutting stone. He placed his left hand on the stone, fingers splayed, and slipped a neatly folded handkerchief under the smallest finger.

The jakuza's fingernails were stained with engine oil. The professor allowed himself a slight frown. No demon, this one. Only bosozoku trash.

A slim knife appeared in Machii's right hand. A swift slash – no sound of blade meeting marble – and the yakuza's left pinky was severed at the juncture of the proximal and middle phalanges.

Beads of sweat erupted on Machii's forehead. Carefully, he folded the handkerchief over the severed finger. Once. Twice.

Hearthstone nearly laughed at the scene. A clean white shroud for a dirty little finger.

A shroud.

Machii peered into Hearthstone's eyes. The professor backed away, fighting the memories that came flooding back.

Hearthstone held out a hand.

The yakuza snorted against the pain. His lower lip quivered. (Hearthstone watching.) Tightened into an agonized grin. (Hearthstone reaching inside his coat.) Parted as he took a very small breath.

His last breath.

His last grin.

A single slug exploded from the barrel of Hearthstone's automatic, and the yakuza slumped forward. His severed digit slipped from the handkerchief and dropped into the elegant dish. A thick line of blood oozed over the filet mignon and puddled beneath the thin teriyaki sauce.

Hearthstone watched the yakuza's face, stiffened when the man sank to the floor.

It wasn't that the man's death disturbed the professor. Behind him, something had begun to growl.

She came each day to Hearthstone's Grant Avenue suite, though she preferred to call the street Dupont Gai, or old Dupont Street, in the manner of the local population. She came with books tucked under one arm, ready to teach the Chinese language to Jacob Hearthstone.

Her name was Anastasia White, and she had grown up in Shanghai. Her father was a diplomat – of what nation she would not say. Her mother was not a topic for conversation, either. But Hearthstone judged that Anastasia's mother must have been a true beauty, for the young woman's complexion was a stunning creamy gold and her amber eyes were as delectable as spiced almonds.

Needless to say, Hearthstone played at being a poor student, ever eager to keep the beauteous Miss White in his employ. Soon they were working their way through the extensive menu at Madame Liu's, Anastasia's favourite restaurant, under the pretence that chatting with the waitresses was good practice for the professor; but before long there was no need of pretence. There were evenings at the opera and excursions to the cinema, though Hearthstone attempted to avoid the latter, especially when the night's

programme included features starring Bela Lugosi or
Boris Karloff. No sense, he thought, in rekindling
unpleasant memories when romance was on his mind.

And then, on a rare, warm afternoon, Anastasia came
to him in tears. 'Professor, I'm afraid that I will be leaving
San Francisco immediately. I've come to refund the balance of this month's lesson payment, as I shan't be able
to instruct you further.'

'My dear, whatever can the matter be?' Hearthstone
asked, strong concern evident in his voice. 'And why so
formal? This isn't like you at all.'

'Please, Jacob. Don't make this difficult.'

'But I must insist—'

'Very well. A man has been visiting my apartment.
A very disagreeable man. He has related several stories
concerning his association with you, stories which I
refused to believe until very recently. And then, just last
night, he threatened to reveal our relationship to the most
sordid members of the press. He demanded blackmail
payments. When I refused, he . . . he forced himself . . .'

Anastasia broke down, and Hearthstone moved to comfort her. 'This . . . this man,' he said, his voice trembling
as he remembered the Shroud. 'You must tell me his
name.'

Anastasia managed to collect herself enough to whisper,
'His name is Thomas Clancy.'

A relieved smile twisted the corners of Hearthstone's
lips. Clancy. The busted policeman who had headed up
the takeover of Chinatown. 'You mustn't worry, my dear,'
he said. 'I will handle this matter. Personally.'

Within the hour, the professor was standing outside a
dingy saloon which, while located in the same city, was a

world away from his Chinatown home. A blood-red scarf was draped around his neck. A target pistol was secreted beneath his camel-hair coat. Four masters of wing chun gung fu stood at his side.

'I'm going in,' he said, his Chinese impeccable. 'Alone.' His subordinates knew better than to argue.

Hearthstone entered the saloon. Yellow light swimming with smoke. The smell of whiskey and beer and the unwashed. A song ringing over loud conversation – the same song he'd heard during the destruction of Sun Lim's Restaurant many months before.

> *When I'm dead and laid out on the counter,*
> *A voice you will hear from below,*
> *Sayin' send down a hogshead of whiskey,*
> *To drink with old rosin the bow.*

In a dark corner, all alone, sat Thomas Clancy. Hearthstone elbowed his way through the crowd, one gloved hand on his hidden pistol.

Hearthstone sat down. Clancy grinned. The Irishman held a bowie knife in his left hand, and he was sawing it gently across the top of his right wrist. There were dozens of small cuts there, some scabbed over, some weeping blood.

'I'll tell you one thing,' Clancy whispered, 'for a high 'n' mighty pris, she was awful lively 'tween the—'

The pistol thundered, time and again, until the chambers were empty.

Clancy still grinned. His voice came in a purring whisper. 'Remember, Jacob Hearthstone, I come for those who are evil . . . Those who are evil must suffer . . . They must suffer, and then they must . . .'

Clancy slumped backward. His jaw slackened and a bloody bubble formed on his lips.

Hands grabbed at Hearthstone's arms. Someone wrestled the empty pistol from his grip.

The bloody bubble burst. A scarlet shadow poured from Clancy's mouth and rippled across the scarred tabletop. It hit the floor and slithered over the professor's shoes. Hearthstone screamed at the icy feel of the thing. The crowd screamed as well, but their screams were for him, for *his* blood.

The professor fought against his subduers, and he saw for the first time that they were policemen. Irishmen like Clancy. A punch thundered into his stomach. Clancy was a busted copper, but there was no such thing as a busted Irishman.

The professor hit the floor. Filthy sawdust caked his bleeding lip and stained his expensive camel-hair coat. He rolled away from his attackers, desperately trying to gain his feet. He didn't fear kicks or punishment. No, he feared the scarlet shadow that had slipped from Clancy's mouth, the shadow that had to be the Shroud.

God. Where were his reinforcements? Where were the wing chun men now that he needed—

The Irishmen pulled Hearthstone to his feet and towed him into the alley behind the saloon – deeper, deeper – the professor's eyes watching the street, drinking in the maddening scene with the sardonic humour of a true masochist, an unabashed cynic.

For in the street, he saw it. The shadowthing that was the Shroud. It expanded like a great net and ensnared the wing chun masters, whose punches and chops proved laughably ineffectual as the thing tightened its grip on their muscular bodies, crushing bones and reducing flesh to bloody pulp.

Then came the true horror.

Once more a snake, the scarlet shadow slithered across the blood-slick pavement. Encircled a creamy gold ankle. Coiled around a delicate calf, a perfect knee, and disappeared beneath the skirt of the woman with amber eyes.

The Dobermann advanced, growling, its nails ticking against the tiled kitchen floor.

'Down, Dempsey . . . Good boy, Dempsey,' Hearthstone whispered, inching toward the centre of the kitchen.

He glanced at Machii's corpse. Damn. For the last few months, the yakuza had been feeding Dempsey, and now the dog thought that Machii was its master, thought that Machii was the one who provided teriyaki-marinated filet mignons.

Hearthstone almost laughed. If only his bride hadn't loved the dog so much. If she hadn't spoiled the animal, and if he hadn't gone along with the spoiling . . . if only he'd complained about the price of filet mignon in the Japanese markets, then maybe Dempsey wouldn't care a damn about the dead man on the floor . . . If only . . .

If only he hadn't been crazy enough to think that Machii was the Shroud returned.

Hearthstone toed the expensive dish and slid it toward Dempsey. Slowly, slowly . . .

'Good boy. Good doggy.'

The dog began to pant.

Sniffed at the teriyaki-drenched finger that floated in the dish.

Parted its lips . . . and grinned.

After three months in the hands of incompetent prison doctors, Hearthstone was happy to join the general population in the penitentiary. His ribs had healed nicely, his back bothered him only when the weather was bad, and he soon accustomed himself to eating solid food despite the absence of several teeth which he'd left behind in a San Francisco alley.

Silly, really. The whole idea. Heal a man in order to fry him whole and hearty in the electric chair.

Though most death-row inmates were not allowed to work or even move among the general population, an exception was made in Hearthstone's case. After all, the warden had never before had the service of a full professor at his disposal.

So, Jacob Hearthstone, prisoner number 37965, was allowed to present lectures to his fellow convicts. These lectures took place in the prison library, and before long Hearthstone had insinuated himself among the library staff. In a few short months he was a member of that staff, charged with the delivery of books and magazines to the prisoners in their cells. This duty gave him a feeling of freedom and took his mind off the execution date which drew closer with each passing day.

Hearthstone wanted to move among the general population for one reason: he wanted to determine if he was a madman. His visits from the demon known as the Shroud seemed increasingly fantastic as time passed, and he often wondered if he had imagined the monster, conjured it up, as it were, out of thin air. As he moved from cell to cell he listened for any mention of the mysterious creature, and sometimes he ventured a question or two with inmates he knew and trusted.

In Hearthstone's seventh month of incarceration a new prisoner appeared on death row, a transfer from a federal pen on the east coast. Hearthstone struck up a conversation with the man soon after, explaining that he was a pipeline to the library and could obtain materials that would help the new fish pass the time.

'Sure.' The man smiled at the suggestion. 'Bring me anything you got on electricity, and bring me anything you got on the human soul.'

Hearthstone thought the requests odd, but he didn't say anything, for he had learned that questioning a prisoner's taste in even the most unimportant matters could be a fatal mistake. He'd seen a con killed with a sharpened spoon for daring to denigrate his cell mate's preference for a certain brand of cigarette.

And apart from all questions of jailhouse etiquette, Hearthstone didn't trust this man's eyes. They were dark green and always moist, almost as if brimming with tears, two fathomless pools that swam on the con's chalky, stretched visage. The eyes were part of the new fish's mystery, and their peculiar cast made Hearthstone all the more eager to investigate him.

So he brought the man a stack of books. Books by Edison and books by Kant. And then he brought more. William James, Descartes. The new fish read them all. And soon they were talking.

Hearthstone called his new friend the Electric Man.

Before long, the Electric Man exhausted the prison

library's meagre resources. 'Just let me talk to you, Jake,' he said. 'You're a professor. You should know all the answers.'

Ignoring the vulgar familiarity, Hearthstone said that he was happy to indulge such a request.

'OK, Professor. I been reading all this stuff, and it just don't tell me what I need to know. I mean, I know about electricity. That stuff I can figure. The stuff about the soul is tougher, but some of it makes sense, too. But what I don't get, what I don't know anything about, is the two things together. Get me?'

'Keep going . . . I'll try to follow.'

'That's jake. Now I'm gonna lay it out flat, and if you don't want to believe me, you just say the word and I'll never look at you again. But what would you think if I told you that the screws strapped me into the electric chair back east two years ago, and one of 'em pulled the switch and gave me a real good ride, and nothing happened to me at all?'

Hearthstone thought of his fast-approaching execution date. 'I'd ask you how you managed the trick.'

The Electric Man grinned. 'Oh, it's an easy one, y'see. All you got to do is get someone to come inside you, swim around in your blood, and steal your soul.'

Hearthstone grinned. 'Where do I sign up?'

'It ain't funny, Jake,' the Electric Man said. 'You ever hear of something called the Shroud?'

'As it happens, I've met the fellow.'

'Uh-huh. I thought you had the look. Well, I'm the world's greatest expert on the son of a bitch. I've had him in my head, and it wasn't what you'd call a barrel of laughs.' The Electric Man shivered at the memory. 'And ever since then I been tryin' to figure it all out. Figure him out. But I just can't do it. I got too many questions. And now I'm startin' to think that it ain't a thing you can answer. It ain't like a puzzle where all the pieces fit.

'Look, Professor, I only want to know one thing: if that devil made off with my soul, and if they strapped me in the chair and it didn't do nothin' but curl my hair, do you think I'm ever gonna be able to die?'

Hearthstone said, 'Before I can answer that question, you must tell me what you know of the Shroud.'

Hearthstone readied his pistol.

The dog's grin gaped into a yawn, and then the animal dipped its huge head and sniffed at the food that the professor had pushed its way.

Hearthstone smiled. 'Oh my, you're jumping at shadows, old boy, jumping at every damn stimulus that fires those very old synapses . . .'

Dempsey began to eat.

Hearthstone relaxed. Remembered.

The Electric Man's voice:

He came after me, y'see. Doesn't matter what I did, doesn't matter that other guys did worse . . . he just came after me. Told me I was gonna suffer, then die. Oh, he kept his word about that sufferin' part. My wife, well, the first night he came around she seen him, and she got so damn scared she went into convulsions and almost bit her tongue clean off. Right on the livin'-room rug. Yeah, that was sufferin' all right, and I ain't even sure the bastard meant for that to happen. Then things got worse. He started stealin' money from me – it'd just disappear right out of my pockets – and I couldn't pay off my boys, and soon they was huntin' for me.

The sounds of Dempsey licking meat, chewing, swallowing.

Yeah, came for me in the morning, he did. I was shavin', looked up and seen him behind me. Well, the razor slipped and I cut myself. Bam! He was on me like a wild animal or somethin' and then he wasn't there at all – outside of me, that is – but I could feel him swimmin' around in my blood, squirmin' in my guts. The devil was inside of me!

The filet mignon was gone. Tentatively, Dempsey licked at the severed finger.

He makes me get all duded up – straw hat, corsage . . . everything. Makes me get my Tommy gun, y'see. Walks me out to a Cadillac, a Sport Phaeton, and there's a dame sittin' behind the wheel. Brown eyes that was almost gold, pretty, a dancer from one of my speakeasies. She don't say nothin', just smiles and drives me over to my boys' digs and drops me off. But that devil's still inside me, see? He trots me upstairs. Makes me open up on my own boys. God, I seen some things . . . but this was awful. These was my friends. And I got mad – crazy mad – thinkin' about what he'd made me do, thinkin' about how he'd hurt my wife.

The dog took the severed digit in its teeth. Flicked its head. Bit.

I started to fight the bastard then and there. I stuck my hand in front of the gun barrel and blasted a few rounds right through it, through my wrist, too – see the scars here? Anyway, I was screamin' – my hand spewin' blood all over me and all over the room and my boys, the awful stink swimmin' in my head – screamin' for the bastard to get the hell out of me. Willin' him to get out of me!

Dempsey swallowed. Panted.

And then came the worst part. It was bad enough back home, lookin' at my eyes in the mirror, lookin' at the little cut on my neck, knowin' that thing was inside of me. But it was even worse seein' it wash out of me in all that blood. God, it was scrambled all over the floor like rotted guts from a slaughterhouse, and it pulled itself together . . . just came together like somethin' out of a nutty cartoon. The damn thing crawled over the bodies of my boys and I started to let it have it with the gun . . . wracked the thing pretty good, wracked up my boys' dead bodies, too, but I didn't even care no more . . . and then it spun around when it got to the window, stood up, holdin' out something black in its hand, a bloody thing that looked like a baby. And it said in that voice it has, 'You live without it, dead man. You just try living without your soul . . .'

Dempsey ducked his head against Hearthstone's shoes and whined, begging for another finger.

So, there was a weakness in the fabric of the Shroud, a weakness that gave Professor Hearthstone hope. Perhaps it was simple fear, and perhaps it was something more complex – something that could not be named. Still, Hearthstone knew that if the riddle of the Shroud could be solved, death might not be inevitable.

Hearthstone considered all the possibilities as his execution date drew nearer. He thought of the Electric Man's state of mind during the Shroud's invasion of his body and decided that the gangster's own fear had allowed the Shroud to control him. And then he remembered how the Electric Man's own anger had grown – anger at what had happened to his wife, anger at what the Shroud had forced him to do to his fellows – boiling to a hateful rage that was pure and possibly quite insane.

When he finished his examination of the Shroud's battle with the Electric Man, Hearthstone was confident that he could form a plan of attack should the demon reappear. He prayed that such a creature as the Shroud could not glory in silent victory. He concentrated on hate, and he was pleased to find that insanity was a prize well within his grasp. And on the night before his execution, the thing came, a nightmarish red-black pudding that sluiced through the bars of his cell and puddled on the brick wall, oozing a great, ugly grin.

'I have supped on your suffering, Jacob Hearthstone,' the Shroud said. 'And now, as I promised, you will die.'

The professor's only reply was a smile. He thought of Anastasia White. He closed his eyes and saw her. Straightened and heard his ruined back pop and complain. Gritted his remaining teeth and pictured bloody molars dotting the slimy cobblestones of a San Francisco alley.

'Tomorrow when you sit in the electric chair, I will be there,' the Shroud said. 'I will be inside the man who wears the hood. Mine will be the hand that pulls the switch.'

Hearthstone wasn't listening. He was deep inside his own head. He saw Thomas Clancy sitting before him, a bloody bubble on his lips. Saw the bowie knife clenched in Clancy's left hand, the thin cuts on the Irishman's wrist.

Suddenly Hearthstone stood and stepped close to the wall, confronting the scarlet grin, sucking the fetid breath that boiled from the Shroud's mouth as if it were the finest perfume in all the world. He removed his glasses, slipped the cover from one of the ear pieces, and drew the rough metal across the back of his right hand. A trickle of blood seeped from the wound.

Hearthstone challenged the Shroud. 'Come in, you bastard. If you dare . . . if you are not frightened.'

The scarlet thing was breathing fast now. It slid away, toward the ceiling, but the smell of blood was too great a lure. The shadow sprang from the wall, poured over Hearthstone's hand, and burrowed inside his wound.

I know you, Hearthstone began. *I know your amber-eyed bitch.*

Great whistling gasps wracked the professor's lungs. He felt claws scrabbling over his heart, fighting for purchase.

Nothing there, devil. No fear to hold on to. Only hatred, strong and pure.

The Shroud twisted in his guts. Hearthstone doubled over.

Oh, you're good. But not that good. Because I remember. I met a man who fought you to a draw, and I learned well the lessons that he taught me.

Teeth ripped at his brain. A fist clenched his heart.

Hearthstone's insanity pushed them away. *I've had your bitch. I've pressed my lips to hers. Felt that creamy skin under my fingertips. And now I have you.*

The Shroud slipped across the condemned man's shoulderblades and down the bones of his arm. Hearthstone pressed his left hand over the wound on his right. *Not so fast*, he thought. *Don't leave me just yet . . .*

The Shroud coiled inside Hearthstone's forearm. The professor felt the thing shiver. Felt it shrink.

Hearthstone laughed. *Your Irishmen were tougher than this. Your bitch had more backbone.*

Footsteps sounded in the corridor. A guard on bed-check duty.

'Now comes the real test,' Hearthstone whispered. 'Let's see who's in control.'

Hearthstone parted his fingers. He willed the Shroud to extend itself in a thin coil that snaked between the bars, and then he unleashed the full power of his insanity, creating a dark monster in his mind, commanding it to grow in the shadow-choked corridor.

Part jaguar.

Part ogre.

Part Kong of Skull Island.

The shadowthing roared. The guard fired his pistol once and was batted against the brick wall by a huge black tail. He lurched to the centre of the corridor, unconscious but still on his feet, and was smashed against the opposite wall by a shadowfist.

Keys rattled. Hearthstone's cell door swung open.

Hearthstone stepped from his prison and joined his ebony escort.

Soon the prison corridors swam with blood.

Later, laughing uncontrollably, the professor wandered the deserted city streets. He twisted the Shroud into a gnarled knot, a feeble arthritic thing. Blew the devil up like a balloon until it was a fat ebony clown. Made the demon crawl on its belly, an armless, legless freak.

Tired of frivolity, Hearthstone ripped the thing's umbilical tail out of his wrist. The Shroud twisted on the pavement, a red-muscled horror that whined like a skinned dog. Hearthstone stomped it, spat upon it, laughed at it, gloried in the way it shrank from the dim glow of the streetlights.

He kicked it down the street, watching it carom like a child's ball. Chased after it, kicked again. It bounced from one kerb to the other, then suddenly sprang claws and raced toward the gutter. Nails clicked on wet pavement, and a second later it disappeared into a drainage opening.

Hearthstone ran to the kerb. 'Run away, coward!' he shouted, his eyes yellow in the glow of the streetlights. 'Run away from the man who turned an electric chair into a throne!'

Dempsey padded forward, secure on a leash that Hearthstone held in his left hand. In his right he gripped the automatic, which he'd reloaded while the dog gobbled a second filet mignon.

No shadows, the professor told himself. No shadows here. And no shadows on the night the thing died. No shadows then, either.

It had been a great change for him, of course. Leaving America. Relocating to Japan. But the country had seemed ripe for the plucking at the close of World War

II, and he'd cashed in his chips in America and reinvested in the land of the rising sun.

It proved to be a wise course of action. Soon Hearthstone doubled his money. Then he tripled it.

He waited for someone to challenge him. No one did. Not the Americans. Not the Japanese.

Not the Shroud.

But did it matter where the shadows hid? His bride . . . the doctor . . . the yakuza . . . even the dog . . . they had all walked among the shadows at one time or another, had they not? And surely they had all bled. Was there not the possibility? Wasn't it always there?

As long as he remembered.

As long as he puzzled over the riddle of the Shroud.

It was.

So, best to be careful.

Eagerly, Dempsey pulled at the leash as they moved down the hall, but the professor held him back. 'Easy boy. Easy, Dempsey.'

The money didn't make him feel much better. He took a young bride, but she didn't make him feel much better, either. He remembered the Shroud's promise that he would suffer before he died. And one evening he looked at his bride and realized that he was making himself suffer.

His bride had beautiful amber eyes. She could have been a sister to Anastasia White. And he had slipped the ring on her finger, not the Shroud. He alone had brought her into his home.

Hearthstone felt the sting of prophecy. He knew that as long as he remembered the past, he would suffer each time he looked into his bride's eyes.

Dempsey stopped at the end of the corridor. Scraped at the closed door there.

'I don't know if we should disturb her.' Hearthstone was unable to banish fear from his voice. 'The doctor says she hasn't much time left.'

The past was always there. Hearthstone was carrying it around, all of it, locked in his heart. All those old failures scrabbling over his innards like the claws of the Shroud.

But there was a way to put an end to it.

He would collect all the pieces of his past, everything that he hadn't destroyed. He would stare at them, make his peace with them. And then he would crush them under the heel of his boot.

And then, and only then, could he begin to live again.

With shaking fingers, Hearthstone opened the door a crack. Closed it and shrank away.

Shadows. The room was full of them.

In there. In the dark, she was sleeping. Though Hearthstone had instructed Taoka to keep the room well lighted at all times, the good doctor had obviously disobeyed his orders.

The professor stared at the black line of darkness where the bottom rail of the door fell just short of meeting the plush rug.

Calm yourself, Jacob. The thing is dead.

No. Not as long as you remember. Memory makes everything alive.

Drawing a deep breath, Hearthstone reached for the knob once again.

The yakuza brought a dozen old Irishmen to Hearthstone's country estate. The professor watched their executions on a grey morning, so early that the event didn't seem quite real. Afterwards, he returned to his bride's bed for a few hours, where he dozed and dreamed of the beating he'd suffered years before. Waking, he talked to her of the executions and of his memories. He was delighted to find that both events seemed unreal, as if they'd happened to another man.

Three doctors followed the Irishmen. They came of their own free will, under the assumption that they were attending a medical conference. It was only while waiting in the cabin of Hearthstone's yacht that they realized something was amiss, for even after the passage of several decades each man recognized the others as old colleagues. None of them remembered Jacob Hearthstone, but he was considerate enough to relate his own memories of his stay in the prison infirmary. When the pleasantries were over, he introduced the doctors to three bosozoku with sledgehammers in their hands.

Hearthstone opened the door. Just a few inches. He slipped his hand into the darkness, his fingers fumbling for the light switch.

Hearthstone felt better after the Irishmen's visit. Better still after his audience with the prison doctors. But on the day the yakuza brought Anastasia White to him, he knew that he was going to feel very fine, indeed.

Hearthstone flicked the switch. Light washed away shadow.

That was all he needed.

Light was the bane of the Shroud.

Pure, clean, electric light.

Electric . . .

A voice from the past – a memory he'd thought erased now – an observation by a man once on intimate terms with the

Shroud: 'And now I'm startin' to think that it ain't a thing you can answer. It ain't like a puzzle where all the pieces fit.'

And then a thought: If hatred could banish the Shroud, if insanity could defeat him, could the same elements, stored deep in the heart for much too long, return him to life when they were finally purged?

Anastasia was still beautiful. Still slim. Still a stylish dresser. But there was a sadness in her amber eyes that was somehow beyond description. And worst of all, she refused to play Hearthstone's games. She refused to reminisce about the old days in San Francisco; she ignored his queries concerning the fate of the Shroud.

Hearthstone's bride rested on the small bed, her black hair fanning over white pillowslips.

Somewhere beneath that hair, dark shadows lurked.

Dempsey growled, snorting at the antiseptic odour of the chamber.

Silently, Hearthstone approached the sick bed. 'My dear, won't you smile for me?'

Anastasia's silence was like stone. Hearthstone's heart sank. She would give him nothing. She knew her life was lost, and she would make no desperate pleas, no bargains that he could betray.

She refused him satisfaction.

He stared at her, thinking of the days when he'd mulled Shroud riddles with such enthusiasm, thinking of all his hypotheses and conclusions . . .

. . . wondering at the fiery glow in her amber eyes.

Hearthstone's bride did not move. He brushed her hair, let his fingers drift to the plastic oxygen mask strapped over her mouth. 'My goodness.' He laughed. 'Of course you can't smile with this thing in the way.'

Hearthstone took the katana from its case, unsheathed the weapon, and showed its silver blade to Anastasia White. 'I have been thinking about our friend the Shroud,' he began. 'I've been thinking about the way it scurried through a sewer grate when I was close to killing it. For many years I thought it was down there, under the city, licking its wounds.' Hearthstone stared at Anastasia's eyes, recognizing the gaze of an unexpected guest. 'Now I don't think that any more . . . Oh, I think it's licking its wounds all right. I still think that. But I think it found another sewer, one that runs with blood.'

His bride's breaths came short and fast without the oxygen mask, and he prodded the corners of her mouth. 'Smile . . . smile . . . '

'I'm not going to kill you, Anastasia. It's the Shroud I want. It's always been the Shroud.'

Her eyes brimmed with tears. She could not keep her silence. 'Leave him alone,' she begged. 'He's tired. He's broken . . . You've beaten him once. Isn't that enough?'

'No, never enough.' Hearthstone raised the katana, held it to her eye, thinking of the way the Shroud used human hosts, recalling the thing's aversion to light and the way it had scuttled for the protection of a dark sewer. He remembered the prison cell where he'd tempted the creature. He remembered the insane hatred he's used to defeat it.

But he hadn't killed it.

It ran. It took refuge.

Anastasia White. The Shroud.

Hearthstone grinned. 'Any port in a storm.'

The professor prodded open an eye. Stared at the amber orb.

Blank. Nothing there. Anastasia was . . .

No. This was his bride.

He lifted his bride's head and examined the white pillow-slip. Next he drew back the sheets and blankets and checked them carefully. Satisfied, he ran his fingers through his bride's hair, but still found nothing there.

He sighed. Stepped back. Impossible. Taoka was dead. And Machii was dead. And Dempsey was loyal.

His bride.

Impossible. But something was here. He could feel it.

And whatever it was, it was more than a memory.

He pulled Anastasia to him. Parted her mouth and kissed her. He forced his tongue against hers, felt it squirm away.

Like that night in the prison, he thought. Like the Shroud, shrinking from my power.

Anastasia pushed at him. 'He's weak.' She sobbed. 'He's nearly dead. Just leave him be. Let him die in peace.'

Hearthstone slashed Anastasia's shoulder with the katana, then drew the blade across his palm. 'Come on, you bastard,' he said. 'It's time to face your master.'

Hearthstone took the stainless-steel scissors from the top of the dresser. He cut open his bride's nightgown, then drew it apart.

He stared down at the purple scar that ran the length of her breastbone.

Black blood oozed from Anastasia's wound. She pressed a hand against it, stemming the flow, her fingers trapping the creature that desperately wanted out. 'You won't have him,' she said, her eyes glowing with defiance. 'Not while I'm alive.'

'Very well,' Hearthstone said.

His bride shivered as the scissors touched her sternum.

Anastasia shivered as Hearthstone drove the katana into her breast. She fell back, slipping off the short blade, collapsing on the floor with hardly a sound.

Hearthstone dropped to his knees and pressed his wounded hand against Anastasia's bloody chest.

Her heart wasn't beating.

She wasn't breathing.

She wore a slight grin that fell somewhere short of a smile.

'Come out, you bastard,' he whispered, his eyes everywhere at once: on the shadows that swam beneath the furniture; on Anastasia's blood; on the hem of her silk dress, which ruffled under a breeze from the open window. Each image burned into his brain as if branded there.

'Come out, you coward.' He closed his eyes but saw the room, the blood, Anastasia's dress. 'Come out and let me forget.'

Hearthstone held his hand to Anastasia's breast, whimpering in frustration, until her blood began to dry.

He sat there alone, but for his memories.

Hearthstone stared at his bride's lips. At the scissors in his hand.

No, it couldn't be.

He wouldn't do this.

His bride was an innocent. She was not possessed. Neither was Dr Taoka. Nor the yakuza, Mr Machii. Nor Dempsey.

This was madness. Time had passed, so much time without incident. The Shroud was dead.

Dead to the world.

Dead, everywhere, but in Jacob Hearthstone's memory.

Anyone . . .

The professor turned toward the mirrored wall and stared at his reflection. What he saw didn't match his memories.

If he had to remember everything, why couldn't he remember how to be the man he once was? Young, strong, confident . . .

Now he was none of those things.

Hearthstone laughed at the feeble old man in the mirror. Here was the true seat of memory. A withered receptacle, nothing more. 'Wipe the slate clean, grandpa. Purge the hatred, the insanity. Make a fresh start.'

Hearthstone turned the scissors on himself and drove the blades deep into his chest.

Anywhere . . .

Blood coursed from the wound.

Any time . . .

The shadows flowed over him, along with the laughter, along with a whispered promise.

Those who are evil must suffer, then die.

Hearthstone pressed cold fingers against the wound and felt warm blood pump from his heart. 'Are you demon or angel?' he asked.

The answer came from the shadows.

I am . . . the Shroud.

Cold as Iron

W. ELIZABETH TURNER

I DON'T USUALLY go for country walks on my own, but Jim had gone off to watch a rugby match, and I really felt the need for some fresh air to chase off the post-Christmas lethargy.

Browsing over the Ordnance Survey map, I worked out a circular route which used a farm track and footpath across fields. It wasn't long enough to have appealed to Jim, but looked a reasonable distance for me to tackle in the time available.

There was a short drive to the start of the track, and I left the car where the road widened to a grassy verge. Tractor marks had patterned the mud, and the churned surface released that cold, sour smell which hangs in the stillness of December air.

I headed uphill, towards a line of trees outlined against the sky. The sunshine was weak and silvery, and gunmetal clouds to the north were already edging the day towards an early close. Setting myself a brisk pace, I passed the signpost indicating where the return path emerged from the field, and tried to familiarize myself with it, so that if

279

the light began to fail I could at least aim in the right direction in order to get back. A couple of scarecrows to one side served to identify the route, and I began to relax into an enjoyable rhythm, warming up and relishing the solitude of the low hills and isolated remnants of woodland.

Some rooks circled irritably over a barn, and shreds of a blue plastic fertilizer bag flapped stiffly where it was caught in a hawthorn hedge. After that the way was quiet again; even a field of sheep seemed oddly muted, their grazing sounds reduced to barely perceived whisperings, and their pale shapes drifting slowly across the dark pasture.

Winter wheat pushed through the ground in lines so straight towards the horizon that the field could have been made of corduroy; it's odd how familiar things take on a different perspective when you're alone. I was looking for the sign to the right, slightly disconcerted that it was not where I thought it should be, when I realized that I had nearly missed it, because the top section had gone. Horses had used the path though, and someone in walking boots, so, with twilight following me, I headed down the side of the field. An old, untidy hedge marked its furthest boundary and a flurry of bird activity there, as I climbed the gate, lured me beside its accompanying ditch. Bramblings, or fieldfares, perhaps, I thought.

Half-way down, a stench crawled out of the dampness which made my body recoil before my mind knew why. It wasn't the ditch. With sickening apprehension, I turned towards the scarecrow, no more than two or three yards away, for its parody of a human form was the source of that appalling reek, an emanation of decay and death.

Two sticks protruded from the coat sleeves, filthy gloves nailed to each end. Trembling with the hope of relief, I looked full at its face. The rotting head was enclosed in a rusting iron grid. It lolled to one side, eyes gone, and thin folds of grey flesh sagging wetly under a sodden hat. The iron cage extended down to the ground, hidden behind rough trousers which had been belted round it. The soil below was stained where foul fluids had dribbled down. Where the jacket fell open, pushed out through the bars, a hand extended, its fingers splayed and curling upwards.

The agony of it was hideous, and the body should not have been there, not in the gentle countryside, and not pinioned in that monstrosity of ancient torture.

Shaking and whimpering, I backed off, the reality of what I had seen fighting my disbelief into cowering submission.

In the cold, dank air, I slid and stumbled, staggering across the uneven ground. Mud was clinging to my shoes, thick and sticky, slowing each step I took. The sound of a motor dragged my mind away from the loathsome thing that I had found. Looking back, I could see headlights bobbing and weaving as the vehicle came down the track, but when it reached the place where the footpath emerged, the engine died and the lights went out.

When the man came into the field, he didn't call out, just moved towards me, slowly. His awareness that I was witness to the evil there seeped along the chill furrows between us.

As I tried to turn, fettered to the cloying ground, the second scarecrow caught at the edge of my vision. Under its grotesque shroud of rags, the iron cage was visible; empty, and waiting.

A Time for Waiting

MICHAEL MARSHALL SMITH

On THE WALL, his pictures. His pride and joy. His only pride and, until tonight, his sole joy.

On the bed, his triumphal robes. To anyone else just a red tie, a white shirt, and trousers of darkest green. But he knew them for what they were, had bought them months ago in anticipation of this night, had neither worn them or even unwrapped them. As he'd come to learn, the waiting was what made something really special, the holding off. The joy of receiving was always fleeting in comparison.

And so today, though the thought of the evening had never left him, he'd spent his Saturday as usual, making another picture, the final one in the set, a set which charted his patience, his waiting. Expressing himself had never come easy, least of all through his face, which he only ever allowed to house a benign indifference. The pictures were his other faces, those of pain and frustration, and hatred: nailed up where he could see them, confront them and one day perhaps master them. Mastering the faces:

that was what it was all about. That was all it was ever about.

The bedroom was cold after the shower and his skin, red in places from the scrubbing off of today's colours, steamed in the half-light. As ever, he put his watch on first, one of his watches: a lady's strap of silver metal with the time inconspicuously huddled in the centre. A slow hour remained before she was due, that was all. The time left for anticipation was running out.

Before starting to dress he stood in front of the mirror, forcing himself to look. Not a body to draw appreciative glances, he knew. What better proof than the fact that it had never drawn any? Not actually unpleasant, just not enough: the short side of medium height, slightly over-weight, manifestly unfit. Just a body, nothing more. Not something to hold, to touch, to covet. And finally, the face.

The face was always most important. In the face you saw the person, and that made him sad. Because no one had ever given his a second glance. He didn't know what was wrong with it, what made it so unattractive. Every-thing was present and correct, the same things everybody else had, so why did women's eyes slide off it as if it wasn't there? What did you have to have inside to make the features come alive? Perhaps he would learn tonight.

Because whatever it took, Julie had it. She'd walked into the office on her first day six months ago and suddenly the corners of the room had seemed to fade away as his eyes had been drawn to her. You fall in love with the beautiful the moment you see them, because their beauty makes you stare and see their faces with a clarity normally reserved for those you already love. And as she'd stood there, shy but confident, he'd fallen.

Then the others descended and she was surrounded, their faces pictures on a wall that shut him out. And of course they were handsome faces, alive faces, and she didn't see his again. Not for a while, anyway.

His body dry, he unwrapped the shirt and carefully put it on, easing the buttons through their holes. Crisp, white. Maybe tonight someone else would undo them for him: maybe it wouldn't just be him again. Wait, and see.

As he put on his underclothes and polished his shoes he could see the faces before him. Only three other people worked in the office, but each had been in front of him. Three faces to beat, to master.

First had been McNeill. Appropriately first, for so he must have been throughout his life. Tall, handsome, a face and body incapable of inelegance. A nose that said he could be trusted, and eyes that showed how far. Beautiful but approachable, his face had moved through the air like a graceful bird.

The tie was perfect on the third attempt. Straker's tie was never perfect, but this was his style, tousled like an actor in rehearsal. A mouth that looked desirable whatever pretension it framed, and an air of not taking himself seriously that made anything easy to forgive. If anything, Straker had been even harder to beat: after McNeill had left it had been months before the mouth and ruffled hair had been mastered.

Fifteen minutes was just enough: sufficient to be ready in, but not enough to leave time for nervousness. But he was already nervous, had been since she'd agreed to come out and the three days of most delicious waiting had begun. In only fifteen minutes she would arrive outside and it would all be over.

Walker had been last, but certainly not least: it was just his luck to work with three of the nicest faces in London. It was fortunate the turnover rate had been so high. Last to go, and not before time: Julie had shown every sign of yielding to his calm and warmth. Moving like a cat, every job finished before it hit his desk, Walker's face had been a still pool whose attractiveness was only enhanced by its minimal imperfections. How the hell did people do that? He'd tried to learn, but Walker's face had never yielded up its secrets.

He pulled on his trousers. The crease was sharp, but as ever they didn't seem to hang as well as he'd hoped. But the colour was her favourite, he knew, and one of his too. Light fingers on the catch tonight, or did that only ever happen to other people?

His hair was dry as he combed it back, and then he stopped and looked once more in the mirror. Surely that wasn't *too* bad. After the time he'd waited, and the trouble he'd taken, please let it be enough. It was still only him, only his face, but he had beaten the others, and he carried their colours as talismans.

The colours of his pictures, too. As he stepped back from the mirror and reached for his jacket, he looked over at the white pictures with the splashes of red and smears of green. Perhaps, if tonight went well, he would show her the pictures, and she would understand him at the last. The jacket just right, the shirt peeping from beneath the cuffs. Because the pictures told a story, like all good ones should do, the story of a waiting. He reached out and touched them, old friends that they were. McNeill's face, sliced off carefully with a scalpel and nailed to the wall through the forehead and chin, drooping elegantly now as the patches of iridescent rot slowly joined. Next to his, Straker's, still with some semblance of three dimensions: beneath the white skin the axe had left the very front of the skull, held to the wall by the nails through its lips. And finally, today's picture, the face of a man missing for three weeks. Sadly excitement had got the better of him that afternoon and Walker's face had come off in three pieces, now fixed to the wall in a row, the edges of each red raw. But he knew what he meant.

The doorbell rang and he hurried downstairs to meet her, past the other rooms with their pictures: each telling a story, as all good ones do.

By Bizarre Hands

JOE R. LANSDALE

For Scott Cupp

WHEN THE TRAVELLING preacher heard about the Widow Case and her retarded girl, he set out in his black Dodge to get over there before Hallowe'en night.

Preacher Judd, as he called himself – though his name was really Billy Fred Williams – had this thing for retarded girls, due to the fact that his sister had been simple-headed, and his mama always said it was a shame she was probably going to burn in hell like a pan of biscuits forgot in the oven, just on account of not having a full set of brains.

This was a thing he had thought on considerable, and this considerable thinking made it so he couldn't pass up the idea of baptizing and giving some God-training to female retards. It was something he wanted to do in the worst way, though he had to admit there wasn't any burning desire in him to do the same for boys or men or women that were half-wits, but due to his sister having been one, he certainly had this thing for girl simples.

And he had this thing for Hallowe'en, because that was the night the Lord took his sister to hell, and he might have taken her to glory had she had any Bible-learning or God-sense. But she didn't have a drop, and it was partly his own fault, because he knew about God and could sing some hymns pretty good. But he'd never turned a word of benediction or gospel music in her direction. Not one word. Nor had his mama, and his papa wasn't around to do squat.

The old man ran off with a buck-toothed laundry woman that used to go house to house taking in wash and bringing it back the next day, but when she took in their wash, she took in Papa too, and she never brought either of them back. And if that wasn't bad enough, the laundry contained everything they had in the way of decent clothes, including a couple of pairs of nice dress pants and some pin-striped shirts like niggers wear to funerals. This left him with one old pair of faded overalls that he used to wear to slop the hogs before the critters killed and ate Granny and they had to get rid of them because they didn't want to eat nothing that had eaten somebody they knew. So, it wasn't bad enough Papa ran off with a beaver-toothed wash woman and his sister was a drooling retard, he now had only the one pair of ugly old overalls to wear to school, and this gave the other kids three things to tease him about, and they never missed a chance to do it. Well, four things. He was kind of ugly too.

It got tiresome.

Preacher Judd could remember nights waking up with his sister crawled up in the bed alongside him, lying on her back, eyes wide open, her face bathed in cool moonlight, picking her nose and eating what she found, while he rested on one elbow and tried to figure why she was that way.

He finally gave up figuring, decided that she ought to have some fun, and he could have some fun too. Come Hallowe'en, he got him a bar of soap for marking up windows and a few rocks for knocking out some, and he made his sister and himself ghost-suits out of old sheets in which he cut mouth and eye holes.

This was her fifteenth year and she had never been trick-or-treating. He had designs that she should go this time, and they did, and later after they'd done it, he walked her back home, and later yet, they found her out back of the house in her ghostsuit, only the sheet had turned red because her head was bashed in with something and she had bled out like an ankle-hung hog. And some-one had turned her trick-or-treat sack – the handle of which was still clutched in her fat grip – inside out and taken every bit of candy she'd gotten from the neighbours.

The sheriff came out, pulled up the sheet and saw that she was naked under it, and he looked her over and said that she looked raped to him, and that she had been killed by bizarre hands.

Bizarre hands never did make sense to Preacher Judd, but he loved the sound of it, and never did let it slip away, and when he would tell about his poor sister, naked under the sheet, her brains smashed out and her trick-or-treat bag turned inside out, he'd never miss ending the story with the sheriff's line about her having died by bizarre hands.

It had a kind of ring to it.

He parked his Dodge by the road side, got out and walked

up to the Widow Case's, sipping on a Frosty root beer. But even though it was late October, the Southern sun was as hot as Satan's ass and the root beer was anything but frosty.

Preacher Judd was decked out in his black suit, white shirt and black loafers with black and white checked socks, and he had on his black hat, which was short-brimmed and made him look, he thought, exactly like a travelling preacher ought to look.

Widow Case was out at the well, cranking a bucket of water, and near by, running hell out of a hill of ants with a stick she was waggling, was the retarded girl, and Preacher Judd thought she looked remarkably like his sister.

He came up, took off his hat and held it over his chest as though he were pressing his heart into proper place, and smiled at the widow with all his gold-backed teeth.

Widow Case put one hand on a bony hip, used the other to prop the bucket of water on the well-kerbing. She looked like a shaved weasel, Preacher Judd thought, though her ankles weren't shaved a bit and were perfectly weasel-like. The hair there was thick and black enough to be mistaken for thin socks at a distance.

'Reckon you've come far enough,' she said. 'You look like one of them Jehovah Witnesses or such. Or one of them kind that run around with snakes in their teeth and hop to nigger music.'

'No, ma'am, I don't hop to nothing, and last snake I seen I run over with my car.'

'You here to take up money for missionaries to give to them starving African niggers? If you are, forget it. I don't give to the niggers around here, sure ain't giving to no hungry foreign niggers that can't even speak English.'

'Ain't collecting money for nobody. Not even myself.'

'Well, I ain't seen you around here before, and I don't know you from white rice. You might be one of them mash murderers for all I know.'

'No, ma'am, I ain't a mash murderer, and I ain't from around here. I'm from East Texas.'

She gave him a hard look. 'Lots of niggers there.'

'Place is rotten with them. Can't throw a dog tick without you've hit a burr-head in the noggin'. That's one of the reasons I'm travelling through here, so I can talk to white folks about God. Talking to niggers is like,' and he lifted a hand to point, 'talking to that well-kerbing there, only that well-kerbing is smarter and a lot less likely to sass, since it ain't expecting no civil rights or a chance to crowd up with your young'ns in schools. It knows its place and it stays there, and that's something for that well-kerbing, if it ain't nothing for niggers.'

'Amen.'

Preacher Judd was feeling pretty good now. He could see she was starting to eat out of his hand. He put on his hat and looked at the girl. She was on her elbows now, her head down and her butt up. The dress she was wearing was way too short and had broken open in back from her having outgrown it. Her panties were dirt-stained and there was gravel, like little b.b.s, hanging off of them. He thought she had legs that looked strong enough to wrap around an alligator's neck and choke it to death.

'Cindereller there,' the widow said, noticing he was watching, 'ain't gonna have to worry about going to school with niggers. She ain't got the sense of a nigger. She ain't got no sense at all. A dead rabbit knows more than she knows. All she does is play around all day, eat bugs and such and drool. In case you haven't noticed, she's simple.'

'Yes, ma'am, I noticed. Had a sister the same way. She got killed on a Hallowe'en night, was raped and murdered and had her trick-or-treat candy stolen, and it was done, the sheriff said, by bizarre hands.'

'No kiddin'?'

Preacher Judd held up a hand. 'No kiddin'. She went on to hell, I reckon, 'cause she didn't have any God talk in her. And retard or not, she deserved some so she wouldn't have to cook for eternity. I mean, think on it. How hot it must be down there, her boiling in her own sweat, and she didn't do nothing, and it's mostly my fault cause I didn't teach her a thing about the Lord Jesus and his daddy, God.'

Widow Case thought that over. 'Took her Hallowe'en candy too, huh?'

'Whole kit and kaboodle. Rape, murder, and candy theft, one fatal swoop. That's why I hate to see a young'n like yours who might not have no Word of God in her . . . Is she without training?'

'She ain't even toilet trained. You couldn't perch her on the outdoor convenience if she was sick and her manage to hit the hole. She can't do nothing that don't make a mess. You can't teach her a thing. Half the time she don't even know her name.' As if to prove this, Widow Case called, 'Cindereller.'

Cinderella had one eye against the ant hill now and was trying to look down the hole. Her butt was way up and she was rocking forward on her knees.

'See,' said Widow Case, throwing up her hands. 'She's

worse than any little old baby, and it ain't no easy row to hoe with her here and me not having a man around to do the heavy work.'

'I can see that . . . By the way, call me Preacher Judd . . . And can I help you tote that bucket up to the house there?'

'Well now,' said Widow Case, looking all the more like a weasel, 'I'd appreciate that kindly.'

He got the bucket and they walked up to the house. Cinderella followed, and pretty soon she was circling around him like she was a shark closing in for the kill, the circles each time getting a mite smaller. She did this by running with her back bent and her knuckles almost touching the ground. Ropes of saliva dripped out of her mouth.

Watching her, Preacher Judd got a sort of warm feeling all over. She certainly reminded him of his sister. Only she had liked to scoop up dirt, dog mess, and stuff as she ran, and toss it at him. It wasn't a thing he thought he'd missed until just that moment, but now the truth was out and he felt a little teary-eyed. He half-hoped Cinderella would pick up something and throw it at him.

The house was a big, draughty thing circled by a wide flower bed that didn't look to have been worked in years. A narrow porch ran half-way around it, and the front porch had man-tall windows on either side of the door.

Inside, Preacher Judd hung his hat on one of the foil-wrapped rabbit ears perched on top of an old Sylvania TV set, and followed the widow and her child into the kitchen.

The kitchen had big iron frying-pans hanging on wall pegs, and there was a framed embroidery that read GOD

WATCHES OVER THIS HOUSE. It had been faded by sunlight coming through the window over the sink.

Preacher Judd sat the bucket on the ice box – the old sort that used real ice – then they all went back to the living-room. Widow Case told him to sit down and asked him if he'd like some ice-tea.

'Yes, this bottle of Frosty ain't so good.' He took the bottle out of his coat pocket and gave it to her.

Widow Case held it up and squinted at the little line of liquid in the bottom. 'You gonna want this?'

'No, ma'am, just pour what's left out and you can have the deposit.' He took his Bible from his other pocket and opened it. 'You don't mind if I try and read a verse or two to your Cindy, do you?'

'You make an effort on that while I fix us some tea. And I'll bring some things for ham sandwiches, too.'

'That would be right nice. I could use a bite.'

Widow Case went to the kitchen and Preacher Judd smiled at Cinderella. 'You know tonight's Hallowe'en, Cindy?'

Cinderella pulled up her dress, picked a stray ant off her knee, and ate it.

'Hallowe'en is my favourite time of the year,' he continued. 'That may be strange for a preacher to say, considering it's a devil thing, but I've always loved it. It just does something to my blood. It's like a tonic for me, you know?'

She didn't know. Cinderella went over to the TV and turned it on.

Preacher Judd got up, turned it off. 'Let's don't run the Sylvania right now, baby child,' he said. 'Let's you and me talk about God.'

Cinderella squatted down in front of the set, not seeming to notice it had been cut off. She watched the dark screen like the White Rabbit considering a plunge down the rabbit hole.

Glancing out the window, Preacher Judd saw that the sun looked like a dropped cherry snocone melting into the clay road that led out to Highway 80, and already the tumble bug of night was rolling in blue-black and heavy. A feeling of frustration went over him, because he knew he was losing time and he knew what he had to do.

Opening his Bible, he read a verse and Cinderella didn't so much as look up until he finished and said a prayer and ended it with 'Amen.'

'Uhman,' she said suddenly.

Preacher Judd jumped with surprise, slammed the Bible shut and dunked it in his pocket. 'Well, well now,' he said with delight, 'that does it. She's got some Bible training.'

Widow Case came in with the tray of fixings. 'What's that?'

'She said some of a prayer,' Preacher Judd said. 'That cinches it. God don't expect much from retards, and that ought to do for keeping her from burning in hell.' He practically skipped over to the woman and her tray, stuck two fingers in a glass of tea, whirled and sprinkled the drops on Cinderella's head. Cinderella held out a hand as if checking for rain.

Preacher Judd bellowed out, 'I pronounce you baptized in the name of God, the Son, and the Holy Ghost. Amen.'

'Well, I'll swan,' the widow said. 'That there tea works for baptizing?' She sat the tray on the coffee-table.

'It ain't the tea water, it's what's said and who says it that makes it take . . . Consider that gal legal baptized . . . Now, she ought to have some fun too, don't you think? Not having a full head of brains don't mean she shouldn't have some fun.'

'She likes what she does with them ants,' Widow Case said.

'I know, but I'm talking about something special. It's Hallowe'en. Time for young folk to have fun, even if they are retards. In fact, retards like it better than anyone else. They love this stuff . . . A thing my sister enjoyed was dressing up like a ghost.'

'Ghost?' Widow Case was seated on the couch, making the sandwiches. She had a big butcher knife and she was using it to spread mustard on bread and cut ham slices.

'We took this old sheet, you see, cut some mouth and eye holes in it, then we wore them and went trick-or-treating.'

'I don't know that I've got an old sheet. And there ain't a house close enough for trick-or-treatin' at.'

'I could take her around in my car. That would be fun, I think. I'd like to see her have some fun, wouldn't you? She'd be real scary too under that sheet, big as she is and liking to run stooped down with her knuckles dragging.'

To make his point, he bent forward, humped his back, let his hands dangle and made a face he thought was in imitation of Cinderella.

'She would be scary, I admit that,' Widow Case said. 'Though that sheet over her head would take some away from it. Sometimes she scares me when I don't got my mind on her, you know? Like if I'm napping in there on the bed, and I sorta open my eyes, *and there she is*, looking at me like she looks at them ants. I declare, she looks like she'd like to take a stick and whirl it around on me.'

'You need a sheet, a white one, for a ghost-suit.'

'Now maybe it would be nice for Cinderella to go out and have some fun.' She finished making the sandwiches and stood up. 'I'll see what I can find.'

'Good, good,' Preacher Judd said, rubbing his hands together. 'You can let me make the outfit. I'm real good at it.'

While Widow Case went to look for a sheet, Preacher Judd ate one of the sandwiches, took one and handed it down to Cinderella. Cinderella promptly took the bread off it, ate the meat, and laid the mustard sides down on her knees.

When the meat was chewed, she took to the mustard bread, cramming it into her mouth and smacking her lips loudly.

'Is that good, sugar?' Preacher Judd asked.

Cinderella smiled some mustard bread at him, and he couldn't help but think the mustard looked a lot like baby shit, and he had to turn his head away.

'This do?' Widow Case said, coming into the room with a slightly yellowed sheet and a pair of scissors.

'That's the thing,' Preacher Judd said, taking a swig from his iced tea. He set the tea down and called to Cinderella.

'Come on, sugar, let's you and me go in the bedroom there and get you fixed up and surprise your mama.'

It took a bit of coaxing, but he finally got her up and took her into the bedroom with the sheet and scissors. He half-closed the bedroom door and called out to the widow, 'You're going to like this.'

After a moment, Widow Case heard the scissors snipping

299

away and Cinderella grunting like a hog to trough. When the scissor sound stopped, she heard Preacher Judd talking in a low voice, trying to coach Cinderella on something, but as she wanted it to be a surprise, she quit trying to hear. She went over to the couch and fiddled with a sandwich, but she didn't eat it. As soon as she'd gotten out of eyesight of Preacher Judd, she'd upended the last of his root beer and it was as bad as he said. It sort of made her stomach sick and didn't encourage her to add any food to it.

Suddenly the bedroom door was knocked back, and Cinderella, having a big time of it, charged into the room with her arms held out in front of her yelling, 'Woooo, woooo, goats.'

Widow Case let out a laugh. Cinderella ran around the room yelling, 'Woooo, woooo, goats,' until she tripped over the coffee-table and sent the sandwich makings and herself flying.

Preacher Judd, who'd followed her in after a second, went over and helped her up. The Widow Case, who had curled up on the couch in natural defence against the flying food and retarded girl, now uncurled when she saw something dangling on Preacher Judd's arm. She knew what it was, but she asked anyway. 'What's that?'

'One of your piller cases. For a trick-or-treat sack.'

'Oh,' Widow Case said stiffly, and she went to straightening up the coffee-table and picking the ham and makings off the floor.

Preacher Judd saw that the sun was no longer visible. He walked over to a window and looked out. The tumble bug of night was even more blue-black now and the moon was out, big as a dinner plate, and looking like it had gravy stains on it.

'I think we've got to go now,' he said. 'We'll be back in a few hours, just long enough to run the houses around here.'

'Whoa, whoa,' Widow Case said. 'Trick-or-treatin'' I can go for, but I can't let my daughter go off with no strange man.'

'I ain't strange. I'm a preacher.'

'You strike me as an all-right fella that wants to do things right, but I still can't let you take my daughter off without me going. People would talk.'

Preacher Judd started to sweat. 'I'll pay you some money to let me take her on.'

Widow Case stared at him. She had moved up close now and he could smell root beer on her breath. Right then he knew what she'd done and he didn't like it any. It wasn't that he'd wanted it, but somehow it seemed dishonest to him that she swigged it without asking him. He thought she was going to pour it out. He started to say as much when she spoke up.

'I don't like the sound of that none, you offering me money.'

'I just want her for the night,' he said, pulling Cinderella close to him. 'She'd have fun.'

'I don't like the sound of that no better. Maybe you ain't as right thinking as I thought.'

Widow Case took a step back and reached the butcher knife off the table and pushed it at him. 'I reckon you better just let go of her and run on out to that car of yours and take your own self trick-or-treatin'. And without my piller case.'

'No, ma'am, can't do that. I've come for Cindy and that's the thing God expects of me, and I'm going to do it. I got to do it. I didn't do my sister right and she's burning in hell. I'm doing Cindy right. She said some of a prayer and she's baptized. Anything happened to her, wouldn't be on my conscience.'

Widow Case trembled a bit. Cinderella lifted up her ghost-suit with her free hand to look at herself, and Widow Case saw that she was naked as a jay-bird underneath.

'You let go of her arm right now, you pervert. And drop that piller case . . . Toss it on the couch would be better. It's clean.'

He didn't do that either.

Widow Case's teeth went together like a bear trap and made about as much noise, and she slashed at him with the knife.

He stepped back out of the way and let go of Cinderella, who suddenly let out a screech, broke and ran, started around the room yelling, 'Wooooo, wooooo, goats.'

Preacher Judd hadn't moved quick enough, and the knife had cut through the pillow case, his coat and shirt sleeve, but hadn't broke the skin.

When Widow Case saw her slashed pillow case fall to the floor, a fire went through her. The same fire that went through Preacher Judd when he realized his J. C. Penney's suit coat which had cost him, with the pants, $39.95 on sale, was ruined.

They started circling one another, arms outstretched like wrestlers ready for the runtogether, and Widow Case had the advantage on account of having the knife.

But she fell for Preacher Judd holding up his left hand

and wiggling two fingers like mule ears, and while she was looking at that, he hit her with a right cross and floored her. Her head hit the coffee-table and the ham and fixings flew up again.

Preacher Judd jumped on top of her and held her knife hand down with one of his, while he picked up the ham with the other and hit her in the face with it, but the ham was so greasy it kept sliding off and he couldn't get a good blow in.

Finally he tossed the ham down and started wrestling the knife away from her with both hands while she chewed on one of his forearms until he screamed.

Cinderella was still running about, going, 'Wooooo, wooooo, goats,' and when she ran by the Sylvania, her arm hit the foil-wrapped rabbit ears and sent them flying.

Preacher Judd finally got the knife away from Widow Case, cutting his hand slightly in the process, and that made him mad. He stabbed her in the back as she rolled out from under him and tried to run off on all fours. He got on top of her again, knocking her flat, and he tried to pull the knife out. He pulled and tugged, but it wouldn't come free. She was as strong as a cow and was crawling across the floor and pulling him along as he hung tight to the thick, wooden butcher knife handle. Blood was boiling all over the place.

Out of the corner of his eye, Preacher Judd saw that his retard was going wild, flapping around in her ghost-suit like a fat dove, bouncing off walls and tumbling over furniture. She wasn't making the ghost sounds now. She knew something was up and she didn't like it.

'Now, now,' he called to her as Widow Case dragged

him across the floor, yelling all the while, 'Bloody murder, I'm being kilt, bloody murder, bloody murder!'

'Shut up, goddamnit!' he yelled. Then, reflecting on his words, he turned his face heavenward. 'Forgive me my language, God.' Then he said sweetly to Cinderella, who was in complete bouncing distress, 'Take it easy, honey. Ain't nothing wrong, not a thing.'

'Oh Lordy mercy, I'm being kilt!' Widow Case yelled.

'Die, you stupid old cow.'

But she didn't die. He couldn't believe it, but she was starting to stand. The knife he was clinging to pulled him to his feet, and when she was up, she whipped an elbow around, and whacked him in the ribs and sent him flying.

About that time, Cinderella broke through a window, tumbled on to the porch, over the edge, and into the empty flower bed.

Preacher Judd got up and ran at Widow Case, hitting her just above the knees and knocking her down, cracking her head a loud one on the Sylvania, but it still didn't send her out. She was strong enough to grab him by the throat with both hands and throttle him.

As she did, he turned his head slightly away from her digging fingers, and through the broken window he could see his retarded ghost. She was doing a kind of two step, first to the left, then to the right, going, 'Unhhh, unhhhh,' and it reminded Preacher Judd of one of them dances sinners do in them places with lots of blinking lights and girls up on pedestals doing lashes with their hips.

He made a fist and hit the widow a couple of times, and she let go of him and rolled away. She got up, staggered a second, then started running toward the kitchen, the knife still in her back, only deeper from having fallen on it.

He ran after her and she staggered into the wall, her hands hitting out and knocking one of the big iron frying-pans off its peg and down on her head. It made a loud BONG, and Widow Case went down.

Preacher Judd let out a sigh. He was glad for that. He was tired. He grabbed up the pan and whammed her a few times, then, still carrying the pan, he found his hat in the living-room and went out on the porch to look for Cinderella.

She wasn't in sight.

He ran out in the front yard calling her, and saw her making the rear corner of the house, running wildly, hands close to the ground, her butt flashing in the moon-light every time the sheet popped up. She was heading for the woods out back.

He ran after her, but she made the woods well ahead of him. He followed in, but didn't see her. 'Cindy,' he called. 'It's me. Ole Preacher Judd. I come to read you some Bible verses. You'd like that, wouldn't you?' Then he commenced to coo like he was talking to a baby, but still Cinderella did not appear.

He trucked around through the woods with his frying-pan for half an hour, but didn't see a sign of her. For a half-wit, she was a good hider.

Preacher Judd was covered in sweat and the night was growing slightly cool and the old Hallowe'en moon was climbing to the stars. He felt like just giving up. He sat down on the ground and started to cry.

Nothing ever seemed to work out right. That night he'd taken his sister out hadn't gone fully right. They'd gotten the candy and he'd brought her home, but later, when he tried to get her in bed with him for a little bit of the thing animals do without sin, she wouldn't go for it, and she always had before. Now she was uppity over having a ghost-suit and going trick-or-treating. Worse yet, her wearing that sheet with nothing under it did something for him. He didn't know what it was, but the idea of it made him kind of crazy.

But he couldn't talk or bribe her into a thing. She ran out back and he ran after her and tackled her, and when he started doing what he wanted to do, out beneath the Hallowe'en moon, underneath the apple tree, she started screaming. She could scream real loud, and he'd had to choke her some and beat her in the head with a rock. After that, he felt he should make like some kind of theft was at the bottom of it all, so he took all her Hallowe'en candy.

He was sick thinking back on that night. Her dying without no God-training made him feel lousy. And he couldn't get those Tootsie Rolls out of his mind. There must have been three dozen of them. Later he got so sick from eating them all in one sitting that to this day he couldn't stand the smell of chocolate.

He was thinking on these misfortunes, when he saw through the limbs and brush a white sheet go by.

Preacher Judd poked his head up and saw Cinderella running down a little path going, 'Wooooo, wooooo, goats.'

She had already forgotten about him and had the ghost thing in her mind.

He got up and crept after her with his frying-pan. Pretty soon she disappeared over a dip in the trail and he followed her down.

She was sitting at the bottom of the trail between two

pines, and ahead of her was a clear lake with the moon shining its face in the water. Across the water the trees thinned, and he could see the glow of lights from a house. She was looking at those lights and the big moon in the water and was saying over and over, 'Oh, priddy, priddy.'

He walked up behind her and said, 'It sure is, sugar,' and he hit her in the head with the pan. It gave a real solid ring, kind of like the clap of a sweet church bell. He figured that one shot to the bean was sufficient, since it was a good overhand lick, but she was still sitting up and he didn't want to be no slacker about things, so he hit her a couple more times, and by the second time, her head didn't give a ring, just sort of a dull thump, like he was hitting a thick rubber bag full of mud.

She fell over on what was left of her head and her butt cocked up in the air, exposed as the sheet fell down her back. He took a long look at it, but found he wasn't interested in doing what animals do without sin any more. All that hitting on the Widow Case and Cinderella had tuckered him out.

He pulled his arm way back, tossed the frying-pan with all his might toward the lake. It went in with a soft splash. He turned back toward the house and his car, and when he got out to the road, he cranked up the Dodge and drove away noticing that the Hallowe'en sky was looking blacker. It was because the moon had slipped like a suffering face behind a veil, and as he drove away from the Cases', he stuck his head out of the window for a better look. By the time he made the hill that dipped down toward Highway 80, the clouds had passed along, and he'd come to see it more as a happy jack-o'-lantern than a sad face, and he took that as a sign that he had done well.

Contributors' Notes

John Brunner's story 'Moths' was first published in *Dark Voices 2* and subsequently selected for *The Year's Best Fantasy and Horror: Fourth Annual Collection*. Since the 1950s, he has become one of the most prolific and influential of science fiction writers, the winner of several literary prizes, including The British SF Award (twice), The British Fantasy Award, the Prix Apollo (France) and the Cometa d'Argento (Italy – twice), amongst others. His novel *Stand on Zanzibar* won the Hugo, science fiction's top honour, in 1969. He is the author of many short stories and such acclaimed novels as *The Sheep Look Up* and *The Jagged Orbit*. Brunner has written mystery, thrillers, and fantasy, as well as science fiction. Recently, Mandarin reissued three of his books, *The Compleat Traveller in Black*, *The Shift Key*, and *Shockwave Rider*.

Ronald Chetwynd-Hayes used to be an assistant buyer for the Army and Navy stores, but this probably had nothing to do with the fact that during World War II he was evacuated from Dunkirk and returned to Europe shortly after D-Day! That's quite a few years ago, and in the meantime he has become one of the UK's most industrious authors of horror fiction. Since 1973 he has edited some thirty-three anthologies (including twelve volumes of *The Fontana Book of Great Ghost Stories*), published nineteen short story collections, nine novels and two film novelizations. Two movies have been based on his work, *From Beyond the Grave* and *The Monster Club*. In 1988, Chetwynd-Hayes was awarded both The Horror Writers of America and The British Fantasy special awards for his services to the genre. Recent short stories can be found in *Fantasy Tales 6*, *The Mammoth Book of Terror*, *The Mammoth Book of Ghost Stories 2* and *The Mammoth Book of Vampires*. His latest novels are *The Curse of the Snake God* and *Kepple*.

Philip J. Cockburn lives in Worcester and writes fantasy, science fiction, horror and comedy, which has been published in various small press magazines, such as *Exuberance* and *Dementia 13*. He has completed two novels, a tale of black humour titled *Count Vodcula*, and the other a slapstick fantasy, *Operation Islandscape*. 'Necrophiliac' marks his first professional appearance.

Peter Crowther works full time as a copywriter/publications manager for one of the UK's largest financial institutions. He has contributed numerous articles, interviews, reviews, and stories to such magazines as *Interzone*, *Fear*, *Fantasy Tales*, *Cemetery Dance* and *Million*. He is the editor of a two-volume original-horror anthology from Macdonald, *Narrow Houses*, and is currently working on a collaborative novel with James Lovegrove, *Escardy Gap*, and on his own full-length work, *April Fool*.

Les Daniels was born in Danbury, Connecticut, and presently lives in Providence, Rhode Island, from which university he graduated with honours in English literature. He has been a freelance writer since 1968, but during this time he has also been a musician, performing with a number of groups. His first book, *Comix: A History of Comic Books*, appeared in 1971, and 1991 saw the publication of *Marvel: Five Fabulous Decades of the World's Greatest Comics*. He also edited the non-fiction title *Living in Fear: A History of Horror in the Mass Media*, and the anthology *Dying of Fright: Masterpieces of the Macabre*. Daniels' debut novel, *The Black Castle*, introduced the vampire-hero Don Sebastian de Villanueva, who he has resurrected in four subsequent books: *The Silver Skull*, *Citizen Vampire*, *Yellow Fog*, and *No Blood Spilled*. A sixth Sebastian novel, entitled *White Demon*, is forthcoming.

Bernard Donoghue is a dentist working full time in a practice in north-east England, where he lives with his wife and two children. He is an avid reader of horror fiction and has written a number of stories. 'A Night with Claudette' is Bernard's first published story, and this has inspired him to continue working in the genre.

Tony J. Forder, who lives in Peterborough, won a local-short-story contest and the result was his first sale to *Dark Voices 2*. Since then he has sold fiction to *Fear* magazine, but is concentrating on writing novels. He usually works on two at once, in case one bogs down, and he has completed four in the past two years. The latest are *The Rites of Cairnhill* and *The Farmer Building*. Currently in progress is *One Dark Summer*, with four more ideas in progress!

Christopher Fowler runs the London film promotional company, The Creative Partnership, and a movie development company, Defiant FilmCorp. He first appeared in *The 28th Pan Book of Horror Stories* and is the author of three collections of short stories, *City Jitters*, *City Jitters 2*, and *The Bureau of Lost Souls*. Two further collections are in preparation, *Sharper Knives* and *Menz Insanza*, the latter a series of graphic comic stories which will eventually develop into a graphic novel. His first novel, *Roofworld*, was published in 1988 and his second, *Rune*, is currently being developed as a movie by *RoboCop* producer Jon Davison. His latest novel is *Red Bride*, and a fourth, *Darkest Day*, is forthcoming. Together the four books form a loose series about an alternative London, which he calls his 'London Quartet'.

Daniel Fox was born in Oxford and sold his first story when he left university. In the intervening fourteen years he has been writing full time. Under the name Chaz Brenchley, Hodder & Stoughton has published four of his psychological thrillers, *The Samaritan*, *The Refuge*, *The Garden*, and *Mall Time*, and he is writing a fifth, *Paradise*. Fox has published some three hundred short stories, and his work includes fiction on cassette for children, three children's books, and two plays. 'High Flying, Adored' is his first horror story.

Stephen Gallagher is an all-rounder in the horror field, working in radio and television, as well as writing short stories and novels. He was a researcher for Yorkshire Television's Documentaries Department before moving to Granada TV's Presentation Department. He became a full-time writer in 1980, and his novels include *Valley of Lights*, *Oktober*, *Down River*, and *Rain*, all of which he has been commissioned to adapt as screenplays for television production companies. One of his earliest books, *Chimera*, was screened as a mini-series in 1991. Gallagher's short stories have appeared in *Best Horror from the Magazine of Fantasy & SF*, *Shadows*, *Night Visions 8*, *Fantasy Tales*, and *Winter Chills*. His latest novel is *Nightmare, With Angel*.

Charles Gramlich grew up on a farm in Arkansas and currently resides in Louisiana. By profession he is a psychologist, and he has published research articles in his field. He sold his first horror story in 1989, and several have been published since in various small press publications, including *After Hours* and *Tales on the Twisted Side*. He recently won the Deep South Writer's Contest for the second year running in the fantasy and science fiction categories. Gramlich also writes poetry, and he has completed a fantasy novel.

Peter James lives in Sussex with his wife, their pet Hungarian sheepdog and the ghost of a Roman centurion. He worked in the USA for a number of years, writing for television and producing such movies as *Deranged*, *Children Shouldn't Play With Dead Things*, and the award-winning *Dead of Night*. James' reputation for serious research into the paranormal has been reflected in four best-selling novels, *Possession* (to be filmed), *Dreamer*, *Sweet Heart*, and *Twilight*, all them translated into fifteen languages.

Joe R. Lansdale lives in Nacogdoches, Texas, with his wife Karen and their two children. In 1990 he won the Bram Stoker Award and the British Fantasy Award for his short story 'On the Far Side of the Cadillac Desert With Dead Folks', and some of his best fiction has been collected in *By Bizarre Hands*. He writes westerns, science fiction, mysteries, thrillers, fantasy, and horror. His books include a Batman novel, *Captured By the Engines*, *The Nightrunners*, *The Drive-In*, and *The Drive-In 2 (Not Just One of Them Sequels)*, westerns such as *Texas Nightriders*, *Dead in the West*, and *The Magic Wagon*, and the mainstream thrillers, *Act of Love* and *Cold in July*.

Graham Masterton's '5A Bedford Row' appeared in *Dark Voices 3*. He describes his early works, such as his first novel *The Manitou*, as partly responsible for the upsurge of new horror which emerged in the 1970s. The author of more than twenty horror novels, including *The Hymn*, *Black Angel*, *Death Trance*, and *Prey*, he has also written numerous thrillers, historical sagas and 'how-to' sex manuals. In 1989, Masterton created the The Scare Care Trust, a registered charity to help abused and needy children through the promotion of modern horror fiction; this resulted in *Scare Care*, a thirty-eight-story anthology for which all the contributors offered their work for free. He recently completed a new novel in celebration of his first full-length work, *Night of the Manitou*.

Kim Newman was educated at the University of Sussex, moved to London in 1980, and describes his personal evolution as, 'weird kid, became psycho teenager, grew up into maladjusted adult'. Author, critic, and broadcaster, his non-fiction books include *Ghastly Beyond Belief* (with Neil Gaiman), the Bram Stoker Award-winning *Horror: 100 Best Books* (with Stephen Jones), *Nightmare Movies*, and *Wild West Movies*. His short fiction has been published widely, including *Interzone* magazine (and all their anthologies), *Fear*, *Best New Horror 1* and *2*, *Fantasy Tales*, *The Mammoth Book of Vampires*, and *New Worlds*, to name only a few. His story 'The Original Dr Shade' won the 1991 British Science Fiction Award. Newman has written several gaming novelizations and a horror novel under the pseudonym 'Jack Yoevil', as well as novels under his own name such as *The Night Mayor*, *Bad Dreams*, *Jago*, and the forthcoming *Anno Dracula*.

Norman Partridge lives in California. He was born in 1958 and grew up watching the Universal horror movies and reading *Famous Monsters of Filmland*. His fiction has been published in the anthologies *Final Shadows*, *Dark At Heart*, *Chilled to the Bone*, *The Earth Strikes Back*, and *New Crimes 3*. Several short stories have also seen print in the small press magazines, such as *Cemetery Dance*, *Chills*, and *Noctulpa*. His first novel, now in progress, concerns the living dead in California, circa 1955.

Nicholas Royle was born in Sale, Cheshire, and began writing in 1983. He has sold around fifty short stories, most recently to *Best New Horror 1* and *2*, *The Year's Best Horror Stories XIX*, *Fantasy Tales*, *Final Shadows*, *Narrow*

Houses, Interzone: The 5th Anthology, and several other publications. Royle has completed two novels and is the editor of *Darklands*, a 1991 small-press anthology of original horror tales by British writers.

David J. Schow's 'Not from Around Here' was published in *Dark Voices 3* and also appeared in *The Year's Best Fantasy and Horror: Fourth Annual Collection*. His novels are *The Kill Riff* and *The Shaft*, while some of his best short fiction can be found in *Seeing Red* (including the World Fantasy Award-winning title story) and *Lost Angels*. Schow also co-authored the non-fiction guide, *The Outer Limits: The Official Companion*, and edited the movie anthology *Silver Scream*. His screenplays for Hollywood include *Leatherface: the Texas Chainsaw Massacre III*, *Critters 3* and *4*, and an episode of TV's *Freddy's Nightmares*. Recent stories have appeared in *Weird Tales*, *Best New Horror*, *The Year's Best Horror Stories*, *The Mammoth Book of Terror*, *The Mammoth Book of Vampires*, *Fantasy Tales*, and *Pulphouse*.

Michael Marshall Smith's debut short story, 'The Man Who Drew Cats' was published in *Dark Voices 2*. It went on to win him the 1991 British Fantasy Awards for Best Short Fiction and Best Newcomer and was reprinted in *Best New Horror 2*. He works full time as a freelance graphic designer, but he also writes music and the text for corporate videos. New short stores have appeared in *Darklands* and *Darklands 2*, and he is working on a horror novel and several screenplays. Outside the genre, Smith writes and performs for *And Now, In Colour*, a BBC Radio 4 comedy show.

W. Elizabeth Turner lives in Northamptonshire, and she recently retired from a career as a speech and language therapist. She began writing short stories and poems in 1989 and had an article in the magazine *La Vie Outre Manche*. 'Cold As Iron' is her first published horror story.